true
stories
at the
smoky
view

Published 2016
Printed in the United States of America
Cover design by Julie Metz/metzdesign.com
Interior design by Tabitha Lahr

ISBN: 978-1-63152-051-8
Library of Congress Control Number: 2015952635

For information, address:
She Writes Press
1563 Solano Ave #546
Berkeley, CA 94707

She Writes Press is a division of SparkPoint Studio, LLC.

Portions of Chapter 12 were published in a slightly different form as "Old Friends, New Eyes" in *Against the Grain*. The story won that year's fiction contest.

Skip's story "Slipping" in Chapter 15 appeared in *Pebble Lake Review*.

true
stories
at the
smoky
view

a novel

JILL McCROSKEY COUPE

SHE WRITES PRESS

chapter 1

❄ ❄ ❄

Vrai wished she had the nerve to leave Skip's ashes and the box of things from his apartment on his mother's doorstep. Why not loop Cassi's leash around the dogwood, ring the doorbell, and run? She didn't regret the phone call to his mother to offer condolences. Skip would surely have done the same for her. But this visit would be downright awkward.

She and Skip had both grown up here in Knoxville. Decades later they'd become close friends while working in the same library in Baltimore. Just up the street from that library, four days ago, Skip had been hit by a car. According to the article in the *Baltimore Sun,* the driver, an optician, claimed Skip had stepped off the curb with his hands over his eyes. The article had his name right, Jasper Pascal Howard, Jr., but said he was fifty years old. Skip was only forty-nine, two years older than Vrai.

Bittersweet Way, Skip had ruefully called this quiet, tree-lined street where his mother still lived, and for

Vrai, too, his old neighborhood was steeped in sadness. Her best friend, Laramie, had lived next door to Skip.

Vrai's own childhood home, in a very different part of town, had been razed—sold to a commercial developer when her parents retired and moved to Florida. She still exchanged Christmas cards with three or four friends here, but hadn't let anyone know she would be coming for Skip's funeral.

Green-shuttered windows scowled down from the second floor of Mrs. Howard's red brick house. The double front doors were also green, also in need of paint. A flagstone walk led to the front door.

"I'm Vraiment Lynde. Vrai Stevens," she said to the tall black woman who answered the doorbell. "Mrs. Howard's expecting me." Something about the woman looked familiar. "Nancy, is that you?"

It was. The Howards' former maid opened the screen door. "You were Laramie's friend. I recognize that red hair. Come on in, Vrai."

Vrai set the large cardboard box down on the hall carpet. Two days ago, in Baltimore, taking some of Skip's belongings home to his mother had seemed like a good idea. His ashes, still in the white plastic bag she'd been handed at Baltimore Cremation, Inc., were on top.

She had played tennis (with Laramie) on the tennis court behind the Howards' house, had been squirted with a hose (by Lloyd, Laramie's older brother) from the front-yard spigot, but she had never before been inside. The downstairs was carpeted, wall-to-wall, in pale luna-moth green. Matching draperies framed the windows.

"Are you still a . . ." Vrai searched for the right word. "A policewoman?"

"I'm retired now. I'm here today as a friend of the family." Nancy looked down at the box. "What's all this stuff?"

Vrai pointed to the white plastic bag. "I brought Skip's . . . remains."

"Lord have mercy." Nancy's hand went to her heart. "Does Mrs. Howard know?"

"The first time we talked, she asked me to bring them. Last night, though, when I called from my motel, she seemed a little confused."

"Her nephew gave her a tranquilizer last night. Don't know what happened. She's still high as a kite." Nancy eyed the ashes. "She won't need those today. It's only a service. There won't be any trip to the cemetery."

Vrai turned toward the door, determined to get the visit over with as quickly as possible. Lloyd had been right. She could've mailed the ashes, or asked the crematorium to do it for her. "I have Skip's dog, too. In my car. Mrs. Howard asked me to bring Cassi down."

"Not in this house." Nancy was adamant. "She's legally blind. How's she going to take care of a dog?"

Lloyd had also wanted her to ship Cassi down by plane. What would've happened to the poor dog then?

"The service is at two, right?" Vrai wished she'd dropped Skip's high-strung purebred off at the kennel along with her own dogs, two laid-back mutts. "Will I see you there?"

"What else is in that box?" Nancy said.

"Some family photographs. A few other things." She'd gone to Skip's apartment building to see about Cassi. The woman who lived across the hall from Skip had taken the dog in and, after some convincing, let Vrai into his apartment.

"Need some help carrying it into the living room?" Nancy said.

"If she doesn't want the dog, then maybe I should just leave."

Nancy picked up the box. "Didn't you say she was expecting you?"

It was inevitable. Even though Vrai and Skip hadn't spoken to each other in well over a year, she was going to have to sit down and try to make polite conversation about him.

The large living room was dominated by a harp, perhaps the very instrument Mrs. Howard had played as a member of the Knoxville Symphony. Vrai remembered her as a tall, imposing woman, dressed always in a long black skirt, even when she wasn't performing.

"I'll set this on the coffee table for now," Nancy said. "Let me have your coat."

Coffee. Would it be rude to ask for coffee?

The table's smooth marble top reminded her of a blank tombstone. After Nancy left the room, Vrai moved the white plastic bag, heavier than she remembered, to a shelf full of standard reference books: Roget's *Thesaurus*, Bartlett's *Familiar Quotations*, Benet's *Reader's Encyclopedia*, Brewer's *Dictionary of Phrase and Fable*. The familiar titles would be good company for Skip, who, until he lost his job, had been head of the Reference Department at the John Joseph Stark Library in Baltimore.

A frail woman with short white hair appeared in the doorway. If not for the black skirt, Vrai might not have recognized Mrs. Howard, whose cheeks sagged now; she looked like a long thin Giacometti frog.

With a deep voice to match. "I don't see too well these days. Please. Tell me where you are."

"By the bookcase," Vrai said. "I put the ashes on the shelf with the reference books."

Mrs. Howard's cane preceded her into the room. "Now, tell me who you are."

"Vraiment Lynde. Vrai Stevens. My father owned Stevens Landscaping. I drove down from Baltimore."

"So you're the one who called. You were dear little Laramie's friend." Mrs. Howard transferred her cane to her left hand, extended her right. Her long cold fingers were surprisingly strong. "Still have that wild head of red hair?"

"It's a little darker now."

"Whatever were you doing in Baltimore? I hope you brought Cassi. She's all I have left."

"Of course I did," Vrai said. "She's out in my car."

"Vraiment. What a beautiful name. I'd forgotten it. Can I offer you something to eat? Someone dies, people bring food. There's an absolutely tasteless lemon meringue pie."

"No thanks. Shall I get Cassi now?"

"What sort of container is he in?"

She's on a leash, Vrai nearly said. But Mrs. Howard was motioning toward the bookcase.

The container inside the plastic bag looked like a movie popcorn box, larger at the top than at the bottom. Was this the equivalent of a plain pine coffin? Had Skip's mother paid for an urn?

"A sort of box," Vrai said. "Do you want to hold it?"

Mrs. Howard did not. "You chose a good place, beside his father's books. My husband loved crossword puzzles."

Dr. Jasper P. Howard, Sr., she meant. Skip and Melody's father. The pediatrician who made house calls.

"I created a shrine for Melody," Mrs. Howard said. "Did you know my daughter?"

"Not well," Vrai admitted. Skip's little sister, the girl who never grew up, never stopped wearing her pale blonde hair in braids, who chirped when she talked and was always a little too happy, as if her brain manufactured natural Prozac. Melody had probably danced into the ocean at Venice Beach the day she died, the day she sent her parents a postcard telling them not to worry, she was simply going to visit her friend Neptune.

"I hardly knew her myself," Mrs. Howard said. "The shrine was Bill Carr's idea."

"The Bill Carr who went to West High?" Vrai remembered a plump, curly-haired boy who'd kept guns in his locker.

"That's the one. Such a nice young man. He's done missionary work in Mexico, you know." With one hand on her cane and the other in front of her, Mrs. Howard moved forward until she touched the harp's strings with her palm. Using the plane of the harp for guidance, she led Vrai to a corner cabinet with glass doors.

"In Mexico, when a child dies, the family makes a shrine." Mrs. Howard recited the contents of Melody's. "I gave her the porcelain ballerina for her tenth birthday. At the time, she wanted to be a ballet dancer. She did have a certain talent; what she lacked was the proper dedication. The photograph is Melody at sixteen. Isn't she beautiful with her hair down? You wouldn't believe the battle we had that day. She liked to wear her hair in braids. Pigtails, she called them. One braid in back is a pigtail. Two braids are just braids. The ribbons and trophies she won in swimming meets. Melody was such a good swimmer. It's so very ironic. You're probably wondering about the Mounds bars. Melody adored Mounds. More than she liked people, I think. I need to sit down."

Vrai had two boys, both in college. Nothing could be worse than the death of a child. Skip's mother had lost her husband and, now, both of her children. Vrai guided her to the couch and sat down beside her.

The house was silent, tomblike. Vrai smoothed the gray skirt of her two-piece dress, its overblouse a Mondrian-like pattern of blue, maroon, and gray rectangles. Three years ago she'd worn this dress out to dinner with Skip. Happier than she'd ever seen him, he excitedly told her, over paella and a carafe of sangría, all about his new girlfriend. Bev was recently divorced and nervous about dating again, Skip said, so they were taking it slow. They'd met by pure chance, in Poe Park, when Bev's daughter asked to pet Cassi. The girl, Vrai later learned, looked a lot like Melody.

She glanced over at Mrs. Howard, who seemed to think the whole world knew about Melody's suicide. Skip hadn't wanted anyone to know, at least none of his co-workers in Baltimore. In a tearful conversation in Vrai's office, he'd confided that his sister had drowned herself and that he was telling Vrai only because she'd known Melody. He then swore her to secrecy, saying he didn't relish discussing his sister's death with people who'd never met her.

That was eight years ago, in 1985. Vrai had faithfully kept her promise, but Skip got it into his head that she hadn't. He refused to believe, or even to listen to, her protestations of innocence. She was still hurt, still angered by the abrupt end to their friendship. True grief, the sort she should be feeling right now, had not yet taken hold.

"Are you sure you want Skip's dog?" A golden retriever, a replacement, Vrai had always suspected, for his golden-haired sister. "Cassi's a bit hyperactive. I could just take her on back to Baltimore."

And then what? Skip's neighbor didn't want Cassi. Vrai had her hands full with her own dogs.

"Cassi belongs here now," Mrs Howard said. "You'd better bring her in."

Not without telling Nancy first. "Where's Nancy? I don't want to leave you alone."

"Dear," Mrs. Howard croaked, "I've spent my *whole life* alone."

Vrai left the room. It was an effort not to run. The visit was turning out to be even more difficult than she'd anticipated. She felt like a fictional version of herself, a character thrust into the wrong scene who didn't know her lines. The very first thing she should've said to his mother was, "I'm so sorry about Skip."

. . . .

By following the aroma of coffee, Vrai found Nancy slumped in a chair at the kitchen table with her head in her hands. "Skip was the sweet one," Nancy said, looking up. "How could Skip Howard get hit by a car?"

"I've wondered that, too," Vrai said. Skip had always had a wacky side. He loved practical jokes. But he was a scientist as well as a librarian—methodical, careful, observant. "We've had a lot of snow. Maybe he slipped."

Nancy's eyes narrowed, and Vrai longed to tell the former cop about the prescription sunglasses she'd found under the shrubbery near the scene of the accident. And the pair of glasses with a loose lens which someone, presumably Skip, had left on top of the television set in his apartment. Had Skip been wearing sunglasses because his other glasses needed to be repaired? Had he, for some reason, or no reason at all, flung the sunglasses aside before covering his eyes and running into the street?

Olmsted Parkway, in Baltimore, carried four lanes of traffic, three going south into the city and one going north. The John Joseph Stark Library (designated JJS on maps of the Stoneham-Knox University campus, and known affectionately to the students as JJ's) was on the east side of the street. When crossing over from that side there was a tendency to look right, towards the three lanes of traffic, the bigger threat, and to forget all about looking left.

She'd once suggested to Skip that Look Left should be painted on the street, the way pedestrians were warned in London. To which Skip had replied, in his best John Cleese voice, "Brilliant. Precisely what they should do."

Vrai had even searched his apartment for a suicide note. But Skip didn't seem to have been planning anything. He'd left his bed unmade, dirty dishes in the sink, newspapers open on the dining room table. The disorder had been reassuring. Didn't suicides tidy up first, plan things down to the last detail? For the visit to Neptune on her thirtieth birthday, Melody had worn an aqua bathing suit with a white trident on it.

Nancy stood up. "How about some coffee?"

"You read my mind." Vrai sat down, said yes to cream and sugar, yes to a cornbread muffin, to butter and honey.

"You live in Baltimore, too?" Nancy said. "How did that happen, you and Skip in Baltimore?"

A good question. The discovery, ten years ago, that they'd chosen the same profession had been a shock to them both. It wasn't until she arrived for her interview at the John Joseph Stark Library that she learned Skip was on the search committee. A lucky break for her, since the other candidates had master's degrees in art history as well as the MLS. Although Skip had denied it, Vrai knew she owed her position as art history librarian to his kind and loyal nature. He'd adored Laramie, and Vrai was Laramie's best friend. Somehow Skip must have convinced the right people that Vrai was the one for the job.

She kept it simple. "Skip and I worked in the same library." Which had been true until a year and a half ago, when Skip's position was eliminated. "Has someone named Beverly DeFazio called?"

"Not that I know of," Nancy said. "Who's she?"

"Skip's girlfriend. I left a message, with her secretary, about the funeral today. Bev may call to find out what time and how to get there." Vrai had left an earlier message, on Bev's answering machine at home, after learning of Skip's death. Neither call had been returned.

"So Skip had a girlfriend." Nancy, leaning against the sink, wiped at her eyes with a dish towel. "What's she like?"

"Bev's an attorney. Mergers and acquisitions. They were talking about getting married." But then she hadn't seen Bev since Skip's Halloween party, year before last, which was also the occasion for what turned out to be Vrai's final conversation with Skip. "Thanks for the coffee. All right if I bring the dog in now? Mrs. Howard asked me to."

"Let me go talk to her first."

Alone in the kitchen, Vrai helped herself to another cup of coffee and sat gazing at a wall calendar. The month of March featured a photo of a stringed instrument. She had to squint to read the caption. The historic mandolin was the handiwork of a slave at Monticello.

Today was Friday, March 12, 1993.

Vrai let her mind wander back to Monday afternoon, March 8. Skip must have had his old Stoneham-Knox University ID with him when he died, because the hospital called the library office for his next of kin. After providing Mrs. Howard's phone number, Margot, the library director's secretary, called Vrai. Everyone knew Skip and Vrai were from the same home town; not everyone knew they'd had a falling out. Margot, sobbing, said she'd heard the sirens and seen the ambulance from her window but had no idea it was Skip.

The Art History Library was across campus from the main library. Vrai had heard and seen nothing. She replaced the receiver and sat staring out her office window into the branches of a dogwood which would soon bloom pink, waiting for Margot to call back to say Skip had been spotted at Baskin-Robbins, or over in Poe Park walking his dog, and so wasn't really dead after all.

And there, floating outside the window, was Skip's face—his balding head, his wire-rimmed glasses, his lopsided grin. He seemed about to say something, when a vivid flash of red shattered the daydream. A male cardinal swooped down to perch on a tree branch. The cardinal cocked his head and stared back at Vrai, as if passing judgment.

Nancy touched Vrai's shoulder, startling her back to today, the day of Skip's funeral.

"Mrs. Howard has a woman who comes in during the week to help out. Evenings and weekends, neighborhood teenagers can walk the dog." Nancy didn't sound too sure about the latter. "But she's asking for you. Something about a shrine. I'm going to make her an egg salad sandwich. Would you like one?"

"No thanks." Vrai left the kitchen and walked through the pale green house to the room with the harp in it.

chapter 2

✸ ✸ ✸

Mrs. Howard was standing with her cheek against the harp's frame, her long arms outstretched, her fingers plucking soft green air. When she sensed Vrai's presence, she stopped playing imaginary music and located her cane. "Shall we make that shrine now?"

As a child, crossing the creek behind her parents' house, Vrai had been able to hop nimbly from rock to rock. Now, halfway across the day of Skip's funeral, she wasn't sure she'd ever make it to the other side.

"A shrine?" she said to Skip's grieving mother. "Where?"

"Why, in the bookcase. Nancy says you brought some photos. That's a start."

But why start now? Couldn't it wait until after the funeral?

She removed a framed photo from the box on the coffee table. "Here's a picture of Skip and Melody when they were little."

"Which one?" Mrs. Howard didn't even try to look at it.

"They're sitting on a diving board."

"Yes, I always liked that one. What else?"

One by one Vrai described the photographs. To free up a shelf, she took down a leather-bound set of Shakespeare.

"How is it you have our family photos? If you don't mind my asking."

Vrai explained about going to Skip's apartment to check on Cassi.

"So you knew I'd want a shrine." Mrs. Howard seemed pleased. "Were you and Skip dating?"

"No ma'am." Vrai heard her accent returning. "Skip had a girlfriend. Bev. It's possible she'll be at the service this afternoon."

Mrs. Howard had no interest in Bev. "Then what were you doing in Baltimore?"

"Pure coincidence." Vrai tempered this lie with a partial truth. "My husband found work there. He's a photographer." Bob lived and worked in Seattle now. They were still married, still speaking to each other, but neither had yet spoken the word divorce. "I value our family photographs. I thought you might feel the same way about yours."

"Photographs, fine," Mrs. Howard rasped. "What else did you bring?"

Vrai began unwrapping Skip's collection of salt and pepper shakers. Salt and pepper shakers in a shrine? Mrs. Howard wrinkled her nose.

Better than candy bars, Vrai thought but did not say. "They show his wonderful sense of humor."

Mrs. Howard held out her hand.

"This one's Popeye," Vrai said.

Long fingers found the two holes in Popeye's head. "Pepper?"

"Yes ma'am. Here's Olive Oyl. She's the salt."

"Well, I'll be!" Mrs. Howard said, sounding exactly like her long-limbed, slow-talking son, who'd never lost his East Tennessee accent. She inspected each pair—Mickey and Minnie, Rhett and Scarlet, Elvis and Priscilla, Johnny and June Carter Cash, John and Yoko, Sylvester and Tweety—before handing them back. "But you used to date Skip. The two of you went to a dance together."

"Once," Vrai said.

"Poor Skip. He'd wanted to be Laramie's escort that night."

"Poor *Skip*?"

"He had such a crush on Laramie," Mrs. Howard said with a sigh.

Which was exactly why Laramie had asked her brother, Lloyd, to take her. She hadn't wanted to get Skip's hopes up.

"I had a crush on Lloyd," Vrai said.

"Lloyd Eisen? Poor you."

I've been sleeping with Lloyd for several years now, Vrai wanted to shock Mrs. Howard by saying. He's going to divorce his wife after his daughters graduate from college. "We double-dated that night," she said. "The four of us, paired off all wrong. It was weird."

"Skip was in the Army then."

Vrai nodded, then realized it was necessary to speak. "That's right."

"I do wish he'd gone to medical school when he got out. Instead he chose graduate work in chemistry, and then he became a . . ."

"Librarian?" Vrai offered.

"I thought he'd completely lost his mind."

Vrai set the last pair of salt and pepper shakers down hard. "I'm a librarian."

"But, my dear. It's fine for you. Skip's cousin Donald is a doctor, an orthopedist in Chattanooga. Skip was twice as smart as Donny." Mrs. Howard gave each item on the shelf a gentle, welcoming touch. "Skip did seem to enjoy library work, though. He was head of his department." She hesitated. "Do you happen to know? Was he on his lunch hour when the accident occurred?"

If Skip had told his mother about losing his job, she'd forgotten it. "He could've been going for ice cream." Vrai wondered if this might be true. "There's a Baskin-Robbins on the other side of the street."

Mrs. Howard nodded. "That boy did love ice cream."

Vrai removed the last item from the box. "You asked me to bring the newspaper article about the accident."

"I'll read that later," the blind woman said.

Realizing the details of Skip's death might be too painful for his mother, Vrai nearly pocketed the newspaper clipping. But Nancy, having overheard, put down the tray she was carrying and held out her hand. Vrai relinquished the clipping and went to find her coat. Fresh air was what she needed. Several dozen enormous gulps of it.

. . . .

Cassi was so eager to leap out of the car that Vrai had difficulty grabbing the leash. Once she had a good grip, she pulled the dog toward the rear of the house, past a gray Dodge sporting a "Clinton-Gore 92" bumper sticker.

In back of Vrai's parents' old house was a creek, and beyond the creek was a railroad track. Behind the Howards' house was a brick patio, with steps leading down to a tennis court.

A tennis court now in ruins, the red Tennessee clay cracked and uneven, the white chalk lines a distant memory. A roller sat rusting in one corner. The drooping net had gaping holes in it. Vrai remembered the feeling of running on a surface like orange velvet, so soft and smooth that each footprint seemed a pale orange shadow.

As Cassi squatted in the grass beside the chain-link fence, Vrai studied the house next door. Formerly a beautifully proportioned Spanish colonial, a lovely white stucco, Laramie and Lloyd's childhood home had been transformed by its new owners into a mustard-colored monstrosity. It was impossible to locate the window through which Vrai had first seen two teenagers named Skip and Lloyd.

She and Laramie had met the first day of seventh grade, when they chose seats next to each other in Algebra I. A few weeks later, while sitting on her new friend's bedroom rug, Vrai had tried to learn the rules of mahjong, a game at which she would never excel, just as Laramie would never be very good at leaping from rock to rock across a creek.

Through the bedroom windows came the rhythmic sounds of a game of tennis, which continued despite a sudden downpour and rumblings of thunder. The girls got up to close the windows and stayed to watch the endless point being played below. Two boys were swatting a soggy tennis ball back and forth, ignoring the lines on the court and the number of bounces, paying no attention to the flashes of lightning and the pouring rain. They were fourteen and had no fear.

The skinny boy with glasses was Skip Howard. His more muscular opponent was Laramie's brother, Lloyd Eisen.

Like her brother, Laramie had hair and eyes so dark as to be nearly black, but there the resemblance ended. Laramie was not terribly athletic, and she was fair-skinned, with permanently rosy cheeks, as if she'd carelessly slapped on some of her mother's rouge. Laramie always seemed to be either blushing or overexcited, a trait Vrai the redhead shared with her best friend. That and wildly curly hair.

Even after a jagged streak of lightning stitched the dark sky, the boys kept playing. It had become a game of chicken, with neither wanting to be the first to stop.

Skip's little sister came quietly down the Howards' back steps. As if oblivious to the thunderstorm, Melody stood on the patio sucking her thumb and twirling a damp pigtail.

After one last forehand Skip ran to his sister, scooped her up, and carried her inside. The good brother. Keeping Melody safe, at least for the moment, from the harm he must have known would come to her.

Of the five young people that stormy afternoon, three were now dead. A year or so after Melody drowned herself in the Pacific, Laramie and her husband, a Chilean poet, were shot and killed while taking a pre-breakfast stroll on Cape Cod.

Dear, adventuresome, fun-loving Laramie, who, as anyone could have told Skip, was not about to marry the boy next door. Instead of staying in Knoxville and attending the University of Tennessee, as Lloyd and Skip and Vrai had done, Laramie went off to the other UT, in Austin, Texas. After graduation she found a job teaching in Chile, where she fell in love, both with the country and with a poet named Miguel. Many thought Miguel Jose Santiago was destined to win for Chile a third Nobel Prize in Literature, following in the footsteps of Gabriela Mistral and Pablo Neruda.

The assassinations were in retaliation for *Lingering Cries*, Miguel's final book of poetry. Each poem was about a victim of torture. The book was published in the U.S. but not in Chile, the home to which the poet was not permitted to return.

His passport had been stamped *Listado*. He and Laramie were on Pinochet's list.

. . . .

After college, Laramie had moved to another continent, another hemisphere. Vrai had ventured only two states away, to Ohio. At first proud of the fact that she was one of the few art history majors in her graduating class to have found a job in art, she soon realized that her responsibilities at the High Street Gallery, in Columbus, consisted of little more than answering the phone and running errands. OSU was UT on a slightly larger scale, exhibiting the same football mania in the fall. She missed the Smoky Mountains.

Then, one morning in December, as she was walking to work in the snow, a man took her picture. "Red on White on High" he planned to call it. Asking her permission beforehand, while admittedly the courteous thing to do, would have been, he explained, artistically self-defeating.

His name was Bob Lynde. Age twenty-four, with laugh lines accentuating his violet-blue eyes. An OSU freshman planning to major in physics. To make up for five years of Army haircuts, he was letting his hair grow.

Six months later, in 1969, Vrai became a June bride.

When developed, "Red on White on High" proved to be out of focus. The photographer figured out what he'd done wrong. Bob Lynde hardly ever made the same mistake twice. It was one of his most reliable qualities.

In September of 1986 Bob took time off from his new job in Seattle to stay with their two boys in Baltimore while Vrai flew off for a week in Spain. She'd traveled solo, intentionally out of touch while moving from hostel to hostel, hoping the varied art and architecture of sunny Iberia would temporarily obliterate the signs that her marriage was unraveling.

She'd been in her job as art history librarian for nearly three years by then. It was the ideal job for her. The boys, too, were happy in Baltimore. She and Bob had bought a large row house. Why move again so soon? And so very far away? Vrai didn't think Bob had exhausted the local job possibilities. Washington, DC, would've been far preferable to Washington state.

Was she being selfish and unreasonable? she kept asking herself in Spain. Which was more important, her marriage or her job? Did she have to choose? Was there a way to keep them both? She planned to have a long talk with Bob when she returned. If they still loved each other, then surely they could work things out.

By the time Bob met her at the airport, Laramie and Miguel had already been buried, in a cemetery near Boston. After learning of their deaths from Skip, Bob had tried, without success, to get a message to Vrai.

Travel-weary, she didn't understand the first time Bob told her. Very gently, before exiting the airport parking garage, he told her again. She still couldn't believe what she was hearing. "Laramie was shot dead," Bob said finally, and Vrai punched him in the arm.

Later that week Skip came to her office to tell her about the funeral. She didn't want to listen, and as it turned out, she didn't have to. Skip broke down and couldn't continue. Laramie had been Vrai's best friend, not Skip's, but it was Vrai who comforted him that day. They stood with their arms around each other—Skip sobbing, Vrai patting him on the back—in full view of anyone on the other side of the glass partition between her office and the library tables and shelving.

It had happened on a beach near Laramie's parents' summer home on Cape Cod. Multiple shots were fired from a boat which then sped off, leaving Laramie and Miguel dead on the sand and orphaning their almost four-year-old son.

From her trip diary Vrai determined she'd been in the Prado at the time. That she had not felt so much as a twinge still bothered her. Somehow she should have known.

She'd vowed to go to Chile and hunt down the killers. Librarians were skilled at locating information. She would brush up on her high-school Spanish well enough to conduct interviews. Those responsible would be identified and brought to justice.

And what had she done so far? On the question of justice for Laramie Eisen Santiago, her oldest and dearest friend, Vraiment Stevens Lynde had done absolutely *nada*.

chapter 3

❆ ❆ ❆

*a*s Cassi pulled Vrai toward the driveway, a blue BMW like Lloyd's appeared. It *was* Lloyd's. He was driving.

Vrai was treated to a second taste of the cornbread muffins. Lloyd was the first person she'd called after learning of Skip's death. In subsequent phone conversations he'd urged her not to come to Knoxville, warning that he wouldn't be able to talk to her at the funeral, not with Marianne by his side. "I'm no good at deception," he'd claimed, "and neither are you."

The BMW came to a stop in front of the Eisens' old house. Lloyd said something to the woman behind him, who rolled down her window, as if that might somehow erase the ill-considered changes and return the Spanish stucco to its former beauty. Vrai hadn't seen Marianne since high school but recognized her instantly.

The young boy in the passenger seat had to be Jonathan Santiago, Laramie and Miguel's child. Ten years old now, he lived with his aunt and uncle in Asheville, North

Carolina. Lloyd had argued against bringing the boy along—Jonathan had never even met Skip—but Marianne thought a funeral might help Jonathan to accept his parents' deaths, or some such nonsense. Obviously Marianne had prevailed.

After Laramie and Miguel were killed, Vrai had wanted to take Jonathan in herself but had been reluctant to offer. She wasn't a relative, and she and Bob no longer lived together. Lloyd and Marianne seemed the perfect couple, high-school sweethearts whose marriage had lasted. When her affair with Lloyd began, Vrai let herself dream. Soon she'd be sharing a house with Lloyd and his nephew. Baltimore? Asheville? They'd work it out.

Jonathan's cousins, two girls, were eleven and thirteen when he moved in. According to Lloyd, Marianne resented having to care for a young child again, especially a headstrong boy with "adjustment problems." As a result, she'd gained weight (blimped up, was how Lloyd put it) and lost all interest in sex.

Was referring to his wife as a blimp unkind? Of course it was. Did Vrai feel a guilty sort of glee upon learning that tiny little Marianne Cox had turned into a middle-aged roly-poly? Yes, indeed. Even good-hearted Laramie had disliked Marianne.

Unwilling to face Lloyd just yet, Vrai tugged hard on Cassi's leash and retreated to the patio, from which steps led up to Mrs. Howard's back door. Nancy heard Vrai knocking and let them in.

Cassi, her toenails clicking on the kitchen floor, sniffed at Nancy's stockinged legs, then jumped up and pawed at her skirt. Nancy responded by giving the dog a swift kick in the chest.

"Oh, don't hurt her," Vrai protested, tightening the leash, but Cassi seemed more chastened than injured. "Is that your Dodge outside?"

Nancy's eyes went wide. "The doctor rammed my car?"

"The orthopedist from Chattanooga? Where is he?"

"At the airport. His wife and daughters were off in the Bahamas. They'd be safer in a taxi cab. That man's a terrible driver."

"Your car's fine," Vrai said. "I noticed your bumper sticker. I voted for Clinton, too." It took courage to be openly Democratic in Knoxville.

"Good for us." Nancy smiled, then shook her head. "Mrs. Howard wouldn't even vote. I offered to take her. Wouldn't even let me send for an absentee ballot."

"I need to get the dog food from my car." Vrai waited a beat, hoping Nancy would offer to go instead. Lloyd might give Nancy a friendly wave. "Could you watch Cassi?"

Nancy backed away.

"Skip really loved this dog," Vrai said.

"Doesn't mean I have to love it, too." Reluctantly, Nancy took the leash.

. . . .

At the front door Vrai hesitated. A part of her hoped Lloyd would be gone. A less cowardly part wanted to give him fair warning. Despite his objections, she would be at Skip's funeral.

She stepped over to the mirror above the hall table and tried to tame her wild hair. My Pre-Raphaelite beauty, her husband used to call her. She didn't consider herself beautiful. Her one good feature? Hemlock-green eyes.

The BMW hadn't moved. Marianne, her chin in the air, continued to peer out the back window. Her hair was still blond, cut short and swept back. In high school, where petite Marianne had had to look up at nearly everyone, she'd somehow managed to look down her nose at most of the world. This imperious demeanor had not changed.

Little Miss Perfect, Laramie had dubbed her.

As Vrai headed toward her own car, Lloyd exited his. Perhaps blinded by the hideous additions to his former home, he didn't seem to have noticed the white Toyota with Maryland license plates parked next door.

One of the hideous additions, Vrai realized with a start, was a garden with a poignantly familiar design. Yes, Luther Stevens himself had laid out those pathways, built the brick walls, and planted the boxwoods.

Rule number one at Stevens Landscaping: a garden should be in harmony with its house. Vrai remembered the gardens she'd seen in Spain, the enclosed patios, the tiled pools and fountains, the large pots of brightly colored geraniums against white walls, the graceful Moorish arches, the eucalyptus and cypress and oleander. Her father had surely made similar suggestions, had tried, in his gentle way, to persuade the new owners toward harmony. She imagined his fatalistic shrug, his wry smile at his rule number two: the customer is the boss, and the boss is always right.

Now Lloyd was coming up his old driveway. Vrai wished she had a camera with which to record his expression the instant he became aware of her. It would be a moment of deep truth, a revelation of his innermost feelings.

But at that exact moment a car door slammed, and Lloyd, his face wild with panic, turned toward the street. Jonathan, his shoes untied, came stumbling up the driveway. His sport coat was several sizes too small, and his slacks barely met the tops of his socks.

Why hadn't Marianne bought some new clothes for her nephew before dragging him across the mountains to a funeral? Lloyd, in a dark gray suit, looked as dapper as ever. He'd once been mistaken at an airport for Arnold Schwarzenegger.

"I thought I told you to stay in the car," Lloyd snapped. He raised his palm, a sign to his wife that he would handle this. He had everything under control.

"I want to see, too," Jonathan said. "Isn't this where my mother used to live?"

A grassy strip between the two driveways separated Vrai from Lloyd and the boy.

As she started toward them, Lloyd gave a barely perceptible shake of his head. No. But she disobeyed him, just as his nephew had done. Like Jonathan, she simply couldn't help it. She crossed the grass, leaned down, and offered the boy her hand. "You must be Jonathan. Your mother was my very best friend. I haven't seen you since you were a baby."

His handshake was firm, his voice solemn. "I've grown up."

"You sure have. My name's Vrai."

He had Miguel's straight black hair and high cheekbones, but his dark eyes were Laramie's—animated and mercurial, with a magnetic pull that made it difficult to turn away. Vrai had to blink to keep her own eyes from tearing up.

Jonathan let go of her hand. "This is my Uncle Lloyd," he said.

"Your mother's brother. Yes, I remember him."

Hello, Vrai. An easy thing to say, a matter of simple courtesy, on a day for simple courtesies, but Lloyd didn't oblige. He'd asked her not to come to Knoxville, but here she was, and he was furious.

"I guess you're in town for Skip's funeral," Vrai said to him.

Lloyd dipped his head ever so slightly in the direction of the BMW. "Didn't expect to see you here." He turned away. The conversation was over. To Jonathan he said, "Let's go knock on their door. Maybe they'll let us see how they've butchered the inside."

Vrai marched to her car and yanked open the back door. Her hands were shaking, her heart pounding. She had perfectly valid reasons for attending Skip's funeral. There would be consequences, though. With Lloyd, there were always consequences.

Next to the bag of dog food was Skip's computer. She'd taken it yesterday morning on impulse, intending to look through his files for any sort of hint that might explain his oddly accidental death. But after the long drive with hyperactive Cassi, she'd been too tired to do anything more than check into a motel and call Mrs. Howard. This morning she hadn't even had time for a cup of coffee.

. . . .

Mrs. Howard and Nancy were on the couch holding hands, their eyes closed in prayer. Cassi, dozing beside the harp, raised her head when Vrai came in, then laid it back down as if drugged.

"I will fear no evil," Nancy was saying.

Vrai waited until they were finished. "So sorry to interrupt. I just wanted to say good-bye. I've left Cassi's bowls and a bag of dog food in the kitchen." She took Mrs. Howard's hand. It was warmer than her own.

"Aren't you coming to the service?" Mrs. Howard rasped.

"Of course I am. I'll be there."

"You driving back tonight?" Nancy said. "There's a big storm on the way."

Bad weather was the least of Vrai's worries. Lloyd's presence was far more unsettling, something she felt a strong need to confide. "Lloyd Eisen's here."

"Don't let that boy in my house." Mrs. Howard was vehement. "I don't care if he *was* Skip's friend."

Was she still angry about a boyhood prank? Years ago, at a Boy Scout cookout, Lloyd had set Skip's hair on fire with a flaming marshmallow that left a permanent scar, but Lloyd was also the one who'd grabbed a canteen and put the fire out.

"He's next door, inspecting his old house," Vrai said. "You don't like Lloyd?"

"I never trusted him," Mrs. Howard said, and Nancy nodded in agreement. "Laramie now, she was a dear, the complete opposite of her brother." She let out a sigh. "Life is so unfair."

Vrai leaned down and patted the top of Cassi's head. Leaving the dog with Mrs. Howard seemed wrong. What would Skip have wanted?

"Good-bye," she said to Cassi.

"Good-bye," Mrs. Howard replied.

Nancy pointed to a pocketbook under the coffee table.

"Thanks," Vrai said, "I'll need that."

The BMW with North Carolina license plates was gone. Under an ominous sky, dozens of purple crocuses dotted the Howards' lawn.

chapter 4

❄ ❄ ❄

Extra rows of folding chairs had been set up to accommodate the overflow crowd at Jordan Funeral Home. Vrai took an aisle seat toward the back, planning to hit the road as soon as the service was over. To keep from looking around for Lloyd, whose BMW occupied a prime parking space outside, she concentrated on the orange-and-white scarf (UT's team colors) wound around the neck of the woman in front of her.

A dark suit appeared beside her chair. Not Lloyd. Not his hands. She moved her knees to the side, so the man could get past, but he wasn't looking for a seat. The deep voice, proclaiming he would've recognized that red hair anywhere, belonged to Bill Carr. In high school he'd been chubby and defiant. Thirty years later this trimmed-down, balding Methodist minister projected the air of a calm believer.

Vrai stood up. They shook hands. Bill suggested she might prefer a seat near the front, then asked her married name. His voice was soothing, persuasive. She let herself be shown to the last available seat in the fourth row, where she sat down feeling trapped.

A woman led her husband and son to empty spaces in the front row. Her husband, yes, Vrai realized, but the boy was Marianne's poorly dressed nephew.

Bill Carr had changed drastically since high school, but Mrs. Lloyd Eisen was still tiny, still slim and trim and cute as a button. For Vrai the sensation was like stepping down hard on a nonexistent stair, that sinking, foolish feeling in the pit of the stomach, like the moment of realization that it's not your train that's moving, silly goose, it's the train beside you.

Lloyd, Lloyd, pants on fire.

Marianne was wearing a navy blue knit dress with a checked bolero jacket. The dress fit her snugly, revealing a total absence of extra pounds. She was beautiful, a successful woman who owned a travel agency and conducted tours, twice a year, to France. In the basement of her home in Asheville was a wine cellar stocked with the French wines she'd begun importing.

During her one visit to Lloyd's house, Vrai had drunk some of Marianne's cabernet sauvignon. It was good.

That was the night Lloyd cajoled her into having sex outside on the patio, in the hammock, claiming he wasn't the least bit worried about what the neighbors might see or hear. All he cared about was having sex with her under the stars. Something his wife, even in her good days, had refused to consider.

As Marianne's trim butt took a front row seat for Skip's service, the back of Lloyd's neck turned a guilty crimson. So he'd noticed where Vrai was sitting.

Lloyd was far too modest. He was actually quite good at deception. The bullshit king of deceit.

Bill Carr walked over to speak to them, and Lloyd, his head down, slunk off with Marianne and Jonathan to search for different seats. Soon Nancy guided Mrs. Howard toward the recently vacated spaces. A couple with three teenage daughters squeezed in beside them.

Reverend Carr stepped up to the lectern and, in a singsong voice, began enumerating Skip's stellar qualities. The world's last honest man. An unwavering faith in the ultimate power of truth. A scholar who chose to serve. A trusted friend, a kind and generous colleague. His life cut short by a tragic accident.

Vrai was barely listening. She longed to tell Skip how sorry she was. Sorry he'd lost his job. Sorry they'd quarreled at his Halloween party. Sorry she hadn't found the right words that night to convince him that she had indeed kept Melody's suicide a secret. Most of all, she was sorry he was dead. She'd always hoped they would run into each other, at just the right moment, and be able to talk things over, forgive and forget.

There were so many memories. The two of them hugging and crying in her office in Baltimore after Laramie was killed. The one kiss they'd shared, here in Knoxville, the night poor Skip had been her date, not Laramie's.

That was the night of the dance at the country club, the big event Laramie had refused to attend unless her best friend, whose parents weren't members, could come, too. The Eisens pulled some strings, and Vrai received an invitation. Skip and Lloyd, who were stationed at Fort Campbell, drove down from Kentucky for an evening of escort duty.

Where was Marianne that night? In France, *peut-être*, where she'd spent her junior year of college.

The four of them—Lloyd and Laramie in the front seat, Vrai and Skip in the back—had arrived at the country club in Lloyd's Pontiac. Males on the left side of the car, females on the right, and nobody saying a word.

Halfway through the evening Lloyd steered Vrai outside, through French doors, to a tiled terrace overlooking the Tennessee River. From the ballroom came the band's rendition of "Only You." Lloyd, tan and handsome in his Army uniform, his dress blues, took her in his arms, and they danced slowly, slowly in the soft night air—the only couple under the stars.

"If you weren't such good friends with my sister, I'd have asked you out long ago," Lloyd whispered, his lips moving against her forehead, his fingers tickling her bare back before slipping under the elastic of her strapless bra.

Skip was also in dress blues that night, also bound for Viet Nam. He found them on the terrace and tried to cut in, but Lloyd twirled Vrai away, saying, "Go dance with my sister. Everyone else is. Your date wants to dance with me."

"Do you, Vrai?" Skip persisted.

Vrai nodded. "I do."

Skip marched off to find his true love, his spit-shined Army shoes clicking on the terrace tiles. But he soon returned, with Laramie in tow, both of them determined to save Vrai from Lloyd and Lloyd from his horny self.

"Follow me," Lloyd whispered. He danced Vrai over to the edge of the terrace, sat down on the stone wall, and pulled her down beside him. River smells mixed with the fragrance of honeysuckle.

"Lloyd," Laramie said, her satin dress glowing in the moonlight, "may I have this dance?"

Lloyd took Laramie's hand, but he didn't stand up, didn't loosen his grip on Vrai. Skip grabbed Vrai's free hand. Lloyd and Vrai were then pulled to their feet, and Laramie and Skip completed the circle by taking each other's hands.

Laramie let out a hoot of laughter, victorious and forgiving. "You put your right foot in. You put your right foot out." The rest of them joined in. "You put your right foot in, and you shake it all about."

A complicated circle of friendship, mismatched siblings, and unrequited love.

Vrai couldn't remember leaving the dance, or switching cars, but they must have done both, because Skip drove her home in his father's Renault. She had to give him directions to Mudlark Street. The perfect gentleman, he got out of the car and came around to open her door.

As he escorted her up the front walk, his hand cupping her elbow, questions flickered in the air like heat lightning. Was Skip going to kiss his date goodnight? Would she kiss him back?

He did. She did. Each of them kissing someone else. Neither caring that the other one knew this.

. . . .

There was a chord change in Bill Carr's intonation, a shift upward to a new key. The just world we all believed in when we were growing up together. His missionary work in Latin America. A belief that the good people in our lives never leave us. They live on in us. Our memories of them will shape our own lives as we carry on for them, try to stand where they stood.

"The dead never leave us," he proclaimed.

While Bill described a custom he'd observed at funerals in Central America, Vrai concentrated on the display of flowers behind the lectern. Hundreds of flowers. Everyone had loved Skip.

To her long black skirt and white blouse, Mrs. Howard had added a black velvet jacket. Concert attire. She was playing an imaginary harp, her arms stretched forward, her long fingers active.

Bill called her name first. "Clara Swann Howard."

Mrs. Howard settled her hands in her lap. "*Presente.*"

"Dr. Henry Donald Swann."

"*Presente*," said Skip's cousin the orthopedist. As did his wife and daughters.

"Nancy Morris."

"*Presente*," Nancy said.

"Vraiment Stevens Lynde."

Surprised to hear her name, Vrai managed to respond, "*Presente*." Confused, thinking her husband was beside her, she expected to hear Bob's name, too. If Skip was able to see her with that third eye of his, what must he be thinking?

Was Bev here? Her name should be next.

Bill paused. "Skip Howard."

"*Presente!*" responded the mourners, joyously hopeful, and Vrai felt a prickle of déjà vu.

"Dr. Jasper P. Howard, Sr."

"*Presente*."

"Melody Howard."

"*Presente*."

"Laramie Eisen Santiago."

"*Presente*."

Tears stung Vrai's eyes.

. . . .

The center aisle was clogged with people waiting to speak to Mrs. Howard, who remained seated. Vrai made her way to a side aisle and looked around for Bev. Had she and Skip broken up? Even so, wouldn't Bev have wanted to be at his funeral?

The noise rivaled that of a cocktail party. Vrai was nearing an exit door when she was accosted by Mrs. McLean, the high school art teacher, who seemed pleased to hear about Vrai's position as art history librarian but confused by the fact that she and Skip had worked in the same library. Vrai managed to extricate herself by saying she hoped to get as far as Roanoke tonight.

Roanoke was halfway home. Halfway to where she could lock all the doors and pretend she was safe. Spend hours alone in a quiet room figuring out what to do and how to feel. About Skip, yes, but also about Lloyd.

The ladies' room was at the end of a carpeted hallway. Just inside the door, combing her hair in front of a mirror, stood a small woman in a navy blue dress.

Vrai considered leaving, stopping at a gas station instead. But she was strangely fascinated by Marianne, who turned around, comb in hand.

"You were at the Howards' this morning." Marianne's smile seemed genuine.

Vrai nodded, too tongue-tied to speak. She'd always been jealous of Marianne. Now, in addition, she felt an uncomfortable mixture of guilt and pity.

"I'm sorry." Marianne turned back to the mirror. "I remember your face but not your name. It's a dreadful failing of mine."

"Vrai Lynde. I was Vrai Stevens in high school."

"Laramie's friend. Of course!" Marianne said to the mirror. "That's how you knew Jon." She didn't provide her own name, expected Vrai to know who she was. "Are you still here in Knoxville?"

A stall door opened, and Vrai moved forward in line. "Baltimore. Skip and I worked in the same library. I brought some of his things down to Mrs. Howard."

"I just can't believe he's gone." Marianne checked her mascara. "So you live in Baltimore, too? Lloyd visited Skip in Baltimore, several times."

Lloyd visited Skip once, Vrai wanted to say; the other times he stayed with me. But mostly we met in DC. And remember parents' weekend at your daughters' college? I drove down to Virginia and checked into a motel. Didn't you wonder why Lloyd was so late returning from his morning run that Sunday? But here's the worst of it. He told me horrid lies about you.

"Lloyd seems the same," Vrai said.

Marianne returned her comb to her purse and stepped back, patting her hair. She turned her small face up to Vrai. "Lloyd *is* the same. Still a teenager, in many ways. You know?"

Yes. Vrai did know. "Jonathan's been with you for a while now. How's that going?"

"Little girls are so much easier!" Marianne rolled her eyes. "It's been seven years, but Jon still misses his parents. I thought attending another funeral might help him to find closure."

Maybe he's not looking for it, Vrai had to stop herself from saying.

A frustrated sigh escaped from Marianne's recently colored lips. "I even bought him a new suit and shoes to wear. What he did with them is anyone's guess. Boys!"

Vrai nodded. "I have two of them." Neither of whom she had ever forced to attend a funeral.

Marianne shrugged her tiny shoulders. "Well, Lloyd will be wondering where I am. Nice to see you again, Fay."

Vrai was grateful when it was her turn to lock herself in a stall. Once seated, she searched through her pocketbook for deodorant (Cinnamon Stick, from the health food store, non-irritating to a redhead's sensitive skin but also not very long-lasting). Marianne had made her sweat.

She was determined not to cry, not here, where crying was such a cliché. She would not do it.

But the tears arrived from somewhere. Again she searched her pocketbook, this time for sunglasses, which weren't there. At the basin she splashed water on her crimson cheeks, her puffy eyes.

chapter 5

❋ ❋ ❋

Newly mulched flowerbeds bordered the curved sidewalk at the funeral home's entrance. Yellow jonquils, their star-shaped saucers holding tiny cups, seemed to glow beneath a dark and threatening sky. Vrai paused under the portico to button her black wool coat, bought years ago on sale and now snug through the chest. Winter, like the day of Skip's funeral, was not yet over.

The BMW, she was relieved to see, was gone. But there on the curb beside the empty parking space sat a young boy with black hair.

She hurried down the sidewalk. "Where are your parents?" she asked in alarm, then corrected herself. "Where are Lloyd and Marianne?"

"Dunno," Jonathan said with a shrug.

"You mean they drove off without you?"

He nodded. "You been crying? I didn't cry. I think she wanted me to, but oh well."

"I knew Skip." That her tears weren't entirely for Skip would remain her secret.

In a large family a child could be left behind inadvertently, but this had to be deliberate. She sat down beside him. "They're coming back for you, right?"

Jonathan's black eyes sparkled. Laramie's eyes, drawing her in. "I didn't want to come to the stupid funeral. I had a soccer game today." He'd exchanged his sport coat for a thin blue windbreaker that fit him, but he wasn't wearing any shoes. "I called her a bitch."

"Marianne? Just now? That's why they left?"

"Happens all the time. Them leaving, I mean."

Short blond hairs clung to Vrai's coat. Had she done the right thing by leaving Cassi with Mrs. Howard? "*Is she a bitch?*"

"She wanted me to ride in back. She knows I get carsick, especially in the mountains." His voice rose. "She keeps calling me Jon. My name is Jonathan. I've told her and told her. A john is what you flush stuff down."

"I like the name Jonathan." Vrai noticed white flecks on the black wool. Did Cassi have dandruff? "Can I wait here with you till we see their car?"

"They were pretty mad," Jonathan said. "Uncle Lloyd got all red in the face."

The flecks on her coat disappeared. New ones took their place. The sky was a thick fleece blanket patterned in camouflage gray. Snow clouds. "Think it might be a good idea to zip your jacket?"

Jonathan complied.

It was nearly four o'clock. She needed to get going. In

good weather it was a five-hour drive to Roanoke. But she couldn't leave an abandoned, shoeless, ten-year-old boy in a funeral home parking lot when it was starting to snow. She was, after all, a responsible mother with sons of her own.

Jonathan licked a snowflake off his wrist.

"Let's wait in my car," she said.

They made an odd pair, Vrai in heels, Jonathan sock-footed, as they crossed the parking lot. She unlocked the passenger door, and he hopped in, Miguel in miniature except for those heart-stopping eyes.

"Why is it called a funeral *home*?" Jonathan said. "Isn't a home where people *live*?"

"Good point." She started the engine to give them some heat. "I never thought of it that way before. I don't know why. Some advice, please. I can't leave you here. I can't take you with me."

"Where you going?"

"I was planning to spend the night in Roanoke. I live in Baltimore. Roanoke's about halfway."

"I've never been to Baltimore," he said, his eyes alert and excited, ready for adventure.

Vrai ignored this.

"Never been to Roanoke, either," he said quickly. "Virginia, right?"

"Where *are* they?" Vrai couldn't hide her impatience.

"Honestly," Jonathan said, "I have no idea."

"Do they do this often?"

"Is the Pope Catholic?"

Vrai burst out laughing. It was one of Lloyd's favorite expressions.

"It's stupid, really," Jonathan said. "They think they're teaching me some sort of lesson, but I'm always glad to see them go. If I had a dime for every time they've driven off like this, I could buy a ticket to the World Cup. Know where it'll be played next summer? The Rose Bowl. I sure wish I could go. I bet Pelé will be there."

"But they come back for you?"

"Last summer they left me outside a shopping mall. I snuck in and saw *Thelma & Louise*."

"No!"

"Not the whole movie," Jonathan said. "I didn't stay to see the beginning. I already knew they drove off a cliff. I guess they didn't want to get shot to smithereens like Butch and Sundance. But it was a crummy ending. They didn't need to die."

Nor did his parents. "The movie theater was in Asheville?"

Jonathan nodded.

"How did you get home?"

"Walked."

Lloyd was, in many ways, a jerk, but he loved his nephew. Teaching the boy a lesson by abandoning him had to be one of Marianne's misguided ideas.

"So, you play soccer?" Vrai said.

"Soccer's in my blood. My Uncle Enrique played World Cup for Chile. My dad met Pelé once."

"I know."

"You do?" Jonathan sounded hurt. This was his story, and he wanted to tell it.

"I think your dad mentioned it in one of his poems. But I don't remember the details."

"Well, I do." Jonathan narrated the tale with enthusiasm. "The World Cup was in Chile that year. My father was in this big room under the stadium, where only players and their families could go, and Pelé came in. He was limping, and very sad, because he couldn't play for his country. He introduced himself to my father. Everyone knows Pelé. He doesn't have to tell people who he is."

Had he read Miguel's poems? Wasn't ten a little young to be reading about torture? "I saw Pelé play once," she said.

"You did?" Jonathan was impressed. "Where?"

"At RFK Stadium in Washington, when he was playing for the New York Cosmos. Even from where we were sitting, which was very high up, you could tell he was an extraordinary person."

"Did the Cosmos win?"

Vrai didn't remember. "I'm sure they did."

"Did Pelé score?"

Vrai couldn't remember this either. "Twice," she said.

"All *right*!" He whistled. "You. Actually. Saw. Pelé. Score."

The snowflakes were small and serious. A fair punishment for their barbaric child-rearing practices would be for Lloyd and Marianne, if and when they returned, to become panicked about Jonathan's whereabouts.

"I must have left my sunglasses at the motel where I stayed last night," Vrai said. "It's just up the street."

Jonathan scrambled to fasten his seat belt.

"I'm sure they'll be here waiting for you when we come back," she said.

"Wanna bet?"

The cleaning staff had gone home for the day. The friendly woman in the motel office wrote down Vrai's name and address and promised to ask about the sunglasses and put them in the mail if they showed up. A total stranger, but Vrai knew this woman would keep her word.

Lloyd was no stranger. What a fool she'd been to trust him.

She dreaded another encounter with still-petite Marianne. This time, with Lloyd listening, Vrai might reveal the ugly truth. *He told me you were fat and frigid. He thought I'd sleep with him then, and you know what? He was right.*

But back at the funeral home, there was no sign of the BMW. The snow was tapering off.

"I'm going inside to ask if anyone's been looking for you," Vrai said. "Mind waiting here, in case they drive up?"

"Waste of time," Jonathan said.

And he was right. No one had reported a missing boy. Vrai left Jonathan's name, and hers, and said she'd check back later.

To Jonathan she said, "I grew up not far from here.

Our house has been torn down, but I'm kinda curious to see what that area looks like now."

"Then we'll go to Roanoke?"

"Then we'll come back here." She would give his irresponsible guardians one more chance to redeem themselves. Clearly, Laramie's child deserved a more loving home.

Less than a mile from the funeral home, she made the familiar turn off Kingston Pike. At the railroad tracks she slowed down. "When I was your age, we'd put pennies on the rails."

"What for?"

"A train comes by, and the pennies get mashed flat. They're warm when you pick them up."

"Cool," Jonathan said.

"You have to be very careful."

"Well, duh."

Beyond a new bowling alley, the road widened to four freshly paved lanes. Mudlark Street had a shiny new sign, but its name was all Vrai recognized. She drove to the end of the street and turned around. Even the ancient maple in her parents' front yard was gone. Without the tree, it was impossible to get her bearings.

She pulled into a Jiffy Mart and parked beside a plumber's van. "This might be where I used to live." Her entire childhood had vanished.

"Wow," Jonathan said. "Did you get free Cokes and stuff?"

Next door was Antique City, a one-story building

with a wraparound porch on which rocking chairs were displayed. If her house had been replaced by the Jiffy Mart, then Antique City must be in the field where Mr. Boyd had kept his goats.

"Think they sell chocolate milkshakes here?" Jonathan asked.

"I doubt it. We passed a McDonald's on Kingston Pike."

"Those are fake shakes."

Lloyd's exact words. "Let's go inside and see what they do have."

Shoes and shirts were required. In the Toyota's trunk, in a box of things destined for Goodwill, she found a pair of boys' hockey skates.

"Too big," Jonathan pronounced.

Vrai laced them up anyway. "See if you can walk."

Jonathan had trouble standing, never mind walking, but she helped him wobble into the Jiffy Mart, where a familiar green-and-white box caught her eye. It had been years since she'd tasted a Krispy Kreme. She and Laramie had wolfed the doughnuts down, a dozen at a time.

From a pile of half-price orange sweatshirts Vrai selected the smallest one. Fuzzy white letters said GO VOLS. "The University of Tennessee Volunteers. This is Big Orange country. Want to try it on? That jacket doesn't look very warm."

"I don't have any money," Jonathan said.

"My treat."

She rolled up the sleeves so that his hands were visible.

"Your mother went to another UT, but the team colors in Texas are also orange and white."

Vrai set their purchases on the counter. "How long has this store been here?" she asked the cashier.

"No idea." The girl had small mean eyes. "This all?"

"Plus the sweatshirt he's wearing." Vrai felt around in her pocketbook for her wallet. "Is there a creek out back?"

"No idea." The girl yawned.

"No brain, either," Jonathan whispered.

Vrai pulled out her sunglasses and waved them around, as if they explained her laughter. "Thank goodness. I'll have to call the motel."

"Twenty-three sixty-four." The girl wanted them to pay up and leave. "Out of thirty. Six thirty-six is your change." Her voice rose proudly, as though she'd done the math herself. "Have a nice day."

It took two trips to get first Jonathan and then their food into the car. Vrai opened the box of doughnuts, inhaled the heavenly aroma.

"Are your mother and father dead, too?" Jonathan said.

"They live in Florida now," she said gently. Marianne should be reported, to someone, for forcing an orphan to attend a funeral. Why had Lloyd acquiesced? What was wrong with them?

"So they got a new house?"

"More like a mobile home, except that they've added on to it so much it can't go anywhere." Luther Stevens had wanted at least ten acres in a location where he could garden year-round. "My father took his rosebushes with him. He has roses there that used to grow here." Also sunflowers nearly twice as tall as he was, twenty varieties of tulips, plus exotic melons and squash. He'd become a fixture at the local farmers' market.

"My father grew goldfish," Jonathan said, his mouth full of popcorn. "They were tiny when he brought them home, but they kept getting bigger and bigger, so I helped him build a goldfish pond."

Vrai was surprised he could remember this. She devoured another doughnut, finished her coffee, and, feeling fortified, headed back to Kingston Pike.

. . . .

The only vehicle in the funeral home's parking lot was not a BMW. Vrai pulled up beside the woman who was unlocking the car door. "I spoke to you earlier, remember?"

"The lost boy," the woman said. "No one called. When did you see him last?"

"I'm not the one who lost him," Vrai said. "I'm the one who found him. He's right here."

"Have you tried calling his parents?"

"They're not home," Vrai said quickly. "He lives in Asheville."

"I see. What you should do then is contact the police. I'm sorry I can't be of more help." The woman got into her car and drove off.

It was snowing again. Lloyd and Marianne had been gone for over an hour. The only way Vrai could get in touch with Lloyd was by calling his work number.

One thing she knew for sure: the last place Jonathan belonged was in a police station.

She could take him back to the motel, check in, and spend the night there, but what would that accomplish?

Nor did she feel like driving him to Asheville and staying there with him until Lloyd and Marianne decided to show up.

If they'd been in an accident, then wouldn't one of them have called the funeral home to say there was a little boy sitting outside on the curb?

Was there any point in bothering Mrs. Howard with this relatively minor dilemma? Vrai couldn't think of one.

What would Laramie want her to do?

"Let's go on to Roanoke," she said. "I'll call Lloyd's voice mail and tell him you're safe. Wherever he is, I know he's worried sick about you."

"They don't give a shit about me."

Vrai was beginning to believe this was true. "That's not so. Of course they care. There's been a mistake, that's all. Some sort of terrible mix-up."

"What's your name?"

"Vraiment Lynde." She turned toward him. "I'm sorry. I should have introduced myself again. Everyone calls me Vrai."

"It's a funny name."

"*Vraiment* is French." She exited the parking lot. "It means really. If you told me, in French, that you were going to the World Cup, I'd say, *Vraiment*?" Her parents had honeymooned in Quebec and, even now, enjoyed speaking French to each other. "It's a girl," her father had informed her mother after the anesthesia wore off. "*Vraiment*?" her mother replied. "Vraiment," her father agreed, and that was that.

The peculiar origins of their names was something Vrai and Laramie had had in common. Laramie had been conceived while her parents were vacationing in a certain town in Wyoming.

"Vrai." Jonathan tried it out. "Is that your computer in back?"

"It's Skip's." She made the turn onto Kingston Pike.

"So. You're stealing it."

"No, I'm planning to take it back. That's not stealing, is it?"

"I was just wondering." Jonathan's voice softened. "Does it have any games on it?"

He was like her younger son Robbie at this age. "I don't know," she said. "Do you like computer games?"

"When I can play them, yeah. But she won't let me have a computer."

Vrai was too busy trying to follow the signs for I-40 to respond. She made a turn onto Northshore Drive. Or was this Papermill? She knew where she was but felt completely lost.

It seemed she was being offered a choice, but she wasn't. I-40 was also I-75, at least for the moment. The two were one. She would be heading east toward Asheville and also north toward Lexington. A logical impossibility, but she merged with hundreds of other cars whose drivers had made the same decision. Were any of them rescuing a child who'd been stuffed into clothes that didn't fit, brought to a funeral against his will, and then abandoned with no shoes?

What was the difference between rescuing and kidnapping? As soon as she stopped for gas, she'd leave Lloyd a message. She had Jonathan. He was being properly cared for.

"Your mother and I used to ride horses on I-40," she said. "West of here, when it was only a roadbed, and all the farmers' fences had come down. On Sunday afternoons we'd pay the stable two dollars, for a two-hour ride, and we'd take our horses out along the roadbed, then turn them around and let them *fly* back to the barn. Man, that was fun!"

"*Santiago!*" Jonathan shouted it.

Vrai was so startled she let go of the steering wheel. "Please. Don't. Yell."

"Sorry. Spanish soldiers do that when they ride into battle. That's what my teacher says."

She glanced over at him. "Promise me. No more battle cries."

Jonathan gave her a small salute. "How much further?"

"To Roanoke? Five hours, if we're lucky." I-75 had split off. They were on I-40 only, heading east. Signs enumerated the declining distance to Asheville.

"What kind of accident was Skip in?"

"He was hit by a car."

"Was he jaywalking?"

"I'm not sure," Vrai said. "Could we talk about something else please?"

It was a while before Jonathan spoke again. "I'm going to join Interpol, soon as I'm old enough. I want to know who killed my mom and dad."

"Good," she said. "I'd like to know that, too."

After a comfortable silence, the sort she and Laramie had so often shared, she added, "I wish I could go to Chile and ask around. Someone there must know."

"You *can*. We'll go together."

Another silence, during which it came to her, the source of her *déjà vu* at Skip's funeral. During her one visit to Boston, Miguel had vividly described another funeral, that of Pablo Neruda, the Chilean poet, who died soon after General Pinochet ousted President Allende in a bloody coup.

Although Pinochet had forbidden a public funeral, Laramie and Miguel joined the thousands of mourners who followed Neruda's coffin to a Santiago cemetery. As the coffin was lowered, a voice cried out, "Pablo Neruda!"

"*Presente!*" came the response from the crowd. "*Ahora y siempre!*"

"*Compañero* Salvador Allende!" another voice cried. "*Presente!*"

Armed guards lined the road leading out of the cemetery. Some of the mourners, intimidated, left through a side gate. Miguel and Laramie followed the rest of the crowd through the main gate, where Pinochet's soldiers were taking names.

chapter 6

❄ ❄ ❄

The gas station, with an oasis of brand-new gas pumps, was surrounded by snow-dusted corn-fields. As Vrai pulled in, strange green lights came on. Hers was the only car.

"Maybe this place has chocolate milkshakes," Jonathan said.

"Maybe not," Vrai said. "I'm desperate for the rest room. Can you wait here for a few minutes?"

"I *can*."

"Well, will you please? I'll come back and help you get inside on those blades."

The pay phone, like everything else, was shiny and new. She left a hurried message on Lloyd's voice mail. In case he was wondering, she had Jonathan. They'd waited and waited at the funeral home. Now they were on their way to Roanoke. She'd call again from there.

Why did you have to ruin it by lying? she wanted to add, but the answer was too painfully obvious.

It's cruel to abandon a child. She didn't say this either.

In the ladies' room she slammed home the bolt on a stall door. Dizzying images swam across the hexagonal floor tiles. Skip's lopsided grin. Pablo Neruda's coffin. Lloyd with his arms around minuscule Marianne.

The Krispy Kremes had not digested well. Vrai was glad to see that the store sold antacids.

"Little boy with no shoes on?" The deep voice belonged to a giant behind the counter. "He belong to you?"

Vrai hurried to the door. Her car was indeed empty. "Which way did he go?"

"Relax, Mom, he's in the can." With a hand the size of *The World Almanac*, the man pointed at a pile of shoe boxes. "Got some nice moccasins over there, just your boy's size. Genu-wine Indian moccasins, made in Taiwan."

"Let me think about it while I get gas," Vrai said.

"Gotta turn the pump on first. What kind you want?" He ogled her heels and stockings, her long black coat. "Soo-preme?"

"Regular."

"Yes ma'am." Two fingers touched his faded Atlanta Braves cap.

Outside, in the eerie light, green snowflakes swirled like moon dust. She inserted the nozzle and squeezed the handle. Jonathan had probably done exactly as she'd asked—waited in the car for a few minutes. Then he'd unlaced the hockey skates, set them upright in the passenger seat, and scurried inside in his socks.

She found him stomping around in a pair of fringed, knee-high moccasins. On his head was a coonskin cap.

"How much for the moccasins?" she asked.

The man's price list seemed to be printed on the ceiling. He stared up at it. "Twenty-nine ninety-five for them high toppers," he said finally.

Vrai knelt down and felt for Jonathan's toes under the rough suede. "They fit OK?"

"Perfect," Jonathan said.

"I'll throw in that coonskin cap for only twelve bucks more," the man offered.

"Please?" Jonathan stroked the long tail.

"But think about that poor raccoon."

"It's only fake fur."

"Then let's not buy it," Vrai said. "Put the cap back, OK?"

Jonathan did as he was told. Her own boys wouldn't have given up so easily. She felt hard-hearted and cruel. Quarts of milk called to her from a refrigerated glass case. A waist-high freezer offered Popsicles and ice cream cups. Her mind was racing.

"Why don't you go on out to the car? I'll be out in a minute." She gave herself some leeway. "As soon as I'm done here."

Jonathan didn't move. Was he trying to come up with a clever answer to the question that wasn't a question? The reason he wasn't going on out to the car was because . . .

"Hey dude," the man said. "You heard your mother."

"She's not my mother," Jonathan said. "She kidnapped me."

Vrai put a hand on his shoulder, turned him toward the door. "Try not to step in any oil spots, OK?" She watched through the glass door as a small, orange-suited astronaut in moonwalking boots moseyed out to the car and climbed in.

A quart of milk and a cup of chocolate ice cream should do the trick. She placed them on the counter and asked for a spoon.

"There's one of those little wooden thingies stuck to the lid," the man said.

She opened the carton of milk and drank from it. "Don't you have something else I can use? He loves milkshakes."

"Got a mouth on him."

"We just came from a funeral."

"Hell, why didn't you say so?" He took a Swiss Army knife from his pocket and pulled out a blade. "Try this."

"Thanks." She cut the ice cream into quarters, speared a wedge, and pushed it into the milk carton. With the man watching in disbelief, she inserted the other three wedges, refolded the spout, and gently shook the carton.

"I must seem crazy, buying ice cream in this weather." She wiped his knife on a napkin and gave it back to him.

"How far you going?" He rang up her purchases.

"Baltimore."

"Hell, you'll never make it to Baltimore. You're crazy, all right. This here's a goddamn blizzard."

"Haven't had any trouble so far." She gave him her credit card.

"You will. You get up as far as Wytheville, 81'll be pure ice. Listen, if I was you, I'd stop at the first motel I come to. There's a Howard Johnson's up the road a bit."

"Bet they have milkshakes. Oh well." Vrai gathered up napkins and straws.

"I don't want to have to read about you and your little boy in the newspaper, frozen to death in some ditch. I mean it. You be careful now."

"I will. Thanks."

Back in the car, she gave the milk carton a final jiggle. "Feel like a chocolate milkshake?"

"That's just plain milk."

"Try it."

Jonathan refused a straw. He opened the spout, peered inside, and took a sip. "Hey, not bad."

The snow was swirling furiously. "That man said we should stop at the first motel we come to."

"He's a total wimp."

The closer they got to I-81, the lighter the traffic was. I-81 would take them north, across the state line, into Virginia. How angry would Lloyd be when he checked his voice mail? Angry enough to press charges?

Jonathan could read the mileage signs. He wasn't shy about speaking up. If he wanted her to drive him home to Asheville, he'd say so.

The exit ramp from I-40 was unusually long, its gradual change in direction barely noticeable. No merging was necessary or even possible. The ramp was also the beginning of I-81's northbound lanes.

"What're *azulejos*?" Jonathan's pronunciation was perfect.

In efficient, repetitive arcs, the wipers cleared snow from the windshield. "They're beautiful, hand-painted tiles," Vrai said. "It's one of the arts the Moors brought to Spain. Why?"

"It's in that poem."

The poem about the tiled room under the stadium in Santiago, he meant. There, as a boy, Miguel had shaken hands with Pelé. Years later, in the same room, men had burned Miguel with cigarettes and broken his jaw and several of his ribs. But he told his interrogators nothing, admitted to knowing no one.

Attending Skip's funeral had made Jonathan think about his dead parents, all right. "You've read your father's poems?"

"Why shouldn't I? I'm his *son*."

"I know," Vrai said softly. "I'm not angry."

"She sure was. She said I wasn't old enough. But you know what? I'm much better at hiding things than she is."

"Your Aunt Marianne?"

The question was too dumb to rate an answer. "She hid my dad's book from me, but I found it, and then I borrowed one from the library, too, just to make her double mad."

The librarian in Vrai was pleased. Her parental instincts, in this instance anyway, were similar to Marianne's.

"How come you know about *azulejos*?" Jonathan said. "I asked my Spanish teacher, and all he said was, must be something blue."

"I was in Spain when your mom and dad died. I didn't even know, till I got home." On the verge of tears, she stopped speaking.

The tractor trailer in front of them slowed down and turned on its flashers. Vrai looked around to her left to see if she could change lanes. A minivan was coming up fast. Too fast. It hit the ice the truck driver had tried to warn them about, did a 180, and ended up traveling southbound along the snowy median.

"Whoa!" Jonathan said.

"I'm going to stop, first motel we come to." She waited for Jonathan to call her a wimp.

"There's one," he said a few minutes later.

The Smoky View Motel was perched atop a steep hill overlooking the interstate. Halfway up the hill stood a big black bear holding a neon VACANCY sign in one paw. Vrai doubted the Smoky Mountains were ever visible from this far north, even on a clear day, with high-powered binoculars. She activated the blinker and took the next exit.

"You zeenk zey have a hrreuuumm?" Jonathan said.

She giggled. Hysteria was setting in. "Inspector Clouseau. Which movie was that?"

"*The Return of the Pink Panther*. It's my favorite."

A crazy quilt of skid marks decorated the motel's steep driveway. She put the Toyota in low. The Smoky View had a restaurant. What she needed was protein. Protein and sleep.

chapter 7

❋ ❋ ❋

The restaurant would be closing early, so that the staff, too, could find shelter for the night. Vrai ordered a beer with her cheeseburger before realizing wine was available, both by the bottle and by the glass. East Tennessee had joined the modern world. Her father had bought booze from a bootlegger. Everyone did back then, even Laramie and Lloyd's father, the taciturn FBI agent. Whenever the question of legalizing liquor was put on the ballot in Knoxville, the Baptists teamed up with the bootleggers to defeat it.

Their dinners arrived while Jonathan was in the men's room. He returned looking solemn and glum.

"Something wrong?" Vrai asked him.

"Maybe."

"Are you ill?"

"Nope. I feel great." He sat down. "But I got something to tell you." A deep breath, followed by a dramatic pause. "The thing is, you did kidnap me."

Vrai took a bite of her burger.

"After the funeral? I called her a bitch, and Uncle Lloyd heard me."

Vrai nodded. "You already told me that. You said they were so mad they drove off and left you."

"Yeah. I've been thinking. That's not exactly what I said, but you thought it was, and I didn't tell you it wasn't, so I guess in a way I lied to you."

A lie of omission, the easiest kind of lie to tell, the hardest to confess. "But you're telling me the truth now?"

"I'm sure trying to. They go off and get coffee. I sit there and hope they won't come back, but they always do. With Styrofoam cups."

"Except that sometimes you don't sit there and wait. You sneak into movies. And then you walk home."

Jonathan looked offended. "I only did that once. They got *really* mad that day."

"OK. They come back with coffee. Then what?"

"Then they don't speak to me for hours. The silent treatment. I love that part."

"So they might've come back while I was asking about my sunglasses at the motel. Or when we were at the Jiffy Mart. They came back, and when they couldn't find you, they started driving around looking for you." Two cars, four people, one French farce. "I guess they're still looking for you. Serves them right, is what I think."

Jonathan's eyes widened.

Vrai sipped her beer. Lloyd would've been too embarrassed—the word *mortified* occurred to her—to have stopped in at the funeral home's office. What was your nephew wearing? A thin jacket and no shoes. Why did you leave him on the curb in the cold? To punish him while my wife and I went for coffee.

"So you knew they were coming back," she said.

"I *hate* living with them." Jonathan upended the ketchup bottle and let a red pool form on his plate. "I want to go home to Baltimore with you."

Was this even possible? She reached over to dip one of her French fries in his ketchup. "What's so awful about it?"

Jonathan picked up his hamburger. "The worst thing? I had to hide the pictures of my mom and dad. She kept messing with them."

"Messing with them how?"

"See, I liked their pictures on the dresser, but face down. That way I knew they were there with me, but they weren't always looking at me and reminding me." He looked down at his plate. "You know."

Vrai drank more beer. Realized she'd forgotten to buy antacid.

"But she kept turning their faces up again. I'd come home from school, or I'd wake up in the morning, and she would've been in my room messing with my pictures. So I hid them where she'll never find them."

"Did you ever ask her to stop?"

"I shouldn't have to. She's a grownup. She knows not to mess with my stuff. Are you taking her side?"

"I think she was being rude and insensitive." The worst

kind of bitch. "Marianne should never have touched your photographs. Not even once."

"But she did. Thousands of times."

"So where did you hide them?"

"A secret hiding place," Jonathan said. "Secret means I'm not going to tell you."

"Fair enough. Are the pictures safe there?"

"I guess if the house burned down, they wouldn't be, but if there was a fire and I was home, I could carry them outside." Jonathan was so wound up the words came tumbling out. "I hid my new clothes in there, too. She bought me this puke green suit to wear to the funeral and some new shoes. I didn't think Uncle Lloyd would care. I had a soccer game this afternoon. The only good excuse for missing a game is a broken bone. But he got just as mad at me as she did. I couldn't believe it."

Vrai wanted another beer. She looked in vain for the waitress.

"She made me wear my old clothes." Jonathan was in free fall. "I thought if I didn't have anything to wear to the funeral, they'd let me go on to school. I don't even know who won the game." He stopped for breath.

"So that's why you were walking around with your shoes untied," Vrai said. "They're too small."

"Yeah. I kinda like those new shoes. She wanted me to get some ugly brown clodhoppers, but I talked her into a pair of black and white wingtips. Uncle Lloyd said his grandpappy used to have a pair just like them. I'm gonna wear them trick-or-treating on Halloween."

"If I'd bought you a new suit, and you hid it, I might've gotten a little angry, too," Vrai said.

"Yeah, but you wouldn't have made me go to a funeral."

Vrai smiled. He had that right.

"You know what the next-to-worst thing is?" Jonathan said. "They make me go to bed at nine o'clock."

Nine seemed a reasonable bedtime for a ten-year-old, even a precocious one.

"It's so they can, you know. Downstairs. Naked." Jonathan spat the words out.

Vrai knocked over her empty beer bottle.

"Sometimes they do it outside in the hammock."

"Noooo," Vrai wailed. "In the hammock?"

"I can see them from my window."

"That's unforgivable." Had Lloyd told her nothing but lies?

Jonathan's lip quivered. She was handling this badly. He thought she was mad at him. "I know I sound angry," she began. "I'm not angry." A lie. "I'm shocked. Not because you told me. Because of *what* you told me. I'm not angry at you."

"You sure sound like it."

"I'm sorry. Truly I am. Have you ever told anyone else?"

Jonathan shook his head.

"Well, I'm glad you told me."

The lights blinked off and on. Libraries used the same

signal to indicate closing time. The waitress, wherever she was, already had their room number. Vrai wrapped Jonathan's uneaten burger in a clean napkin and stowed it in her pocketbook.

"I wish I could live with Grandmama and Granddaddy." He lifted his hands, palms out, to show how powerless he was in this game called life.

It was like seeing a ghost. "Your mother used to do that," Vrai said softly.

"What?"

"That thing you just did with your hands." She stood up. "Ready to go?"

Not yet. "Summers, I go up to Cape Cod, and they always say they'll take me down to Boston, to the cemetery, but then that day is always a scorcher, and they say we'll go another time, but we never do."

"They want us to leave so they can close up," Vrai said.

Jonathan got slowly to his feet. "I've never even seen their graves."

"That makes two of us." Vrai put an arm around him.

. . . .

It was a blizzard all right. The motel's empty swimming pool was filling up with snow. The gas pumps at the bottom of the hill resembled snowmen. On the interstate, cars and trucks were creeping along in a single line, like slow white ducks.

A covered walkway led from the restaurant to the motel office. After that they were out in the open. Vrai had changed into sneakers, but her feet and ankles were soon numb. The travel umbrella she kept in her car provided little protection from the swirling snow.

"Those moccasins keeping you warm?" she said.

Jonathan had other concerns. "How come you know about Uncle Lloyd's voice mail?"

"Lloyd and I talk sometimes. His sister was my best friend, remember?"

"He's addicted to his voice mail."

"Is he?"

"That's what she says."

Vrai slipped, grabbed Jonathan's shoulder for support. "I left Lloyd a message, back at that gas station, saying I'd call him again from Roanoke."

"But why?"

"So they'd know you're safe."

"Where are we, anyway?"

With a flourish, she unlocked the door to No. 17. "Still in Tennessee."

chapter 8

❄ ❄ ❄

arlier, when they'd carried things in from the car, the motel room had been a musty and drab disappointment. Now its pine paneling and worn beige carpeting felt almost like home.

Warm air from the dented, noisy radiator stirred the brown plaid curtains. Above each headboard hung a framed print of obscenely long pine cones. A TV with rabbit ears sat atop an old oak desk. Next to the TV was Skip's computer.

In his eagerness to please, Jonathan had even brought in the paper grocery bag containing the eyeglasses from Skip's apartment and the sunglasses Vrai had found under the azaleas near the scene of the accident. Librarians tended to group like entities together. A possible "see also" reference was in her wallet. While searching in vain for Skip's obituary, she'd come across one for Gussie Morgen, the former psychology librarian, who'd died two days before Skip.

Jonathan tore off his snow-caked sweatshirt and damp windbreaker and set them on the radiator to dry. Vrai's own coat, its sodden weight requiring the support of three wire hangers, went into the small closet. She helped Jonathan peel off his moccasins and socks and made room for them on the radiator.

"Want to take the first shower?" she offered.

"I don't need a shower."

"Not even to get warm?"

"Not even."

"Well, I do." She unzipped her small suitcase. "How about a pair of dry socks?"

These Jonathan accepted, along with a lilac turtleneck. He then padded over to the desk, pushed up his sleeves, and began connecting the monitor.

"Hey! No!" Vrai said. "Please don't play with Skip's computer."

Jonathan straightened up, the better to present his case. "But it might have Solitaire."

"It might have private files. Material Skip wouldn't want you to see."

"Oh all right." He peered into the paper bag.

Vrai didn't even try to hide her irritation. "Leave Skip's belongings alone now, will you? That bag could've stayed in the car."

"I was just trying to help. How come you have Skip's glasses?"

"The sunglasses may not be his." From the suitcase

she retrieved a nightgown and matching robe. "I'm going to take a hot shower. Want the bed by the radiator?"

Jonathan went obediently to the bed and pulled down the covers.

"Don't you want to take your damp slacks off first?" she said.

"In a minute."

When she wasn't looking, he meant. At the bathroom door she paused. "I can trust you, can't I? About the computer?"

He gave her a solemn nod.

. . . .

The gown and robe had been Lloyd's favorites, a deep green that matched her eyes. He'd liked to undo the robe's pearly buttons, unwrapping her like a present.

After hanging the silky duo on the bathroom door, she removed her watch. It was nearly ten o'clock. Seven in Seattle. She longed to call her husband. Bob knew she'd planned to drive to Knoxville and might possibly be worried about her.

Their row house in Baltimore was too large for one person, but in order to sell it the joint owners would have to decide to make a decision. Either knit their marriage back together, or sever the thread from which it dangled. Vrai had been prepared for the latter. Now she would opt for the former.

She stepped into the shower and made the water hot hot hot, as hot as she could stand. Dirty was how she felt. Permanently stained.

Why were little packets of soap so hard to unwrap? She let the hot water pummel her until steam surrounded her like fog.

A familiar face appeared in the mist. Laramie was *presente*.

Pleease, pleease, Laramie sang. *Can you pleease take Jonathan home with you?*

"I'll try," Vrai whispered. "I'll do what I can."

Laramie's voice was fading, her response faint. *That's all I'm asking. Pleease.*

Frantic, Vrai looked for a way to turn up the volume, extend the conversation. "I promise." She said it out loud. "I'll do my best."

No audible reply. She turned off the noisy shower and waited.

But Laramie was gone. Had perhaps never been there in the first place. A fig newton of your imagination, Skip might have said of the conversation. Perhaps what Vrai had heard was the fierce wind outside. Or the Smoky View's outdated plumbing.

Still, as she toweled dry, she couldn't shake the feeling that she and Laramie had communicated. Reached an understanding.

. . . .

Lloyd had made it perfectly clear that he didn't want her to come to Knoxville and would ignore her if she did. So why had she packed his favorite nightgown? Because for the past two years, whenever she and Lloyd had been within fifty miles of each other, they'd somehow managed to have sex.

Playing tennis in a thunderstorm was nothing compared with Lloyd's risky behavior as an adult. He loved taking chances. It would've been easier for her to visit him in Asheville during the summer months, when Marianne was in France and Jonathan was with his grandparents on Cape Cod. Instead, Lloyd invited her for a weekend in October. Marianne would be driving Jonathan to a two-day soccer camp in Charlotte and spending Saturday night there with a cousin.

Vrai had wondered if Lloyd *wanted* to be caught.

Some women, made careless by passion, leave behind an earring, a comb, a lipstick. For Vrai, that Sunday in Asheville, it was her Cinnamon Stick deodorant. She didn't realize the deodorant was missing until she was back in Baltimore. She'd last used it in the kitchen, a quick swipe under each arm, before the mad dash to the airport.

It must be on the kitchen counter, she told Lloyd's voice mail.

A few days later a package arrived. A Post-it Note on the Cinnamon Stick read: "No harm done."

By which Lloyd meant he'd gotten away with it. Adultery in the hammock. Adultery in the marriage bed. Adultery before breakfast in the shower. And a final quickie against the kitchen counter, while his wife and nephew were on their way home.

....

Skip hadn't approved of her affair. It was one of the reasons his friendship with her had cooled. Maybe he'd felt guilty, partially responsible.

When she arrived at Skip's apartment that night, Lloyd was already there, having taken the train up from Washington, where he was attending a conference. Before Lloyd even helped her off with her coat, Vrai knew. The magnetism was as strong as ever. You look great. You haven't changed a bit. The undercurrents were electric.

During dinner Skip was too preoccupied to notice the rekindled sparks. The library had a new director. Skip didn't like him.

"The guy's clueless," Skip said. "The very first thing he tells you is that he'd really rather be a history professor, but he didn't get tenure. He wants you to feel sorry for him. It's like he's saying, 'That's my excuse for having to work in a library, what's yours?'"

Bev tried to calm Skip down. "If this guy's as bad as you say, then he won't last long."

"Mark my words," Skip said. "Heads will roll. Frank lost a job he really loved. He'll want others to know exactly what that feels like."

"Then tread carefully," Bev warned. "Remember, sweetie, you'll never have tenure. You and Vrai don't even have contracts. Don't let this man push your buttons."

"No ma'am." Skip grinned at the woman he'd told Vrai he might marry. "My buttons, every single one of them, are reserved for you."

From across the table Lloyd gave Vrai a sly smile.

"I'm dead serious," Bev said to Skip. "What would you do if you lost your job?"

"I won't," Skip said. "Don't worry."

"Hypothetical question," the attorney persisted. "What would you do if you could no longer be a librarian?"

Skip thought this over. "I've always wanted to try my hand at writing fiction."

Bev gave him the sort of look she might give her daughter. "Not much money in that."

While Skip and Bev cleared the table, Lloyd examined the salt and pepper shakers, Elvis in tails and Priscilla in a bridal gown. With a mischievous smile Lloyd Eisen, headmaster at a private school in Asheville, covered the holes in Priscilla's head and turned her upside down, looking for extra holes. Vrai was blushing when Skip came in with dessert.

The rest of the evening Skip kept frowning at her and shaking his head. As if he already knew how readily Lloyd would accept Vrai's offer of a ride to the train station and how long they would spend necking there (parked for over an hour in a ten-minute zone, during which Lloyd missed two trains back to Washington). Had Skip also guessed what would happen, three weeks later, on a king-size bed in a Comfort Inn on Connecticut Avenue in DC?

What Skip most likely did *not* know was this. Daphne, who'd been Bob's favorite jogging buddy in Baltimore, had recently picked up and moved to Seattle.

....

Jonathan was fast asleep in Vrai's turtleneck. He'd neatly draped his slacks over a chair, as if to show how trustworthy he was, how little trouble he'd be when he moved in with her. Had Laramie visited Jonathan, too?

Vrai longed to smooth his hair, as she'd so often done with her own boys. Robbie would usually wake up with a sweet smile. Larry, the deep sleeper, never even knew she was there. She hesitated, then leaned down and gently lifted Jonathan's dark hair off his forehead. He stirred but didn't open his eyes.

"Goodnight, little one," she whispered.

"*Azulejos*," he mumbled.

There was the tick tick tick of snow blown hard against the window. The shrill wind sounded upset about something, sad and disillusioned.

When she covered him with an extra blanket, Jonathan spoke again. "Tiles in Lugash," he said clearly. Laramie, too, had talked in her sleep.

"Goodnight," Vrai whispered again.

No reply.

She put another blanket on her own bed. Halfway down the long green hill to sleep, she saw Jonathan's father, naked and tied to a tree. Men with whips began beating him, but he didn't cry out. Whatever it was the men wanted to know, Miguel refused to tell them. He had the courage of an angel.

. . . .

She woke during the night after hearing the toilet flush. "You warm enough?"

"Yep," Jonathan said. "Are you?"

"I am." The wind had ceased its complaining. "Still snowing?"

He lifted an edge of the curtain. "I'll say. Wish I had my sled."

"Wish I had some boots." A flannel nightgown. Bob's old wool bathrobe. "Did you know you talk in your sleep?"

"Do not."

"Do so. What's Lugash?"

"Lugash? That's where the Pink Panther diamond was stolen from, remember?"

Vrai didn't. "Are there tiles in Lugash?"

"A bazillion of them."

Taking Jonathan home with her wouldn't make up for the trip she'd never made to Chile. Still, justice wore many cloaks, balanced a variety of scales. Doing what was right for a child orphaned by murderers should count for something.

chapter 9

❅ ❅ ❅

I promise.

The words surfaced, like a phrase floating in a Magic 8-Ball, then sank back into the murk of sleep.

Vrai woke up in a strange room lit only by a computer screen. In front of the computer sat a young boy with dark hair.

"Hey!" She sat up. "You said you wouldn't."

"I was bored." Jonathan turned around. "I've been up for hours. I was afraid the TV would wake you."

She switched on the bedside lamp. It was nearly nine o'clock. "Did you find a game?" she said, relenting.

"It's a library tour. I'm learning things. Psychology is BF. Religion is BS. Science is Q."

"I'm impressed." She patted his shoulder on her way to open the curtains.

The world had been transformed. Her Toyota was indistinguishable from the other snowy mounds in the motel's parking lot. "It's a blizzard out there. Come look."

"In a minute."

Another kind of snow filled the television screen. Eventually a picture appeared. The stations were providing live, local coverage of The Blizzard of the Century, a gigantic storm extending from Cuba to Nova Scotia. Twelve people had died from tornadoes in Florida, where several homes had been destroyed.

The phone on the table between the beds had a rotary dial. Near panic, Vrai realized she knew her parents' number only as a spatial sequence on a touch-tone phone. Using the small note pad and pencil beside the phone, she drew a diagram of the numbered buttons, then reconstructed her parents' number and wrote it down.

Her father answered after the first ring. "Where in the world are you?"

"In Tennessee, at a motel. Skip Howard died. I came down for his funeral."

"Skip died? Oh honey, I'm so sorry."

"Are you OK?" Vrai said. "I heard there were tornadoes."

"The walls shook some, but the roof stayed on. The worst damage was on the coast. Now tell me about Skip."

"Automobile accident." Vrai said this gently. Her Uncle Sam, her father's brother, had died six years ago after a head-on collision in Kentucky.

"Oh." Her father didn't ask for details. "Are you stranded?"

"Looks that way," she said. "How's Mother?"

"Now that we know you're OK, she's much better. I'll put her on."

Vrai pictured him handing the blue receiver across the blue-and-white-tiled kitchen counter. Her mother, who hadn't wanted to move to Florida, had chosen the decor to remind her of the Smoky Mountains. Tallahassee, Tennessee, her father would joke, not a dime's worth of difference.

"We've been calling your house," her mother said, and Vrai felt guilty as charged: she should have told them she was going to Knoxville. "Daddy says Skip Howard died?"

"Automobile accident," Vrai said again, knowing her mother, with her father listening, would leave it at that. "His funeral was yesterday, in Knoxville."

"I'm so very sorry. Was it a nice funeral?"

Were funerals ever nice? "There was a huge crowd," Vrai said. "Remember Bill Carr? He did the service."

"Bill *Carr*?"

"He's a minister now."

"I always thought he'd end up in prison." An audible sigh from Tallahassee. "Where are you, exactly?"

"I'm not sure. Somewhere south of Bristol."

"All by yourself, I guess."

Without a husband, she meant. Vrai knew the lecture by heart. She should do something. Get a separation. Get a divorce. Get back together. *Quelque chose.*

"Actually, Laramie's son Jonathan is here with me."

"For goodness sake. Does he look like her?"

"More like Miguel." Vrai glanced over at Jonathan, who seemed engrossed in the library tour.

"Daddy's telling me to get the telephone number at your motel."

Vrai complied. "It's snowing like crazy here," she added, wanting to make up for all the secrets she'd kept from her mother. "In Knoxville, the dogwoods were almost ready to bloom."

"I do miss those dogwoods," her mother said, as if the dogwoods in Tallahassee weren't equally beautiful. "Please be careful in this storm."

"You, too," Vrai said, and they hung up.

"Tough luck, Frank," Jonathan muttered.

"I thought you were learning the LC classification."

"The what?"

"The Library of Congress classification system."

"It's a True Story," Jonathan said.

"A story about a library where Frank Leigh's the director?"

"So you've read it, too?"

"I haven't read any of Skip's files. I asked you not to, either. It's snooping. Like reading someone's mail."

"Oh," he said.

"Let me read it."

"Snooping's OK if you do it?"

"I knew Skip. I know Frank. He's my boss." Even to her this was illogical.

Jonathan gave her a look, but he relinquished the

computer. "You have to promise. Out loud. You can't *ever* reveal the secret. Ever."

A Magical Library Tour

Good evening, fellow magicians. Or should I say, Good midnight?

You're entering the John Joseph Stark Library on Ground Level. Well, of course you are. From the outside the building seems to be only one story. But this library actually has many stories, most of them underground, some of them true.

Please, no flashlights! We don't want anyone to know we're here. Once everyone's inside, I'll lock the door.

There's usually a guard beside the turnstile, checking ID's. Down that hallway are the library's administrative offices and also the Poole Room, where staff meetings are held. Anyone can visit those.

Now, one by one, come on through the turnstile. Careful—I don't want any injuries. We have important work to do.

That was the deal, remember? I give you an after-hours tour of the library, and in return you help me with a secret project. Pretty simple, really. We're going to make objects disappear.

Abracadabra. Poof.

Before we start, I need to know that our se-
cret project will remain exactly that: a secret.
Do you promise never to tell a living soul about
your tour of the library? Do you promise? Say
it out loud, then.

With Jonathan reading over her shoulder, Vrai spoke
the words. "I promise."

All right, then. Shall we begin? This is the
Circulation Desk, where you check out books,
and next to it is Interlibrary Loan.

Let's take the elevator down to Level Six. I
like to start my tours down there and work my
way upward.

Voilà! I'll turn on some lights.

The north end of Level Six is where the library's
current periodicals are shelved. This is one of my
favorite spots in the library. Outside that wall of
floor-to-ceiling windows is an ivy-covered well, a
big hole in the ground that lets in natural light. Yes
indeed, on a sunny day, this area is sunlit!

No, the windows don't open. Please don't
even try.

The rest of Level Six is Audio-Visual. Lots
of microfish swimming around in these cabi-
nets, heh, heh.

*We had this stairway up to Level Five spe-
cially built. The scientists wanted to be able to
zip back and forth between their bound jour-
nals and the current issues.*

*Level Five is science and technology, in-
cluding psychology. Psychology is BF. I like to
think of it as Blame Freud, but Gussie Morgen,
who used to be the psychology librarian, never
liked my little joke. Religion is BS, by the way.
Hey, not my fault. I don't think the Library of
Congress meant anything by it, but who knows,
maybe there was an atheist involved.*

*Science is Q, a long long way from religion,
which is up on Level Two with the other B's.
Mnemonically it may help to think quark, a
word coined by James Joyce in Finnegan's Wake.
Medicine is R (think Rx, for prescription); S
(seeds) is Agriculture; T is Technology. So this
floor is Q through T, plus BF.*

*The office with the Cal Ripken poster on the
door used to be Gussie Morgen's. I'll unlock it
so you can peek inside. The office was a mess
when Gussie had it—papers piled to the ceiling—but what looked like total chaos to everyone else was in perfect order for her. It was the
Gussie Morgen system of classification.*

*Gussie used to work in the old library at
Stoneham Women's College before this library*

was built. Some people turn bitter as they get older, but Gussie's as upbeat now as she ever was, always eager to see what's around the next bend in the road. You hate to see a person like that get hurt.

In this corner she kept an aquarium with celestial goldfish, so-called because their eyes are on top of their heads. Most fish look sideways as they swim along, but Gussie's fish were always gazing heavenward.

A moment of silence, please, for Gussie's goldfish. They were flushed down the toilet, I happen to know. Six months later she gave in and, very reluctantly, retired.

Now then. Let's take the elevator up to Level Four, where we'll find L (Education, think learning), M (Music), and P (Literature, think, oh I don't know, poetry and prose?).

N (Art) should be on this floor, but the Art History Library is in another building.

N for nudes? Good one, why not?

Looking for O? O can mean nothing, zero, which is why there is no O. It would be too confusing.

Anyone recognize this piece of sculpture by the windows?

Edmund Muskie? No, though I do see a resemblance.

Not Sir Isaac Newton, either.

Think literature. This gentleman has been placed on Level Four for a reason.

Prince Machiavelli? Isn't that a perfume? No, it's not Machiavelli. Machiavelli wasn't a prince. Machiavelli wrote The Prince. *But you're getting close. Right country. Right city, even. Florence, Italy, is where this gentleman was born. But when he was thirty-seven he was expelled from Florence for his political views. Along with—here's a bit of trivia for you—several members of the Bonaparte family, who ended up moving to Corsica.*

This gentleman had lived in Florence all his life, and then suddenly he was told to leave town. Get out and stay out. I wonder if he had to turn in his keys. I was supposed to turn in my keys when I left. As you can see, I managed to keep a few.

Me, after they kicked me out, I went for long walks. Read a lot. Played chess with Gussie's son, Justin. Tried to do a little writing. But what this gentleman did was truly amazing. Seven hundred years later, people are still reading the product of his exile.

Who said Galileo? Are we on the science floor? We are not. Think literature.

Boccaccio? Close. Very close. Come on. You all know this fellow. The first great Italian poet.

Think about Gussie's fish. Think celestial. Think opposite-of-celestial. Think circles. Think hell-fire and damnation.

Did someone say Dante? Congratulations!

Yes, indeed, folks, this poor ol' lovesick gentleman is Dante Alighieri.

I agree. He does look sad. Could be he's missing Miss Beatrice. Occasionally, students will put him in the elevator and let him ride up and down. Some idiot applied lipstick and rouge a few years back. We sent the bust out to a professional marble cleaner, but, as you can see, traces of pink remain. During the daytime the light coming in off the ivy outside the windows turns Dante a weird shade of green.

Am I giving you a tour of hell? You mean, am I your Virgil? Is this underground library a modern-day version of hell I'm guiding you through?

No, that's not my intent. Anyway, Dante's hell has nine circles. The library has only seven levels. Eight, I suppose, if you count the Art History Library. Dante put different categories of sinners in his different circles of hell. The worse the sin, the farther down the person went. The lower the circle, the greater the suffering. Wrath, for example, was worse than gluttony.

Don't you just love the word wrath?

The very worst sinners, those way down at the bottom of the icy ninth circle, were slurped up by Satan. Eaten alive. What had they done? They betrayed their friends.

If I were making comparisons, which I'm not, I suppose I'd call the Art History Library the ninth circle of hell. A betrayer works there.

Not so! Vrai wanted to yell at the computer screen. She didn't even whisper it. Jonathan was standing at the window, either mesmerized by the falling snow or pretending to be.

OK, time to say good-bye to Dante. Ciao!

Quickly now. Everyone back in the elevator. We have a job to do.

Level Three is the social sciences. The only thing I'm going to show you here is this storage closet full of empty boxes. One overhead light bulb. No ventilation. No electrical outlets. No place to plug in a phone.

For six months this closet was Gussie's office. The library director, a certain Frank Leigh, had the desk and chair from her office down on Level Five moved up here. Gussie was in Hagerstown at the time, visiting her brother, who'd had a heart attack. Anything that wasn't in or on her desk—all that stuff she'd collected over the years—was hauled off to the incinerator. I've already told you what happened to her celestial goldfish. Doug Duesberg flushed them down the toilet.

I'd called Gussie beforehand, to warn her. Still, it was a terrible shock when she returned to work. The office she'd had for years was so empty it echoed. Not even a paper clip remained.

Gussie's tough, though. Knowing Frank wanted her to retire made her all the more determined not to. She pretended having a storage closet for an office didn't bother her one bit.

I even went to see a lawyer. Know what he said? "I'm sorry, Mr. Howard, but there's no law against an employer being a son of a bitch." Makes you see vigilante justice in a whole new light, doesn't it?

Gussie finally did retire. Frank wore her down. She lives with her son, my friend Justin, who was badly wounded in Viet Nam. Gussie's worried she'll die before he does. I've assured her that if something does happen to her, then Justin can move in with me. She doesn't want him to be institutionalized. I've promised her he never will be.

But I digress. Time for us to get down to business. Let's fill both elevators with the empty boxes from this storage closet.

Thanks. That's great. Will the elevator doors close? Fantastic. I'll leave the remaining boxes here in the hallway.

As for us, we'll have to take the stairs the rest of the way.

Level Two is mostly history. And oh yes, philosophy, including some books labeled BS. I'd show you Frank's doctoral dissertation, Napoleon in the Twentieth Century: An Annotated Bibliography. *But we have important work to do.*

Here we are on Level One. The reference collection. Notice the dual staircase curving from Ground Level down to the reference desk.

Now, before I turn out the lights, please study the brass handrails on the left staircase. We're going to have to climb those stairs in the dark. No flashlights, please. We cannot, at this stage of our endeavor, run the risk of attracting attention.

OK, then. Let's go!

Congratulations, everyone! Here we are back at the Circulation Desk.

Now, let's form a human chain. We'll take the empty boxes out of the elevators and pass them over the turnstile.

Yes, the full moon does help. But remember. Campus Security patrols all night long. I can't emphasize this enough: we can NOT be seen.

All right, time to carry the boxes into the administrative offices.

Fantastic!

Everyone remember the promise you made? This is a secret mission. Secret means don't tell. Ever.

The big office to the left there is Frank's.

I have a key to Frank's office and a key to his desk. I have keys to his filing cabinets. I even have a key to the little closet next to his private bathroom.

How come? Can I just say that I have friends in low places?

Note the huge windows in Frank's office. Isn't this moonlight glorious?

Don't pack the boxes too full. We need to be able to close them well enough to stack them on top of each other.

Then what? You mean you haven't guessed? Then we take the boxes full of Frank's stuff back down to the storage closet. We'll put a few empty boxes in front, so that no one, least of all Frank, will have a clue as to where the contents of his office have gone.

His antique fountain pen. His Napoleon books. His nameplate. His desk calendar. His sneakers and sweats. His mail. His phone messages. The pile of reports he's using to prepare this year's budget. The performance appraisal he's doing on his poor secretary, Margot.

His files. His files. His files. Every single one of them.

His paper clips. His pencils. His pencil sharpener. His Rolodex. His toothbrush and toilet paper. His mouthwash and deodorant. His Stoneham-Knox University Phone Directory. His Baltimore phone books. His computer disks. Every single one of them.

His computer? Too big for a box, but maybe we could stash it in the very back of the closet.

His trash can. His telephone. His business cards. His framed diplomas from LSU. His family photos. His teapots and teacups. His imported French tea.

His oil portrait of Napoleon? Absolutely. It can go back there with his computer.

In a few hours Frank will unlock his office door and discover he has nothing.

Zip.

Zero.

Zilch.

All gone.

What does he look like? Franklin Benjamin Leigh, PhD, MLS, is a short, pudgy, gray-haired guy with a deep, sonorous voice and bad breath. When he gets angry, his eyes glisten and his cheeks turn fiery red. I'm guessing that's exactly what'll happen at a little after eight this morning.

There was no mystery about what happened to Gussie's things. But for Frank we'll leave not a single clue.

He'll call Campus Security.

"Do you have good working relationships with your staff?" they'll say. "This looks like an inside job. We patrolled last night as usual. We saw no one.

"What time did you leave your office? Are you sure nothing was missing then? Did you forget to lock up?

"Who has keys to the library? More importantly, who has a key to your office? A key to your desk?"

"No one," Frank will say.

"Someone had keys last night," they'll point out. "Who, Frank? Are you in the habit of leaving your keys lying about?"

"I keep my key ring in my pocket at all times." Frank will pull out his keys. "See, they're all here."

"Someone must have had them duplicated. Who could it have been, Frank?"

The questions will wear Frank down. Finally, he'll give up and admit it. He is completely clueless. Dumber than a doorknob.

C'mon everybody, to the theme from Drag-net: *dumb de dumb dumb . . . dumb de dumb dumb . . . DUMB!*

chapter 10

✻ ✻ ✻

T hat's not a true story," Vrai said, exiting the file.
"Frank's office was never cleared out like that."
And the art history librarian betrayed no one.

When she turned around, Jonathan had an index finger pressed to his lips. "Shhh!" he said. "You promised not to tell."

"I'm really sorry to disappoint you. It's like a fairy tale." A revenge fantasy. She had to agree with Bev. Skip wouldn't have made much money, not from stories like this one.

"How do *you* know?" Jonathan said.

"If something like that had happened, then everyone who works in the library would've known about it by lunchtime."

"So the world's last honest man was lying?"

"Is *Winnie-the-Pooh* a lie?"

Jonathan frowned, considering this. "You're saying Skip made the whole thing up?"

"Not all of it. The library's real."

"How come you and Skip worked in the same library?"

Why was that such a problem for everyone? "It just sort of happened."

She turned back to the computer screen. The subdirectory, True Stories, contained three files. She opened the one labeled Guillotine.

The Guillotine in the Cloakroom

Let's call him Dr. Hyde.

Dr. Hyde wears a white academic robe to preside over staff meetings. We assume the robe's fur collar implies dead white rabbits. With his cold gray eyes darting this way and that, searching for any sign of insurrection, Dr. Hyde steps up to the lectern and begins to recite his catechism.

We respond, as he has trained us to do.

"Do you believe in transformation?" he intones in his deep bass voice.

"We believe in transformation," we reply.

"Will the library be fully prepared for the twenty-first century?"

"Yea, verily," we reply, row after row of us, seated on folding chairs arranged with a center aisle, like a church.

"In the twenty-first century will there be any need for reference books?"

"In the twenty-first century, reference books will be obsolete. The reference collection will consist entirely of CD-ROMs," we reply.

"In the twenty-first century will there be any need for reference librarians?"

"In the twenty-first century, reference librarians will be obsolete," we reply. "In the library of the future, a jukebox of CD-ROMs will replace the reference librarian."

We say this because we must.

His eyes dart, Nixon-like. His cheeks turn scarlet. "We are transforming ourselves."

"The future is now," we reply.

"Non-reference books will never be obsolete."

"Long live the circulating collection," we reply. "Long live rare book purchases."

"Automation will not replace the book."

"Long live the book," we reply.

"Automation will merely replace the reference librarian."

"Long live automation," we reply.

Dr. Hyde has been director of our library for nearly a year now. At his second staff meeting, someone dared to disagree with him. Begged to differ. Duane Marshall was the unfortunate fellow's name, a tall dude from Okla-

homa, who at the time was head of the reference department. Good ol' Duane was of the opinion that, due to the increasing multiplicity of formats, libraries were getting more difficult to use rather than easier, and he thought this trend would hold, right on into the twenty-first century. Duane believed there would always be a need for reference librarians.

Duane sat down when he'd spoken his piece. A dreadful silence followed. Then Dr. Hyde gave two deputy directors the nod, and they stood up and drew their guns in practiced unison. Poor ol' Duane, his hands in the air, was marched into the cloakroom to the left of the lectern.

The library of the future contained an ancient relic. We couldn't see the guillotine. All we heard was a whoosh followed by an ominous thump.

Duane's head rolled, ear over ear. Out the cloakroom door it came, leaving a bright red trail on the floor. Our first moments of shocked disbelief were followed by screaming pandemonium.

So we say whatever he wants us to say.

Someone made an anonymous complaint to the library's Board of Trustees about a guillotine in a cloakroom and the missing head of reference, Duane Marshall, not to mention Duane's missing head. A security officer was sent to investigate and hasn't been heard from since.

That's why we have agreed to agree with Dr. Hyde. About the twenty-first century and any other damn thing.

"OK, this one's better," Vrai said. At least Skip had changed the names.

"Can I read it?"

"It's pretty gruesome." She remembered the ketchup-soaked hamburger in her pocketbook. "Are you hungry?"

"I was, while I was waiting for you to wake up, so I ate the last two doughnuts."

"I thought this keyboard felt sticky."

"I like gruesome," Jonathan said.

"Have at it, then."

As she set the soggy burger on the cold windowsill, a man in a parka came into view, his breath visible, his puffy gloves gripping a shovel. Was he clearing the way to a coffee machine?

She dialed 0 for the motel office. A friendly man assured her he had plenty of coffee, as well as some stuff he'd scrounged from the restaurant kitchen, which was closed. He warned her to be careful opening her door, due to the drifting snow.

Jonathan looked up from the computer. "What's a gill-o-tine?"

"It's a contraption with a big blade that chops off people's heads." Capital punishment. Heads will roll, Skip had predicted.

"Ouch!"

"The French used it to execute people. The Germans, too, I think."

"Did you know Duane?" Jonathan asked.

"What do you think? Let's go get some food."

Jonathan's moccasins were still wet. He left them on the vent and took the dry sweatshirt into the bathroom.

Vrai placed a call to Seattle, forgetting until Bob's phone was already ringing that it was still early there. After giving his answering machine the number for the Smoky View Motel, she left a similar message on Lloyd's voice mail.

Jonathan came out looking like a devoted fan of the University of Tennessee Volunteers, and she went into the bathroom with the jeans and turtleneck she'd worn for the long drive down from Baltimore. The phone rang while she was brushing her teeth. She raced for it, but Jonathan had already answered. He held the receiver out to her, his expression unreadable.

"Who's your friend?" Bob said.

Relieved, she sank down on her bed. "Jonathan Santiago, Laramie and Miguel's boy." In Seattle it was seven fifteen on a Saturday morning. Had Bob just arrived home?

"I thought he lived with his aunt and uncle," Bob said.

"He does." Or did. "They brought him to the funeral yesterday, and now he's stranded here with me."

Who is it? Jonathan mouthed.

My husband, she mouthed back.

"I take it he's listening," Bob said. "Then tell me about the blizzard. Sounds pretty bad. I've had the radio on."

While driving home from Daphne's? During their years of living apart, Vrai and Bob had developed an unspoken rule. She never asked him to account for his whereabouts, and he returned the favor. "It just keeps on snowing," she said. "Remember I-81? Completely deserted. Not a tractor-trailer in sight."

"Good to know you're safe," Bob said. "Sorry I missed your call. Had to take the dog out."

"I didn't know you had a dog." She was still his wife. Why hadn't he told her about something as important as a new member of the family? "What kind?"

"Mostly blue tick, I think. Still a pup. Got him last week at the Humane Society."

Had Daphne gone with him to pick out the puppy? "But blue ticks are Appalachian hounds."

"Seattle's full of immigrants. You should come out sometime. I'm thinking about calling him Picasso, because of Pablo's blue period."

Was he asking her to come to Seattle? "Picasso wasn't very nice to women," she said. "Just call him Blue."

"Blue? That's not much of a name."

"Did you just invite me to come out?"

"Would you like to?"

A question in response to a question? Vrai was tired of

games, tired of secrets, tired of pretending. Bob didn't know about Lloyd, how could he? But Vrai did know about Daphne. At least she thought she did. "What about Daphne?"

Bob took an audible breath. "Texas. For about a month now."

Daphne had been there with him and now was gone. Bob was admitting it. He was telling the truth, as Vrai had known all along he would. If she'd asked him earlier, it would have been a different truth, one she would have reacted to in a vastly different way.

She curled herself around the receiver, as if it were a priceless jewel, once lost, now found. Warm blood suffused her cheeks. "I'd love to come to Seattle."

"We'll talk," Bob said. "Later, when you're alone. I'll call again tomorrow to see how you're getting along. Don't leave without letting me know first."

"We're not going anywhere. You should see the parking lot. I can't tell for sure which car is mine." Vrai was reluctant to hang up. "Could you please tell Larry and Robbie about Skip? I should have, I know, but I just couldn't." Skip had been a friend to both of their sons.

"I did tell Larry. He took it hard. Robbie's away on spring break, I think, but I'll try to track him down."

Very gently, she replaced the receiver, then sat transfixed by the falling snow. This blizzard was changing everything!

Bob wasn't a perfect husband, but he was a good father. Together, they could give Jonathan the sort of home Laramie would approve of.

She opened the door a crack. New snow was quickly obliterating the recently shoveled path to a cup of coffee. Alien shapes populated the monochromatic landscape. The black bear holding the Smoky View sign had been transformed into an enormous polar bear.

"Moccasins dry yet?" She shut the door.

"Nope." Jonathan sounded delighted. "Guess I'll have to stay here."

"I can bring the hockey skates in from the car. Just let me put my sneakers on."

"You can't get into your car."

"Maybe not," Vrai agreed. She donned her damp coat and tested the umbrella. Still functional. A bath towel made a decent head scarf. "Uncle Lloyd might call. I left him a message. He has the number here."

"But why?" Jonathan made a face. "Why did you do that?"

"I told you why. They'll want to know you're safe." She went to the computer and turned it off. "I'm unplugging this. Please keep your promise this time."

"But what am I supposed to do?"

"Watch television. Those temperature listings are fascinating."

. . . .

The friendly voice belonged to Dave, the night manager, who was working the day shift as well. A fellow redhead, he'd cheerfully risen to the occasion. And was still rising, fueled by caffeine.

According to Dave: The man with the shovel, the only one of the Smoky View's guests prepared for a blizzard, was on his way back to Toronto after wintering in Miami. Vrai was the third woman who'd come in wearing a towel on her head. Two of the men had chosen ice buckets.

Vrai headed straight for the coffee machine. Never had java tasted so good. She drained the Styrofoam cup and re-filled it. Somewhere in her car was a thermos bottle. If only she'd brought that inside and left the computer and its files to freeze.

Had Skip *ever* been her friend? All these years she'd felt she owed her job to him, forgetting that Dr. Brill, Chair of the Art History Department, would've had the final say.

The doughnuts Dave had provided were the cakey kind, some with chocolate icing. Vrai ate one and put several more in a plastic bag. Loaves of Wonder bread and slices of ham and cheese were also available. While she was making sandwiches, there was a loud rumble.

"That can't be thunder," Dave said.

Vrai threw the sandwiches and two juice cartons into the plastic bag. She glugged the last of her coffee and thanked Dave as she hurried out the door.

The parked cars resembled white whales stranded on a glacier. A biting wind quickly turned her umbrella inside out. Icy needles stung her face. Each step forward was a small victory.

The room numbers were barely visible. As she passed No. 13 (or was it 15?), lightning illuminated the charcoal-gray sky. The devil's pitchfork, Skip used to say. Thunder growled.

The door to No. 17 opened as she approached. "Can you believe this?" Jonathan shouted.

Her fingers numb, she handed him the bag full of food and stumbled inside. Someone's teeth were chattering. She could hear them. After Jonathan helped her struggle out of her coat, she sat down on her bed and lifted a snow-caked sneaker for him to untie.

Forked lightning raked the sky. The accompanying crack of thunder came seconds later. Jonathan went to turn off the TV.

"Close the curtains, too," she stuttered.

"Don't you want to watch this?"

"I want. Hot shower."

He knelt down and excavated one of her shoe laces. "I got something to tell you."

"Hurry up, then."

"Uncle Lloyd called."

Vrai felt a convulsive twitch between her shoulder blades. "Tell me. Every word of it." She grabbed the extra blanket and tried to wrap it around her.

"He asked how I was. I said I was fine. He asked about you. He called you Mrs. Lynde, and at first I didn't know who he was talking about. I told him you'd gone to get coffee but you'd be back. You wouldn't abandon me."

"And?"

"And then I hung up on him."

"Nooo." Vrai was regaining the use of her fingers. She combed ice from her hair. "Why'd you do that?"

"Because I remembered something." Jonathan gave up on the double knot she'd tied before venturing outside. "If you don't talk too long, the police can't trace the call. Uncle Lloyd used to be in the Army. He still has friends at the Pentagon. They might send a helicopter down here. It could land right outside in the parking lot."

"Whoa." She pointed at the food. "Eat something." Little boys could come unhinged when they were hungry.

"I wish you hadn't told him where we are."

"If one of my boys was out in a blizzard, I'd sure want to know he was safe."

Jonathan scowled at her.

"Take a good look outside. Not even Interpol could find us here."

"She could."

"Marianne? How?"

"On her broomstick." Jonathan opened his mouth, leaned down, and blew warm air on the frozen knot.

"I have some nail scissors." The sneakers had to come off before her jeans could.

. . . .

The shower stung as painfully as the snow had. Vrai quickly turned it off, patted herself dry, and put on her nightgown and robe.

Jonathan had used the closed scissors to pry the knots loose. Even without nourishment he was thinking more clearly than she was.

"Mind if I turn the heat down a little?" he said when she opened the bathroom door. "I'm sweatin' bullets in here."

Another of his uncle's expressions, and truer than Lloyd knew. After sex Lloyd smelled like a wet tin roof.

"Fine with me," she said. "I'm going to get under the covers."

The phone rang. Jonathan tried to keep her from answering it, but she swatted his hand away. Her voice when she said hello was ice cold.

"Where the hell are you?" Lloyd said. "Not in Roanoke, I can tell that much from the area code."

"Then you know I'm in Tennessee," Vrai said. "Where are you?"

Jonathan, sullenly nursing his hand, sat down on his bed.

"You drove off with Jonathan? Just drove off with him? Why would you do a thing like that?"

"It was snowing. He had on a thin jacket and no shoes. We'd waited for over an hour." These were at the top of her list. "I didn't know where you'd gone off to or how to find you. What would you have done?"

A smile flickered on Jonathan's lips.

"But he knew we were coming back. Taking him was the wrong thing to do. Did he con you into it?"

Vrai was fully prepared for a discussion of right and wrong. "Marianne hasn't changed a bit since high school."

A short silence from Lloyd. "Is that any reason to kidnap our nephew?"

"You left him out in a blizzard. We got in my car so he'd have some heat."

"Oh, stop exaggerating. He could've gone inside the funeral home. We did come back for him, but he wasn't there. Please try to imagine the worry you caused us. You didn't wait for an hour, not even close."

"We were gone for ten minutes," Vrai said. "I thought I'd left my sunglasses at the motel. You couldn't wait ten minutes?"

"He'd been fascinated by my old house. We thought maybe that's where he'd gone. So when he wasn't at the funeral home, we drove over there."

We, we, we. The parlance of a thoroughly married man. He'd never intended to divorce Marianne.

"How would Jonathan have made it all the way to your old neighborhood?" she said. "Fly?"

"He could've managed. Little bugger has a few tricks up his sleeve, believe you me."

Trust Lloyd? Believe a single word he said? Never again.

"While we were over there looking for Jonathan, Cassi got loose, and I twisted my ankle chasing after her. Pretty badly. Ducky taped it up."

"Ducky?" Vrai said.

"Donald Swann, MD. We used to call him Ducky. He made me promise to have an X-ray. It's my right ankle, so I can't drive."

"Is Cassi OK?"

"She can still walk. Marianne drove back to the funeral home, but by then it was closed."

"Where are you now?" Vrai said.

"Stuck in Knoxville, in a goddamn Holiday Inn. I'm down in the lobby at a pay phone. I'd called the police to report a missing child, so we couldn't very well leave town."

"And at some point you checked your voice mail." What sort of message, she wondered, had he been expecting to hear?

"That's right. Marianne's furious with you. Never mind that she can't figure out why you had my work number. How are we going to get Jonathan back?"

"Not sure we can discuss that now."

"Why the hell not?" Lloyd said.

"It's a blizzard out there."

"After it stops snowing, I mean."

"Jonathan's safe," Vrai reminded him. "Isn't that what matters most?"

"You're right. Of course it is," said the reigning king of bullshit. "But where the hell are you?"

"Just off I-81." Fingers of lightning clutched at the sky.

"Jesus!" Lloyd said. "What was that?"

The monstrous thunderclap had caused Vrai to hit her funny bone on the corner of the bedside table. Jonathan was on his feet. "Thunder," she said.

"We should hang up," Lloyd said. "I'll call again tomorrow to make some arrangements. Bye, now."

Before the thunder had ceased its ragged roll, the lights blinked off. The electric radiator fell silent.

chapter 11

❄ ❄ ❄

"Time to close the curtains," Vrai said. "Preserve what heat we already have."

"Don't you want to watch the storm? This is so cool."

Didn't he want to hear about his aunt and uncle? "Lloyd and Marianne are still in Knoxville. They were so worried about you that they called the police to report you missing. They're glad to know you're safe."

Safely stranded in a second-rate motel, with wet clothing, no heat, and no light. Three sandwiches and two containers of juice to last them for how long? Car immobilized. A nonstop thundering blizzard outside.

"I'm never *missing*," Jonathan said. "I'm always *somewhere*."

"They came back while I was asking about my sunglasses." Vrai explained about Lloyd's injured ankle. At the window, she found the cord and, with a dramatic swish, closed the curtains.

"Now what?" Jonathan said.

"We wait."

"In the dark?"

She returned to her bed. Already the sheets felt cold.

"Wait for what?" Jonathan said.

"Sounds like they want you back." She'd promised his mother to do her best, and she would, but she couldn't do the impossible.

"You're changing your mind, aren't you?"

"Changing it from what? Don't go putting words in my mouth. Anyway, there are lots of reasons why it wouldn't work out. What about school?" As the public schools in Baltimore went downhill, the private schools became more and more expensive. "You must have free tuition now, with your uncle being the headmaster."

"So what?"

"Sew buttons."

"I think my mother used to say that." Jonathan sniffled.

"She did," Vrai said softly.

"I hate Marianne."

"I know you do. But I can't wave a magic wand. I'm not your fairy godmother."

Silence from Jonathan.

"Anyway, you might hate Baltimore," Vrai said. "And me."

"You better not hit me again."

"You better let me answer the phone when it rings. Who's paying for this room?"

A fierce flash of lightning brightened the edges of the curtains. The subsequent thunder seemed a little farther away.

Vrai rubbed her feet together. "Are you under the covers?"

"I am now."

"Let's talk about the Library of Congress classification. If I told you my dogs were named Elsie and Dewey, would you get the joke?"

"What joke?"

"LC for Library of Congress. Dewey for Dewey Decimal."

"I'm glad you have dogs. I've always wanted a dog."

It was futile to tell a child not to get his hopes up. "Lloyd hurt his ankle running after Skip's dog. A golden retriever. I left her with Mrs. Howard, but I'm afraid that was a big mistake."

"So why'd you do it?"

"She asked me to," Vrai said.

"Skip's dog can talk?"

"Eloquently. Her name's Cassi."

"It's a great name for a dog," Jonathan said. "Short for Cassiopeia?"

"Short for *Chemical Abstracts Service Serials Index*. An important reference book for the sciences. Want to know what it's used for?"

He didn't. "Got any games? A deck of cards, maybe?"

In her car, in the box of stuff for Goodwill, was an old Parcheesi game. "It's a little dark in here for games."

"Ray Charles plays chess."

"Does he?"

"All the time."

Jonathan was quiet for so long that she hoped he'd fallen asleep. Thunder rumbled, an ancient automobile engine trying to turn over.

"How come there wasn't a coffin at the funeral?" Jonathan said.

"Skip was cremated."

"In Boston there were two huge coffins."

To a three-year-old, any coffin would look gigantic, especially one with a parent inside.

"I puked in the church," he went on. "Someone took me home. That's why I've never been to the cemetery."

"Who took you home?"

"Don't remember. The church had a stone floor. I made a yellow puddle."

"Let's talk about something else."

Silence.

"What kind of dogs do you have?" he said finally.

"They're mutts. My younger son, Robbie, found them one Sunday afternoon while he was hiking with friends." Vrai started to tell him the story—how three puppies, mangy and malnourished, had been left in the woods to die—but then realized she'd circled right back to the subject of death. By the time Robbie found a vet willing to see him on a Sunday evening, one of the puppies, a male, was already dead.

No comment from Jonathan, who seemed to have fallen asleep.

. . . .

The night before she left them at the kennel in Baltimore, Vrai had taken the dogs out for their usual walk. Only three nights ago that was. She'd worn her cold-winter-night, dog-walking clothes—Bob's corduroy cap with ear flaps, Robbie's outgrown fur-lined gloves, and an old raincoat with a wool lining.

It was colder than she'd anticipated, a damp, penetrating cold that subdued even Elsie and Dewey. The dogs had trotted meekly beside her, perhaps sensing from her mood that something was wrong.

On Monday, the day Skip died, the moon had been ripe and round and full, a floating melon. Two nights later it was hidden by puffy clouds.

The streets in her neighborhood were lined with sturdy brick three-story row houses, each with a gabled slate roof and a small front yard. Heavy shutters framed the windows. On nearly every porch a light was burning, would burn all night.

Because of the cold she took the shortest route to Poe Park, down Daphne's old street. The Daphne with the insincere smile and the overly muscular legs. You could know something without being aware you knew. Spend time looking for a pencil, when you'd already done the math in your head.

Skip's apartment building was visible from the park. While Elsie and Dewey got down to business, Vrai located Skip's dark windows, three floors from the top. She thought about poor Cassi. Dogs had emotions. Humans weren't the only ones.

Suddenly the moon appeared, looking forlorn and misshapen. In its faint light Vrai saw a golden retriever pulling a man toward the statue of Edgar Allan Poe. Skip, she thought, with Cassi! Of course Skip was alive. He'd come back, from wherever he'd been hiding, and was taking Cassi for a walk. Vrai expected her own dogs, who knew and loved both Skip and Cassi, to want to hurry over and say hello.

But Elsie and Dewey were ready to leave. As if a shade had been lowered, the moon disappeared behind swirling clouds. She let the dogs lead her home.

Her sighting of Skip and Cassi that night could've been a trick of the moon. What seemed more likely was that she'd come slightly unhinged.

A sense of balance was as important in a person's life as it was in a work of art. The year before Laramie's murder, Bob had moved across the country. Then, one by one, Larry and Robbie had left, too. With these jagged rocks in her path, Vrai had stumbled a bit. Lost her balance, but then found it again.

That night in Poe Park she'd seen things that weren't real. Two nights later she'd spoken to Laramie in the shower. The difference between these incidents was that throughout the conversation with Laramie, Vrai had known she was speaking to a dead person.

Skip, though, she had imagined back to life. Even with his ashes in her car, her clothes already packed for his funeral, she'd seen Skip alive and in motion, walking his dog in the moonlight.

The betrayer, he'd called her, when in fact she had faithfully honored his request. Though she'd never understood the need for secrecy, Vrai had told no one about Melody's suicide. Not even Bob.

She had not told Frank.

chapter 12

❄ ❄ ❄

On a warm September afternoon Frank had brewed tea for Vrai in his office. Six months into his job as director, he was in the process of visiting each department for a let's-get-acquainted meeting. Because the Art History Library was in a separate building, and Vrai its only employee, he'd asked if she'd mind coming to him instead.

Eager to make a good impression, she hid her surprise when Frank shut his office door, walked over to the credenza beside his desk, and plugged in a hot plate. "Please sit down," he said, motioning to two upholstered chairs.

Vrai chose a chair and sat.

"I'm delighted you could come. I'm finding these departmental meetings enormously helpful." He gave her a sheepish smile. "As you may have heard, I've never been a library director before. May I brew you some tea?"

"Oh please don't go to any trouble."

"No trouble at all." His light gray suit matched his eyes

and beard and hair. "I find the ritual immensely soothing." He flourished a round black tin. "This is French tea,
Empereur Chen-Nung, from Mariage Frères, named for
the Chinese emperor who discovered tea long before the
birth of Christ." Frank spoke with the flair and enthusiasm of a TV chef. "The ancient Chinese texts say to use
water from a fast-running stream, thought to be more
pure than river water. But the tap water here in Baltimore is really quite good." He took an aluminum kettle
into his lavatory and turned on the tap.

The kettle sizzled when he set it on the hotplate. As
the water approached the boil, he poured some into a
blue china teapot and swirled it around. "This step is
called 'rinsing.' It warms the pot." After emptying the
rinsed teapot into the lavatory sink, he returned to spoon
in tea from the tin. "Four teaspoons." He then rinsed another teapot, a white one, and two teacups.

Vrai was fascinated. Her husband sometimes drank
tea, but Bob used tea bags.

"There are different stages of boiling." Frank popped
open the kettle's lid. "I like to follow the ancient advice of
Yu Lu. In the first stage, the water is quiet and resembles
fish eyes. In the second, audible bubbles look like pearls
on an eternal string. I wait for the third stage—loud,
majestic ocean waves." He lifted the kettle and poured
boiling water into the blue pot. "Enough water to cover
the leaves. And then a little bit more. The leaves expand,
you see, while steeping." He set the kettle on a trivet, un-

plugged the hotplate, and looked at his watch. "Steep the leaves for three and a half minutes."

Vrai started to say something polite and appreciative, but Frank was so intent on his watch that she was afraid to interrupt. Finally he transferred his attention to a silver gadget with a wooden handle. With great care he strained dark tea from the blue pot into the two cups. "Fill each cup halfway," he said. He then strained the rest of the tea into the white pot. To the tea in the cups and the tea in the pot he added just the right amount of recently boiled water.

"Sugar?" he asked. "My wife takes sugar in her tea."

"Please," Vrai said.

Using small silver tongs, Frank selected a sugar cube and released it into one of the cups. The elaborate ceremony was making Vrai uncomfortable. Was Frank planning to move the art history collection to the main library? If so, then he was brewing tea for the wrong person.

Years ago, when construction of the John Joseph Stark Library began, Dr. Rupert Brill, longtime chair of the Art History Department, took one look at the huge watery hole in the ground and declared that none of his department's books would ever be housed in a building that was sure to leak. They weren't his books, of course, any more than Vrai was his employee, but Dr. Brill wielded such power on campus that he usually got his way.

"Thank you," she said, accepting the cup and saucer from Frank. She stirred the fragrant liquid with a tiny little spoon.

After handing her a small white napkin, Frank settled carefully into the other chair with his own cup and saucer. "I taught my dear wife to brew tea. It's the secret, I believe, to our long and happy marriage. Whenever we need to have a serious talk, one of us brews tea. We have the obligation then to be completely honest, no matter how painful the truth may be. One cannot lie while drinking tea. Brew rhymes with true."

Venetian blinds divided the sky into strips of deep sapphire blue. Frank's desk faced away from the windows, toward a large oil painting in which a red-jacketed Napoleon frowned down from a white horse.

Vrai decided not to inquire about the artist. She sipped her tea. The true brew.

"Delicious," she said.

"*Vraiment.*" Frank rolled the r. "It's a lovely name."

"*Merci,*" she replied.

"*Parlez-vous français?*" he asked excitedly.

"*Un peu,*" she admitted. "But badly."

"Then we'll stick to English today."

They sipped their tea. Frank hadn't even mentioned his failure to receive tenure, had perhaps mellowed since sharing his disappointment with Skip.

"I understand you and I have something in common," he said. "A commuter marriage."

Was he coming on to her? Lloyd had spent the previous weekend at Vrai's house. She felt her cheeks redden.

With smooth courtesy Frank rescued them both.

"My wife is still in Philadelphia. Our younger son wanted to finish high school there. But Celeste will be joining me next summer. We're counting the days."

Celeste. Babar's wife. Vrai noticed the photograph on Frank's desk of a smiling young woman with a round face.

"Yes, that's my Celeste." Frank was beaming. "We plan to buy a house here in Baltimore. Right now, as you may know, I'm renting a place nearby.

"It's been difficult living apart, as I'm sure you and your husband have discovered. Each spouse worries about the other." Balancing the teacup and saucer in his left hand, Frank straightened his right leg, reached into his pants pocket, and withdrew a key ring. "Isn't this clever? A gift from my dear wife." He fingered a small red flashlight. "Looks like a flashlight, but it's really a pepper spray. I left the car with her, and she worries about me walking home at night." He re-pocketed the key ring. "More tea?"

"Not yet, thanks. It's really very good."

"You have two sons in college." It wasn't a question. Frank had done his homework.

"That's right," Vrai said.

"Our older son graduated from Penn State. He's a computer programmer in New York now. And I think our younger son's planning on college. I dearly hope so, anyway. But our daughter." Frank shook his head. "The day after her high school graduation she followed a drummer to Milwaukee. She calls every now and then, asking for money. I tell her I'll send her money for college tuition, or for a plane ticket home, but that's it."

"I've been lucky." Vrai knew this was true.

"I understand you grew up in Tennessee. Knoxville, is that right?"

Vrai nodded. Was he even going to mention the Art History Library?

"Then you and Skip Howard must be old friends."

"Skip lived next door to my best friend," Vrai said. "That's the only connection we had back then."

"I see." The warm tea was turning Frank's cheeks pink. "Before we talk about your department, I was wondering if I might ask your help with a problem I'm having."

"Of course."

"It's Skip, actually."

Vrai raised her empty cup to her lips and pretended to swallow.

Frank frowned into his own cup. "Skip seems angry about something. Resentful. I hope you won't think I'm prying. It's not my nature to pry. I'd like to suggest counseling, but I'm not sure how to go about it."

Maybe it wasn't the tea. Even Frank's forehead was pink.

"I've had my own share of professional disappointments," he went on. "I used to be a history professor, a Napoleon scholar. You may have heard of my Napoleon Project. My plan was to develop a CD-ROM database listing everything ever written by or about Napoleon. I have thousands of index cards.

"But the head of my department and I didn't see eye to eye. Angelo Papanikolakis is his name. It's Angelo's unenlightened opinion that bibliography is not scholarship. He saw to it that I was not awarded tenure."

Here it comes, Vrai thought.

"Every man has his Waterloo. That, I'm afraid, was mine. So I ended up in library school. At least I wasn't exiled to the South Atlantic. No, I was fortunate indeed. What more beautiful body of water is there than the Chesapeake Bay? Did you know that Napoleon's youngest brother lived in Baltimore for a time? Jérôme was his name."

With his napkin Frank dabbed at his mustache, his beard, his perspiring brow. "At first, I admit, I resented having to change careers, but now I couldn't be happier. I'm earning more money already than that little Greek olive ever will. I'm determined to make a success of my new profession. I'm optimistic about the future of libraries. But Skip. I can't help wondering if he suffered some sort of disappointment, as I did, and needs help finding his way."

I don't *think* so, Vrai stopped herself from saying. "Nothing I'm aware of."

"You think I'm asking you to rat on a friend." Frank nodded his strange little beard. "I told you it wasn't my nature to pry, and what am I doing? I'm prying. Let me assure you that anything you say this afternoon will be held in strictest confidence. Ready for more tea?"

He refilled their cups from the white pot. "Sugar, yes?"

"Please."

They sat and sipped. Frank's face was an alarming shade of red. He was breathing heavily.

"If you're willing," he said, "tell me a little about Skip's family."

She told him as little as possible. "There's just Skip's mother now. His father and sister are dead."

"Did they die together? An automobile accident?"

It had been a mistake to mention Melody. "I think his sister died first."

"Had she been ill?"

Vrai took a long sip.

"Cancer?" Frank pressed. "There's so much of it these days."

To tell him Melody drowned would only invite more questions. "I hardly knew her. She was much younger."

"Too young to die." Frank's tone was solemn. "Skip must have been devastated."

"He was."

"So Skip discussed her death with you?"

"Not really," she lied, her cheeks flushing warm and pink.

"Do you remember his sister's name?"

Of course she remembered. He'd get this from her and no more. "Melody."

"Melody." Frank was elated. "How difficult it must be to lose a little sister named Melody! I have a dear friend whose wife recently committed suicide. He, too, was devastated."

Vrai set the cup and saucer in her lap to stop the rattling. He was fishing; he couldn't possibly know for sure. "Frankly, I'm a little uncomfortable with this conversation." She cringed at her choice of words. Skip liked to joke, in a mock Clark Gable voice, "I'm Frank Leigh, my dear, and I don't give a damn."

"The last thing I want is to make you uncomfortable." Frank studied her with his steely eyes. "Let's talk about the real reason for our meeting today. I hear nothing but good things about the Art History Library. Rupert Brill sings your praises."

"Thank you." Her mouth was dry. She lifted the cup and drained it.

"I imagine it must be difficult, at times, managing a unit physically separate from the main library. Is there anything I can do to make your job easier?"

A golden opportunity, and she seized it. Who wouldn't have? "Having an assistant would help tremendously, even part-time." This was a request she'd been making for years.

"Well, I'll certainly look into it." Frank stood up. The meeting was over. He took her empty teacup. Thanked her for coming. Asked her to keep their conversation in strictest confidence. Said he knew he could trust her.

. . . .

A couple of weeks later a memo to all staff announced that Skip's position as Head of Reference had been eliminated. There were rumors that Skip had been told at noon to clean out his office and return all keys by two o'clock. Vrai learned of his departure the following morning and, worried about him, left several messages on his answering machine at home. He didn't return her calls.

In early October, on a beautiful Sunday afternoon, she spotted him in Poe Park. But instead of returning her wave, Skip leaned down and spoke to Cassi, and the two of them took off running.

So Vrai was surprised when an invitation to Skip's annual Halloween party arrived. The address label was computer-generated. Perhaps he'd forgotten to delete her name. Or was he finally ready to talk?

Skip looked ridiculous that night. The scar on top of his balding head, the result of the incident with Lloyd and the burning marshmallow, had been turned into a third eye, complete with eyeliner and false eyelashes. "A pineal eye," Skip kept explaining, bowing deeply to his arriving guests, "sensitive to light in some reptiles but vestigial in humans."

Skip and Gussie swore they hadn't consulted about costumes beforehand. Gussie had sewn two eyes on top of the hood of an orange bathrobe and come as a celestial goldfish, its eyes gazing upward.

Did Gussie's son Justin, who was there in his wheelchair, know that both his mother and his host were sporting extra eyes? Justin couldn't see out of either of his. No one dared ask if his faded camouflage shirt was his costume, if Justin had come dressed as the disabled vet he actually was.

Bev, too, seemed to have come as herself. The busy lawyer. So busy that all the costume she'd had time for was a plastic pumpkin tied to each earring.

Vrai and three catalogers had arranged to meet in the lobby of Skip's apartment building. After tying themselves together at the wrists with twine, they boarded the elevator as a string quartet. Vrai planned to joke with Skip that she'd been roped into coming.

The initial hilarity of shaking hands with the other guests was replaced by consternation when the string quartet wanted to visit the punch bowl. While the catalogers—Alice, Rachel, and Martina—discussed the logistics, Vrai's attention was drawn to a framed photo of a woman braiding a young girl's hair. The girl was seated in a white wicker chair on a flagstone patio, her chin lowered, her eyes closed.

But the woman in the photo was Skip's girlfriend, not his mother. The girl with blonde hair was Bev's daughter, not Melody. Startled by the realization, Vrai raised her right hand in surprise, bringing Rachel's left hand up with it, and Alice, the one whose idea the string quartet had been, the one with the scissors, carefully severed the twine joining Vrai to Rachel.

In the dining room Vrai ladled orange-colored vod-ka punch into four cups. Stacked on a chair were Skip's party favors for the guests, white T-shirts proclaiming in blue letters: WE HAVE BEEN TRANSFORMED.

Alice and Martina, forced to coordinate sips of punch with the other two, were eyeing the guacamole when Skip appeared with a pair of kitchen shears. He refused to look at Vrai, hadn't met her eyes all night. Snip, snip, snip went the shears. No more string quartet.

Vrai followed Skip into the kitchen. "Anything I can do to help?" she said.

Skip opened a cabinet and took down a large bowl. "Help? Surely you jest."

"Please, Skip," she said. "Turn around and look at me."

Instead, he opened the top door of the refrigerator in her face. Taped to the door was a quote in his hand-writing. "'Most men have found friendship a treacherous harbor.' Sophocles, in *Ajax*."

"Congratulations," Skip said. "I hear you finally have an assistant." He made a lot of noise emptying a tray of ice cubes into the bowl. "And somehow our new direc-tor—sorry, your new director, your confidant—knows all about my little sister. Who could possibly have told him?"

"Look at me, Skip. If you'll just look at me, I'll tell you exactly what happened."

But Skip refused. He refilled the ice trays at the sink and returned them to the freezer.

"I swear to you," she said, "I told Frank nothing."

"Did he charm it out of you? I happen to know just how susceptible you are to the charms of married men."

Vrai was stunned. "Is that what this is about?"

"This is about trust. This is about betrayal of trust."

"Skip. I give you my word. I've never told anyone."

As he left the kitchen with the bowl of ice, Skip bowed low, giving her a good long look with his third eye.

Vrai's response was equally childish. She stormed out of the kitchen and found her coat. Halfway home she realized she'd forgotten her WE HAVE BEEN TRANSFORMED T-shirt.

chapter 13

❄ ❄ ❄

"You awake?" Jonathan asked softly.

"I am."

"Did you ever see Gussie's goldfish? Before they got flushed down the toilet, I mean?"

"I'm not sure that actually happened."

"But the goldfish were real?" Jonathan said.

"A lot more real than that guillotine."

Skip's depiction of the atmosphere at staff meetings, though, was fairly accurate. Like a preacher at a revival, Frank would get himself all worked up, saying over and over, in evangelical tones, *You must transform yourselves.*

"What's Gussie like?"

Vrai had been afraid he might ask. She didn't want to lie. "I'm so sorry. Gussie had a heart attack and died. Last Saturday, I think it was."

"Noooo."

She wished she could take it back, he sounded so upset. "I saw her obituary when I was looking for Skip's."

"So who's feeding the goldfish?"

"Justin, maybe," Vrai said. "Gussie's son."

"Wait! Who's taking care of Justin? Skip was supposed to, if something happened to Gussie."

"You have a really good memory."

"Isn't there something wrong with him?" Jonathan's voice rose. "Where's Justin now?"

"I don't know."

"We need to find him."

"Not much we can do from here," she said.

"Is Gussie's brother still alive?"

"I think so." The surviving relatives were listed in the obituary.

"Maybe Justin's with his uncle. Maybe that's where the goldfish are, too."

"I bet you're right," Vrai said. "Glad that mystery's solved."

"Nothing's sol-ved," Inspector Clouseau snapped. "This is so mixed up." He took a breath. "Gussie died on Saturday? When did Skip die?"

"Monday afternoon."

"Skip and Gussie were good friends?"

"Gussie may have been a substitute mother for Skip." A mother who saw some value in librarianship.

"Don't you think it's suspicious? Two deaths in two days?"

"Not really." Vrai had already given this some thought. "Here's what might've happened. On Saturday, Gussie had a heart attack, and Justin called his friend Skip. On Monday, Skip was on campus making arrangements for a memorial service for Gussie. He took the short cut back to his apartment, along the path beside the tennis courts, and he was so upset he started to cry. He was wearing sunglasses, because his other glasses were broken, and he took them off to wipe away the tears, and that's why he didn't see the car coming."

"Or hear it?"

"He was upset."

"Is that a true story?" Jonathan said.

"It makes sense, doesn't it?"

Silence from the other bed. The dark room felt like a sensory deprivation chamber. No fan dispensing heat. No footsteps, no voices. No more thunder and lightning. She closed her eyes.

"Speaking of Skip," Jonathan said.

"Mmm?"

"Where was Frank when Skip was killed?"

"I have no idea. Why?"

"Why do you think?" Jonathan said. "Frank could've pushed Skip in front of that car, because Skip knew Frank killed Gussie. Justin might be dead, too."

"Whoa!" Vrai opened her eyes. "Want to eat one of those sandwiches?"

"Where are they?"

"I gave them to you, remember?" Another item she should've brought in from the car was the little flashlight in the glove compartment.

"What kind of sandwiches?"

"Ham and cheese."

"What kind of cheese?"

"Yellow." She heard Jonathan get out of bed and then the rustle of a plastic bag.

"You want one?" he asked.

"Not right now." Her stomach was in turmoil. "There's juice, too."

. . . .

On Wednesday, after her initial phone conversation with Mrs. Howard, Vrai had e-mailed Doug Duesberg to tell him she'd be taking Thursday and Friday off to attend Skip's funeral. She'd then walked down the hall to see if Dr. Brill was in. Rupert Brill liked to be asked in person.

Despite his secretary's protest that he was busy, Dr. Brill beckoned Vrai into his office. He was a heavyset Texan with soft white hair and impeccable manners, the sort of man Oscar Wilde had in mind when he defined a true gentleman as someone who was never unintentionally rude.

"Let me offer my condolences," Dr. Brill said. "I know Skip Howard was a good friend of yours."

Vrai longed to tell him the truth. The friendship had blown up in her face.

"There's a service on Friday in Knoxville," she said.

"Of course you must go."

"I can ask my assistant to work extra hours."

Dr. Brill leaned back in his white leather chair. On the wall behind him was a painting of horses, by Degas; the painting had belonged to his mother. "Don't give the library another thought. Will you drive down?"

Vrai nodded. "I have to take his dog. And the ashes." Her voice was a hoarse whisper. "I have no idea where the ashes are."

Dr. Brill buzzed his secretary, who placed the call for him to Maryland Memorial Hospital. Each time he was transferred to a different person, Dr. Brill insisted he was related to the deceased and needed to locate the remains at once, since they had to be transported to Tennessee immediately.

"Skip's mother said the doctor who called her was named Hashish." Vrai shrugged. "Not sure she heard that right."

"An autopsy?" Dr. Brill said into the phone. Then, "I see." On hold again, he explained that in Maryland an autopsy was required when the deceased was DOA.

He turned back to the phone. "The Medical Examiner's Office?" He wrote down the number, hung up, and placed the call himself. Again he was transferred, again he was put on hold. He tapped his pen on the desk in annoyance.

"Finally!" he said. "What's your name again? Well, Cindy, please tell your boss for me that you deserve a substantial bonus." He placed yet another call and, his tone brisk, told Greater Baltimore Cremation, Inc. that a young woman named Vraiment Lynde would collect Mr. Howard's remains within the hour. Yes, he supposed she could wait until five thirty, but no later. Greenspring Avenue, just north of the zoo. Yes, she did know where that was.

Dr. Brill handed Vrai his notes. The o's in "zoo" had bars on them, like cages.

"I don't know how to thank you," she said.

He brushed this away with the back of his hand and turned to gaze out his windows at the cold, rainy day. There was a rumble of thunder.

"Skip once played tennis in a thunderstorm," she began, but her throat tightened up, and she couldn't continue.

Dr. Brill gently changed the subject. "How long have you been in this job?"

"Ten years," she managed to reply.

"*Ten years*? When you get to be my age, the years go by so quickly it's like walking fast past a picket fence." He turned back around. "What happened to the Little Corporal?"

Vrai was glad she recognized this reference to the Napoleon scholar. "Dr. Leigh's away at a conference." A staff meeting scheduled for Tuesday had been cancelled because Frank had decided at the last minute to go to New York.

"I saw him Monday night at the Giant," Dr. Brill said. "Tuesday morning, to be exact. On nights I can't sleep I like to make use of that time, not waste it, so I went out to do some grocery shopping. Frank was there, buying a steak. Only a frozen steak would've done that black eye of his any good, and I started to tell him so, but he pretended he hadn't seen me and walked off."

"Frank had a black eye?"

"A beaut. Perhaps he was celebrating St. Patrick's Day a wee bit early? Ran into a fist in a bar? I've heard he has a terrible temper." Dr. Brill rose from his chair.

"Please do drive carefully."

She promised she would.

. . . .

"Frank could be a double murderer," Jonathan said, his mouth full.

"I truly doubt that."

"You *like* Frank, don't you?"

"Not any more." At his first staff meetings, when Frank had gone on and on about transformation, he'd looked enough like M. C. Escher to make her think of fish being transformed into birds and birds into horses. Skip had felt threatened. Vrai had been intrigued, willing to give the new director a chance.

"That tour of the library said where Gussie's brother lives, but I forgot," Jonathan said.

"Me, too. Gussie's obituary might say."

"Where is it?"

"In my wallet. But it's too dark in here to read." Again she wished she'd brought the little flashlight in.

"I'm going to open the curtains."

"No you're not."

"But this is important. We need to find Justin, make sure he's OK."

"What's more important is to stay warm. Wherever he is, Justin's not going anywhere. He's snowbound, just like us."

Goose bumps crawled along her arms. Frank had a flashlight on his key ring. Not a real flashlight, a fake one containing pepper spray. Pepper spray would make a grown man cry. Maybe fling his glasses aside and run into the street while rubbing his eyes.

chapter 14

❄ ❄ ❄

The phone rang, as startling and insistent as a fire alarm but difficult to locate in the dark. "How did it happen?" Robbie wanted to know.

"He was crossing Olmsted Parkway," Vrai told her son.

"This was in broad daylight, right? I mean, Skip hadn't been drinking or anything?"

"Early afternoon, yes," Vrai said. "I told his mother he might've been going for ice cream."

"Killed for an ice cream cone? Skip? Not a chance."

Vrai had to agree. "Where are you? I am so glad to hear your voice."

"Baton Rouge, with Gloria."

She'd never met Gloria. Larry, too, had a girlfriend. Charlene or something. Her sons were becoming adults without her. "Is there snow there?"

"A few inches, yeah." He took a breath, and Vrai knew he was struggling not to cry. Robbie had always taken things hard. He'd been failing chemistry in high school until Skip began helping with the homework. "I can't believe it."

"The blizzard?"

"Skip."

"Me neither," she said. "How long will you be in Baton Rouge?"

It took a while for Robbie to answer. "Driving back tomorrow."

"All the way to Nebraska?"

"All the way, Mom. I think I need to hang up now. I'll call again tomorrow night."

But he didn't hang up.

"Robbie, honey, I'm so sorry," Vrai said, "about Skip."

"Me, too." There was a click, and the phone went dead.

. . . .

With Bob in Seattle, both boys had kept a close watch on the scales, never allowing them to dip for too long toward one parent or the other—trying not to show favoritism, refusing to take sides. For Vrai, the parent in residence, this had been both difficult to watch and, quite often, maddening.

Larry, thirteen when Bob moved away, reasoned that since he'd spent the next four years in Baltimore with his mother he should spend his four college years in Seattle. Larry would soon graduate from the University of Washington. Robbie, two years younger, decided on the University of Nebraska because, as he demonstrated on a map, Lincoln was almost exactly halfway between Baltimore and Seattle.

The family continued to gather at Christmas and

Thanksgiving, often in Baltimore, sometimes in Talla-
hassee with Vrai's parents, and sometimes in Chicago at
Bob's sister's. The previous Thanksgiving they'd met in
Lincoln, Nebraska. Because of its equidistance.

"Robbie's your son?" Jonathan said.

"The younger one. He wants to be called Robert now,
but I keep forgetting."

"He lives in Baton Rouge?"

"Lincoln, Nebraska. He's in Baton Rouge visiting his
girlfriend."

"What's your other son's name?"

"Laramie. After your mother. We call him Larry."

"Oh." Jonathan took some time to think this over.
"How did Robbie know where you are?"

"My husband must have given him the number."

"What's your husband like?"

"He's a photographer."

"I don't mean what he does, I mean what's he like?
Will he try to order me around?"

"He's in Seattle," Vrai said. "Works for a newspaper there."

"He lives there? I thought it was some kind of business trip. You said you were married."

"I am married. We live in different cities."

"Sooo. You're bi-coastal."

Laramie's articulate kid. "Sort of."

"That's why you didn't know he had a dog," Jonathan
said. "I couldn't figure that out. I don't think Daphne's a
good name for a dog."

Vrai thought back to her conversation with Bob. Jonathan had heard every word of it.

"Where does Larry live?"

"Seattle," she said. "He and Robbie are both in college."

"You miss them?"

"Yeah, I sure do." She waited for him to call her an empty-nester.

"I guess you have an empty bedroom in Baltimore."

"Two of them." She wondered what time it was. "I think I could eat a sandwich now."

"OK if I have the other one?"

. . . .

After they'd eaten, there was nothing to do but talk.

"You know Doug Duesberg?" Jonathan said.

"He's the deputy director of the library. Sort of like a vice president." Deputy Dawg, Skip had called him, though probably not to his face.

"Is he as mean as Frank?"

"He pretty much does what Frank tells him to do," Vrai said.

"Like flushing fish down toilets?"

A rhetorical question.

"What Level is your office on?"

Vrai had known this was coming. "I'm the art history librarian. My office is in a different building."

"Nooo. So you're the betrayer?"

"I didn't betray anyone. Skip asked me to keep a secret. I said I would, and I did."

"So Skip was wrong about you?"

"Skip jumped to conclusions. He didn't have all the facts."

"Why should I believe you?"

"Believe what you want," Vrai said.

"What was the secret?"

"I promised Skip I wouldn't tell. He thought I told Frank, but I didn't. I never told anyone, not even my husband. I'm not about to break my promise now."

Silence from Jonathan.

. . . .

"When someone calls the motel, who answers?"

"Dave does," Vrai said. "Today, anyway. He then sends the call to the right room."

"So if Uncle Lloyd called to get directions to the motel, Dave would just give them to him?"

"I suppose so, but you've seen the interstate. How would he get here?"

"Army helicopter," Jonathan said.

"Are you afraid of your Uncle Lloyd?"

"I'm afraid he'll make me go back to Asheville."

"That's entirely possible," Vrai said.

. . . .

"Know what I'd like to do?" Jonathan said.

"Tell me."

"Make snow angels on my parents' graves."

"It's a lovely idea," Vrai said.

. . . .

"So can we go?"

"Go where?" she said.

"Boston. To the cemetery."

"Can we wait till the snowplow comes?"

"There aren't any snowplows down south."

"They plow the interstates." She hoped this was true.

"OK. So is this a promise then?"

"I promise that sometime soon, unless your Uncle Lloyd and Aunt Marianne object, I'll take you to Boston to see your parents' graves."

"Why would they object?"

Vrai couldn't answer, due to salty tears in her throat.

. . . .

"You warm enough?" she whispered, hoping he'd finally fallen asleep.

"Not really."

"Want to come over here with me?"

There was the rustle of covers thrown back. "Good idea."

"Bring your blankets." Vrai slid over to give him the

warmer side of the bed. "If we move our arms and legs around under the covers, we can generate our own heat."

"Good practice for making snow angels," Jonathan said.

. . . .

"They'll never make a movie about my mom and dad," Jonathan said.

"Why not?"

"Because they didn't do anything wrong, like Thelma and Louise did."

"Thelma and Louise didn't start out as criminals," Vrai said. "It just sort of happened."

"Oh," Jonathan said. "I didn't see the beginning. Butch and Sundance robbed banks. But my mom and dad? Why did they have to die?"

"They didn't. I completely agree with you. All your dad did was tell the truth. In his poems."

"That's no reason to kill people."

"Of course not," Vrai said.

. . . .

"I'll have to take French," Jonathan said, "so I can join Interpol after high school."

"Your parents would've wanted you to go to college."

"They'd want justice even more."

. . . .

"Have you talked to your grandfather about Interpol?"
Mr. Eisen was an FBI agent.

But Jonathan was finally asleep.

chapter 15

❄ ❄ ❄

Sunday was living up to its name. The sun was out, the sky completely cloudless.

The lights and the radiator had come on before dawn. A few hours later, despite looking rumpled and weary, the local television announcers were giddy with the excitement of so much news. Church services had been canceled. Sunday papers would not be delivered. The Knoxville airport was closed. The Tri-Cities airport was closed. I-75 was closed. I-81 was impassable in places, especially around Wytheville, Virginia. Groups of hikers were stranded in the Smokies.

Vrai stood at the window gazing out at the snow, the blinding white lie that changed everything, the pristine coverup, the blanket denial. No signs of life in this alien landscape. I-81 was as quiet as a river frozen in its banks. Where, she wondered, did cardinals go in a blizzard?

And where was the Canadian with his shovel? She longed for coffee but was sane enough not to attempt another trek to the motel office. At what point would she and Jonathan become desperate enough to finish off the day-and-a-half-old hamburger?

"Can I read Gussie's obituary now?" asked Jonathan.

What else had she promised, or offered, or hinted she might do? She located her wallet, then sat down on her bed with the square of newsprint. "OK if I re-read it first?"

> **Morgen, Augusta Papastefanos**, *age 75, suffered a fatal heart attack on March 6. Preceded in death by husband Thomas Justin Morgen. Surviving are son Justin P. Morgen of Baltimore and brother George N. Papastefanos, sister-in-law Grace Papastefanos, and nephews Andre and Louis Papastefanos of Hagerstown. Dr. Morgen recently retired from the John Joseph Stark Library at Stoneham-Knox University after a long and distinguished career. A memorial service will be held in the library's Poole Room, 4500 Olmsted Parkway, on Friday, March 12, 1993, at 3 p.m. In lieu of flowers, contributions may be made to the Maryland Library for the Blind and Physically Handicapped.*

Had Gussie died with her Reeboks on? An irreverent thought, but then Gussie had never much cared what people thought of her. For forty years she'd walked to work, the same route each morning, through a neighborhood that had changed over the years and was no longer safe at night. She'd refused Skip's offers to drive her home, even on dark winter nights, telling him he was a paranoid worrywart and she'd be fine. Off she'd go in her pink-and-white Reeboks, her ponytail bouncing with each step. Heads would turn. Gussie Morgen had been a striking, noticeable woman.

To have worn her graying hair in a bun at the nape of her neck would have been unimaginative, stereotypical. Gussie preferred a high ponytail, anchored with a ruffled pink elastic which matched her Reeboks and was precisely positioned, the psychology librarian would point out, at the juncture between the occipital and parietal lobes.

For Gussie, changing into flats or heels once she got to work would have been a silly waste of time and footwear. She wore her Reeboks all day long.

"My turn," Jonathan said.

Vrai handed over the obituary. Skip could've simply called Campus Events to reserve the Poole Room for Gussie's service. Why had he even been on campus the day he died?

She went to the desk and plugged in the computer. "I'm worried the lightning might've erased Skip's files."

Jonathan didn't even look up. "Pa-pa-ste-fa-nos. George Pa-pa-whatever. So let's call Hag-gers-town."

"Hagerstown. Long a. What's the big hurry?"

"No hurry," Jonathan said. "I guess we've got all day."

"Whew," she said as the computer booted itself up. In her search for possible explanations, there was one stone left unturned. She located the subdirectory True Stories and selected Slipping.

Slipping

The Venetian blinds pulse with bright bars of sunlight. Too bright. The woman blinks. She stands up, intending to take a different chair.

"Don't move," the man says quietly. "Stay where you are." He's seated across the table from her, his back to the window.

The woman raises her hands, as if he's pulled a gun on her. He's not armed, of course. He doesn't need to be. He's her boss, his voice smooth as velvet, silky with power. In front of him is a blank piece of paper. His office door is closed.

She sits down again, stares into her lap.

"Look at me," he says.

"The light hurts my eyes." She doesn't raise her head.

"Perhaps you should see an ophthalmologist," the man purrs, loosening his tie. His suit coat hangs on the chair behind his desk. He's warm in the sunlight, his cheeks flushed. "Years of library work can take a toll on one's eyes. A woman your age should wear glasses. You may be getting cataracts."

"There's nothing wrong with my eyes," she says.

"What about your memory? They say the short-term memory is the first to go. What did you have for dinner last night?"

"Chili," the woman says.

"Canned or homemade?"

"Homemade."

"Who made it?"

"I did."

"What did you put in it?" the man asks.

"I can't imagine why you need to know a thing like that."

"I've been told you're slipping," the man says. "You're seventy-three years old. Most people your age are glad to stop working and begin enjoying what time they have left in this world."

"I enjoy my job," the woman says. "There's no set retirement age at this university. You can't force me to retire."

"I am the director of this library," the man says. "You are my employee. May I remind you that as a librarian at this institution you have no contract? I've learned, in fact, that you're not a professional librarian at all. You have a PhD in psychology but no MLS. Your salary is that of a librarian when you are, in fact, a fraud. What did you put in the chili you made last night?"

"*Ground beef, onions, green peppers, toma-toes, garlic, chili powder, kidney beans.*" List-lessly, the woman lists the ingredients.

"*No salt?*"

"*Yes, of course. A little salt, a little pepper.*"

"*How many cans of kidney beans?*"

"*Two.*"

"*Of course I have no way of knowing if you're telling the truth. You may not know yourself. Women your age tend to be forgetful. Maybe last night you poached a salmon.*"

"*I made chili.*"

"*Was there any left over?*"

"*Yes. We'll have it tonight.*"

"*We?*" The man's voice swoops up, like a gull with a fish. "*You live with someone?*"

The woman stares down at her hands.

"*I asked you a question,*" the man says. "*Look at me.*"

Against the Venetian blinds his face is a blur. She turns away. "*Why did you wish to meet with me today?*"

"*I'd like to get to know you better. It's impor-tant for a library director to have good working relationships with his staff.*"

"*If this is a social visit, then I'd like to sit in a different chair.*"

"*Stay where you are,*" the man says. "*Are*

you slipping? I've been told you're slipping."

"By whom?"

"It was told to me in the strictest confidence. Surely you don't expect me to betray a trust. Since this particular bit of information was conveyed to me, I've spoken with your immediate supervisor. Is it the new technology? Women your age are often afraid of computers."

"I have more experience with online databases than you do," the woman says. "In the sixties, I worked with the American Psychological Association to develop the Thesaurus of Psychological Indexing Terms, the backbone of PsycInfo."

"So you say. Yet you lack the MLS. As you may know, I myself have a PhD. Unfortunately, I wasn't awarded tenure. Is that something we have in common? How did you go from a PhD in psychology to library work?"

"It was the fifties," the woman says. "Psychology departments weren't hiring women."

"You could have gone into private practice."

"I'm not a clinical psychologist. Besides, I happen to enjoy library work. We have an excellent psychology collection."

"Yes. I'm curious," the man says, "about your husband. Was he able to find work in the fifties? How long were you married? Do you have children?"

When the woman doesn't answer, the man gets up and strides around the table. He stops behind her chair and grabs her ponytail. "Stupid old biddy," he says. "Do you think this silly ponytail makes you look any younger?" He gives it a yank. "Tell me who you live with."

"Let go or I'll scream," the woman says.

"If you scream, I'll say you became hysterical. Old women often do, you know. Lose their minds. Get to be a problem for the other employees. Forget how to do things. Forget what they did ten minutes ago. Do it again. Repeat themselves. Tell me who you live with."

"Whom," the woman corrects him.

The man gives her ponytail another yank. "Whom," he concedes.

The woman will not give in. Why should she say one word about the son she loves so dearly? "I'd like to go now," she says.

"I need to know about your living arrangements," the man says, moving her ponytail from side to side.

"What are your living arrangements?" she asks. "With whom do you live?"

"No one, at the moment, but my family plans to join me soon. I have a wife and three children, two sons and a daughter. Now then. Do you have children? I believe your parents

were of Greek heritage, but your surname sounds German. Did you have a husband at some point? Did he like Greek olives?"

The woman tries to stand up, but he forces her back into the chair. He raises her ponytail up over her head and pulls. She feels the beginning of helpless tears. But tears are exactly what he wants, a sign of weakness on her part. She takes a deep breath, regains control of herself. She will tell him nothing. She'll be strong, the way the Chilean poet was strong.

On September 11, 1973, General Augusto Pinochet seized power in a bloody coup. Thousands of Chilean citizens were ordered to report to the National Stadium. They went willingly. Obediently. Naively. Thinking nothing bad would happen to them. Chile had been a democracy for years.

The poet went. His wife, a U.S. citizen, stayed home.

Inside the stadium were hooded informants. One of these encapuchados *stopped in front of the poet, who was seated in the bleachers, and gave an ominous nod. A soldier took the poet into the bowels of the stadium, where interrogators demanded the names and addresses of all his friends. When the poet refused, they tortured him. He told them nothing.*

*After three days an army officer came in.
"Can he still walk?" the officer asked.*

The poet was made to stand, then to walk.

*"Release him," the officer said. "This is the
wrong poet."*

*Sometime before dawn he was driven to
a deserted street, reminded of the curfew, and
released. To avoid being shot, he lay shivering
in damp grass until the sun came up. Then he
walked the four miles home to his wife, who
had been afraid to report him missing. Whom
could she tell, officially, who didn't already
know? No one would be willing to make inqui-
ries. An entire country had closed its eyes. Curfew at eleven p.m. and everyone safely inside.
The newspapers didn't use the word* tortura.

*The next day, his jaws wired together, his
nose swollen, his broken ribs taped, the poet
went to warn his friends. At the University he
found armed guards on patrol. They were en-
forcing the signs that said "Keep off the grass."
They were sending girls in jeans home to put
on skirts. They held down boys with long hair
and attacked them with scissors. They arrested
students for kissing.*

All the poets were gone.

*The man has returned to his seat in front of
the Venetian blinds. "I asked you a question,"*

he's saying. "Are we having a little problem with the short-term memory? Difficulty paying attention?" He picks up the pen beside the blank sheet of paper and writes: forgetful and inattentive. "Did you even hear me?" He adds: hard of hearing.

"You asked me several questions," the woman says. "I was thinking about a friend of my supervisor's. He's dead now."

"Your supervisor? Dead? But I saw him this morning."

The man taps his pen on the table, writes: delusional, incoherent. "I've been so very fortunate," he says. "Everyone in my family is healthy. No problems whatsoever, either physical or mental. Your husband. I can't help wondering if you had a husband at some point. I believe you have a son who's disabled, though you refuse to discuss him with me. I feel no such reticence about my own family."

The woman stares down at her hands.

"Please look at me when I'm speaking to you," the man says. "You're being rude."

"The light hurts my eyes." The woman gets up and moves to a different chair.

"Your husband," the man continues. "Did he run off with another woman? Neglect to marry you? Take his own life?"

The woman says nothing.

"Where did you go on your honeymoon? Were you a virgin when you married? Was he? At what age did you have your first sexual experience? Was it with him?"

A lawyer would advise, It would be your word against his. She wishes she'd brought a tape recorder.

The man writes: rude and insubordinate. "Suicide," he muses. "The suicide of one's spouse must be a very difficult burden to bear. I suppose one tends to blame oneself. I have a dear friend whose wife committed suicide. He's pretty much a basket case by now. The University has a counseling program for staff who are experiencing personal difficulties. I'd like for you to go. I'll grant you time off each week for counseling sessions."

The woman will not give him the satisfaction of responding.

"Your supervisor. You mentioned your supervisor a moment ago. He's quite concerned about you." The man's purring again, his voice solicitous, falsely kind. "He asked if you might be permitted to work part-time."

The woman doesn't believe this for a minute. Her supervisor is someone she trusts implicitly. He knows she loves her job.

She hesitates. Part-time would be better

than not working at all. "I'm willing to consider it," she says.

"Well, I'm not," the man says. "I don't want my staff cluttered up with part-timers."

"When you were interviewed for the position of director," the woman says, "you said you were in favor of part-timers."

"Did I say that? Well, I've changed my mind. There will be no part-timers in this library."

The woman starts to point out that there are several part-timers on staff but stops. He might ask for their names.

"Were you about to say something?" The man taps his pen on the table. Tap. Tap. Tap.

The woman stands up. She re-anchors a few strands of hair in her ponytail and turns toward the door.

"Sit down," the man orders. "I'm not finished with you. Sit down, I said. Come back here."

The woman walks to the door and opens it. The secretaries look up from their desks. She's not the first, their sad eyes say; she won't be the last.

She turns to the man. "You horse's ass. You shit-for-brains."

The man scribbles furiously on his sheet of paper.

Vrai stared at the computer screen. Had Frank hassled Gussie into retiring? Possibly. Had Gussie's husband killed himself? Surely not.

Horse's ass? Shit-for-brains? Skip himself would've told Frank off using far more colorful language.

She closed the file, exited DOS, and turned off the computer.

"Wait." Jonathan leapt up from his bed. "Is that another story? Let me read it."

"I can't. It reveals the secret I told you about, the one I promised Skip I'd keep." This wasn't entirely true, but she didn't want Jonathan to read about his father's torture. Skip had known the details of it only because Vrai had told him, never dreaming he'd claim the story as his own. Skip had never even met Miguel. The dishonesty was unsettling, especially since this story seemed more "true" than the other two.

"But Skip told," Jonathan said.

"He told his computer, not us. We should never have invaded his privacy."

"Did Frank know the secret?" Jonathan said.

"Skip thought he did."

"But how? How did Frank find out?"

She remembered the way her teacup had rattled when Frank mentioned his friend whose wife had committed suicide. "Diabolically."

"Huh?"

"Frank is an evil sneak."

chapter 16

❄ ❄ ❄

The phone rang. Jonathan let Vrai answer it.

Dave, sounding dangerously over-caffeinated, was calling to say that the day manager was still stranded at home, or claimed to be, but Corrie the cook was here, thanks to her Uncle Bud, who'd brought her on his tractor. Corrie was going to cook up a mess of grits and scramble some eggs. It was bitter cold outside, two degrees below zero. Best not try to open the door, with the snow drifted up against the motel the way it was. The people in No. 9 made that mistake, and it took them an hour to close their door again. Uncle Bud was going to try to deliver breakfast from his tractor but, due to the amount of shoveling involved, there might be a long wait.

Vrai ordered two breakfasts at five dollars each. "Thanks. That's really nice of you."

"Least we can do. I know it's been hard, with the electricity off and all."

She replaced the receiver. "Room service will bring our breakfasts."

"How?" Jonathan looked dubious.

"By tractor. Want to put your slacks on?"

"Not really."

She tested the moccasins. Still damp, as were her sneakers and jeans. She gathered up her dress, pantyhose, and heels and headed for the bathroom. "I'm going to change into what *I* wore to the funeral."

"And then we'll call Hagerstown." It wasn't a question.

While trying to pull a comb through her hair, Vrai weighed the pros and cons. A phone call might upset Gussie's grieving brother. If he was willing to talk to her, then she might learn that Justin had been carted off to a VA hospital with his uncle's approval. Or that Justin's whereabouts were unknown. Or that Justin, too, was dead. What Jonathan wanted to hear was that Justin had moved in with his aunt and uncle, both of whom loved him and would provide excellent care for him. What were the chances of that?

Knowledge was power, true. Also true: ignorance was bliss.

Where, in his vision of hell, had Dante placed the murderers? Were they down there at the bottom with the betrayers?

Jonathan looked up expectantly from yet another recital of snow accumulations, and Vrai changed the channel. On PBS Audrey Hepburn was gazing wistfully at—could it be?—Henry Fonda.

"It's *War and Peace!*" she said. "Let's watch this."

"I thought we were calling Hagerstown."

"After breakfast."

"You don't *want* to find out where Justin is, do you? You don't even *care* about what happened to Skip."

Vrai picked up the ringing phone. Her father's voice was full of concern for his only child. They traded storm details—three inches of snow in Florida, fifteen inches in Knoxville, thirteen in Birmingham. Two feet, she guessed, at the Smoky View.

She said good-bye and joined Jonathan at the window. A tractor, pushing a snowplow, rumbled back and forth across the parking lot. The driver wore a puffy green jacket and a red-plaid hat with ear flaps. Soon he disappeared, leaving a ridge of snow behind the parked cars.

"How am I supposed to back my car out?" Vrai grumbled.

They went back to watching *War and Peace.*

Eventually the tractor returned and came to a stop. The driver stepped off onto the ridge of snow, grabbed a shovel, and cleared a path to the room next door. He then carried what looked like an insulated pizza case inside.

"That must be Uncle Bud," Vrai said. "Don't you want to put your slacks on? You'll freeze when we open the door."

Jonathan looked down at the gap between his sweatshirt and her socks. He went into the bathroom and came out wearing her robe.

"Who's that?" He pushed back a green sleeve and pointed at the television screen. With the robe trailing behind him he looked like a dark-haired, bespectacled version of Saint-Exupery's Little Prince. "This one. Who is this man?"

"It must be Napoleon."

"Nooo. I know who it is! It's Chief Inspector Dreyfus."

"It's Napoleon." She was sure of it. "Napoleon Bonaparte. He invaded Russia. He's the war in *War and Peace*."

"Yeah, well, maybe he's Napoleon here, but he's Chief Inspector Dreyfus in the Pink Panther movies."

The scowl was familiar. "You're right," she said. "It's Clouseau's boss."

"'How can an idiot be a policeman?' It's him all right. Does he win?"

"Not this time. He has to retreat in the snow all the way back to France."

"Good," Jonathan said.

As Henry Fonda was staggering around in the snow during the Battle of Borodino, the tractor rumbled up, clattered, and went silent. Uncle Bud shoveled a new path, flinging most of the snow onto Vrai's car. He then returned to the tractor and exchanged his shovel for the pizza case. Vrai met him at the door.

"Howdy," he gasped.

She shut the door behind him. "That's pretty strenuous work they have you doing."

With the computer and TV taking up most of the

desk, Uncle Bud set the pizza case on Jonathan's bed. Inside were two plates wrapped in aluminum foil. Napkins and silverware. Two cups.

"Is there coffee?" Vrai said.

From the pocket of his jacket Uncle Bud extracted a thermos. "Can't leave the thermos here," he said. "Everyone wants me to, but this is the only one we have. Good Lord. Where's that? Chattanooga?"

"Russia," Vrai said. "It's a movie." Napoleon's army was in retreat.

"Shucks," Uncle Bud said. "I thought you had the news on." He was close to her father's age, a tall, gaunt man.

"Wouldn't you like to sit down for a minute?" Vrai said.

"I sit down, I might never get up." Uncle Bud smiled. He was missing several teeth. "Cute little girl you have. What's your name, sugar?"

"Jonathan," Vrai said quickly.

"Nah. That's a boy's name."

"He's wearing my bathrobe."

"Criminy! Guess I can't get nothing right this morning. Where y'all from?"

"Baltimore." She frowned at Jonathan, who'd begun to giggle, and he glided into the bathroom and shut the door.

"Baltimore? Why, I was stationed up there in my Navy days. Didn't have more breakfasts to deliver, I'd tell you some wild tales about Baltimore."

Jonathan had turned on the shower.

"You got yourself one helluva drive ahead of you," Uncle Bud said.

"We sure do." From the thermos Vrai filled both cups and put them on the bedside table. "Do I pay you? Or can they put it on my bill?"

Another gap-toothed smile from Uncle Bud. "Don't pay me. Goodness sake. I'd just spend it on my girlfriends."

Uncle Bud didn't want to sit, but he didn't seem to want to go back outside either. She took out her wallet.

"Nah." He put his hat back on and retrieved his gloves. "Can't take no tips. Dave's paying me handsome."

"You sure you don't want to sit for a spell?" It was her grandmother's expression, a phrase from the grave.

"Now don't you worry. Dave makes me rest between deliveries. If my heart craps out, he's the one'll be doing all this shoveling."

"You take care then," Vrai said. "We're mighty grateful for the food."

"You are nothing but welcome." His hand on the doorknob, Uncle Bud turned around. "Almost forgot. Dave says to tell you he's hoping one of the waitresses will make it in. He'll give you a call when the restaurant opens up."

She pushed the door shut behind him and watched from the window until he was safely back on the tractor. The sun on the snow was blinding.

The bathroom door remained shut. Vrai knocked softly. "You can come out now."

"In a minute," Jonathan said. "I'm powdering my nose."

She put cream and sugar in one of the coffees, unwrapped a plate, and covered the other cup with the aluminum foil. The coffee was lukewarm, but this was no time to be picky. Napoleon/Dreyfus was in tears, overcome with grief at the fate of his poor soldiers.

"Good Lord," Jonathan chirped, "it's Chattanooga." He'd left her robe in the bathroom.

"Do you drink coffee?"

"Yuck."

"Can I have yours then?"

Jonathan uncovered the second plate. "You want my grits, too?"

"Someone told me once that I eat grits like a Yankee, because I put butter and sugar on them."

"Good idea." He peeled open a pat of butter.

"Save some of your sugar, please," Vrai said, "for my second cup of coffee."

They ate in silence.

"Done with breakfast yet?" Jonathan said.

Vrai sipped her coffee. "What's the rush?"

"I want to know if Justin's OK."

"But what if he isn't?" Vrai said.

"I want to know that, too."

"Can we wait till *War and Peace* is over?" She kicked off her heels, sat back in her bed.

"What's wrong with you?"

"I guess I just don't see the urgency." When stranded by the Blizzard of the Century, wasn't responsibility for one orphan enough? She barely knew Justin. Jonathan didn't know him at all. Damn Skip and his True Stories. "Even if we do find out something has happened to Justin, there's absolutely nothing we can do about it today. Maybe not ever."

"I trusted you." Jonathan's lip quivered. "You said we'd call Hagerstown after breakfast. You promised."

chapter 17

❋ ❋ ❋

V rai asked for Information in Baltimore, not Hagerstown. "Morgen, Augusta." She spelled Gussie's last name.

"What're you doing?" Jonathan said.

She covered the receiver. "Why bother Justin's aunt and uncle if we don't have to? Justin might still be in Baltimore."

The operator gave her the number for an A Morgen and an A P Morgen. Vrai tried them both but got no answer, so she called Information again and asked for the number of the VA Hospital on Greene Street. No one named Justin Morgen was a patient there.

"I told you he wasn't here the first time you called." The woman sounded annoyed. "I'm really sorry we can't help you."

"This *is* the first time I've called," Vrai said. "He's blind. His legs were amputated. He would've been admitted during the past week."

"I know. That's what you said before."

Vrai felt a chill. "Could he have been taken somewhere else? How can I find out where he is?"

"You already asked me that. And I said, 'You can't. It's Sunday.' It still is." The woman hung up.

Jonathan's eyes were wide. "Someone else is trying to find Justin?"

"Not sure what's going on."

"No legs? Can't see? Justin's a sitting duck."

This time Vrai asked for Information in Hagerstown.

"Unusual name, Papastefanos," the operator said. "That's why I remember it. Maybe you should write down the number this time."

Vrai thanked her and, avoiding Jonathan's intense scrutiny (Laramie's eyes on hyperalert), concentrated on the slo-mo mechanics of the rotary dial. "Maybe the lines are down," she muttered as the phone in Hagerstown rang and rang. Then, "Mrs. Papastefanos?"

"Speaking."

Vrai introduced herself and explained that she'd worked in the library with Gussie Morgen and was trying to locate Justin.

"He's not here." Mrs. Papastefanos said this slowly, enunciating each word.

"I'm not the one who called before," Vrai said. "I'm a friend of Skip's. Skip Howard."

"What's your name again?"

"Vrai Lynde." She spelled both names and was put on hold.

"It's Frank." Jonathan was pacing back and forth between the beds. "Frank's looking for Justin. That means Justin's alive, don't you think?"

Vrai shook her head. "The other caller must be female. It could be someone wanting to locate Justin to offer condolences."

"Huh?"

"To say she's sorry his mother died," Vrai said.

"Does Frank have a secretary?"

"Yes, but she doesn't work on Sunday."

A man came on the line. "This is George Papastefanos. Justin's not here with us. Who's calling, please?"

Vrai remembered her manners. She was sorry to bother them at such a difficult time. She'd worked in the library with Gussie and also been friends with Skip Howard, who'd played chess with Justin. Skip had died two days after Gussie did, under circumstances that seemed unusual, and she'd become a little worried . . .

"Skip died?" Mr. Papastefanos cut in. "Skip Howard?"

"Yes, I'm sorry. Did you know him?"

"Of course we knew Skip. When did he die?"

"Monday afternoon. He was hit by a car. I'm sorry to have to give you more bad news." Vrai stared into one of the empty coffee cups. Even with practice, this would never be easy.

"It's terrible news."

"I'm calling from Tennessee," she went on, relieved that Mr. Papastefanos seemed willing to talk to her. "I came down for Skip's funeral, and then I got caught in this blizzard. Do you happen to know where Justin is?"

Again she was asked to hold. She mouthed it to Jonathan: I'm on hold. She lifted her shoulders, implying she doubted she'd learn anything useful.

"Sorry to keep you waiting," Mr. Papastefanos said. "Where is it you're calling from?"

"Tennessee. I'm not sure where exactly. I'm snowbound in a motel." She laid it on with a trowel. "I'd known Skip since junior high. I drove down here from Baltimore for his funeral. I took Skip's ashes to his mother."

"I was able to speak to Justin. On another line. Can you give me your number, please? He'd like to talk to you."

"Of course." Vrai gave him the number for the Smoky View. "Do you have any idea when he might call?"

"Pretty soon, I expect."

"It's room 17. Last name Lynde. L-y-n-d-e."

"Got it. And Ms. Lynde? We very much appreciate your call."

Jonathan had ceased his pacing. "So Justin's going to call here?" He gave her a thumbs up.

But fifteen minutes ticked slowly by. When the phone finally did ring, Vrai answered with a neutral "Hello." The caller might be Dave, it could be Lloyd, there were multiple possibilities.

"Could I speak to Vrai Lynde, please?" Justin spoke ver-y slow-ly, his voice deep as a foghorn.

"Hi, Justin. This is Vrai."

"Skip's *dead*? Please. Tell me exactly what happened."

"All I know is, he was hit by a car. Monday afternoon. You know how tricky it is to cross Olmsted Parkway." But of course a blind man in a wheelchair didn't know the first thing about the traffic patterns on Olmsted Parkway or anywhere else.

"Where?" Justin said. "By the tennis courts?"

"My god," Vrai said. "How did you know?"

Justin spoke softly, as if afraid someone might be listening in. "On Mondays, Frank takes the shortcut to the Faculty Club for lunch. Creature of habit, Skip said. Skip was going to wait for him there, by the tennis courts." Justin paused, cleared his throat. "To tell Frank the police knew." Another pause. "About the phone calls."

What phone calls? Vrai almost asked, but she looked over at Jonathan and realized it was the sort of blunder Inspector Clouseau might make. "I see," she said.

"So you know, too?" Justin sounded alarmed.

"Actually I don't. I don't know anything. Except that Skip Howard was much too cautious to get hit by a car. Even if he was upset about something. I know he must have been very upset about Gussie." What was wrong with her? "I'm so sorry about your mother. Everyone loved her."

It was a few seconds before Justin replied. "Thank you."

"I wish I could have gone to the memorial service. But Skip's funeral was Friday afternoon, too, and Mrs. Howard asked me to bring his ashes to Knoxville."

"My mother's service was on Friday?"

She had made yet another mistake. "That's what the obituary said. Did Skip write the obituary?"

"He did. He was also going to arrange for a service, at the library."

Justin's wasn't a Southern drawl, but it had a similar effect. Get on with it, Vrai found herself thinking.

"When Skip didn't call me," Justin went on, "I called him, and left a message, and then my uncle showed up, and there was so much to tend to."

Vrai had noticed the light blinking on Skip's answering machine but had been reluctant to listen to his messages. Some detective she'd make!

"I think Mother would've been pleased by the memorial service Skip was planning." Justin was almost whispering. "She hadn't wanted a church funeral, but Uncle George insisted, and I didn't have the heart to argue." Again he cleared his throat. "She's buried in the Papastefanos family plot here in Hagerstown. I hear the views are to die for."

Vrai laughed. "Sorry." So Justin was in Hagerstown after all. "What was it Skip was going to talk to Frank about?"

Justin whispered it. "Frank killed my mother."

With Jonathan listening, Vrai chose her words carefully. "The obituary said she suffered a heart attack."

"She did. Caused by Frank."

"Go on." What looked like ants in the coffee cup were actually coffee grounds.

"Do you have any idea why Frank hated my mother?"

Vrai had a small clue. Didn't the professor who de-nied Frank tenure have a Greek name? Was Frank really so petty?

"I'm sure he didn't hate her." She was no longer sure of anything.

Jonathan sat perched on the edge of his bed, his ex-pression grim.

"Have we ever met, Vrai?" Justin said.

"At one of Skip's Halloween parties."

"OK. So you're aware of my situation."

"Yes."

"Do you know Bev? Does Bev know about Skip?"

"I left her several messages," Vrai said. "I assume she got them."

"They'd stopped seeing each other, I think, but I'm glad you told her," Justin said. "And good god. Cassi. What about Cassi?"

"She's with Mrs. Howard in Knoxville." Vrai refrained from telling Justin how reluctant she'd been to leave Cas-si with a blind person.

"That's good. Cassi's all she has left."

It seemed the only thing Vrai hadn't screwed up. "I don't want to alarm you, but someone else may be trying to find you."

"I know," Justin said. "A woman called earlier. Wouldn't give her name, so Uncle George got suspicious." He took a breath. "Poor Skip. I should never have let him go to meet Frank like that. Skip was so angry."

"Someone may have given Frank a black eye."

"A black eye?" Justin sounded delighted.

Vrai imagined the scene. Frank knocked on his butt in the snow. Skip leaning down to offer a gentlemanly hand up. Frank's other hand going to his pants pocket to retrieve the key ring, activate the pepper spray.

Had Frank given Skip a shove through the gap in the azaleas, or did Skip run through blindly on his own? Where was Frank at the moment of impact? Hiding behind the shrubbery? Fleeing the scene of the crime?

"There's a Sgt. Bailey I want to talk to," Justin said. "In Baltimore. I may need help with transportation."

"I'll be glad to do what I can." She owed Skip at least that much. "If they ever clear the roads down here, I may drive a friend up to Boston. Maybe we could stop in Hagerstown and give you a ride to Baltimore."

Jonathan raised his arms. Vrai had scored the winning goal.

chapter 18

❄ ❄ ❄

"So Frank killed Gussie, too?" Jonathan said. "He murdered them both?"

"Gussie had a heart attack. Skip was hit by a car." Had Frank been involved in both deaths? Justin seemed to think so.

"Are you thinking about your parents?" she said gently.

Jonathan sat down on the end of his bed and turned his back to her. "Don't you *ever* ask me that again. Ever." His right hand, the one Vrai could see, had become a fist. It sat coiled on his thigh, ready to strike. "And don't you dare tell me it'll help to talk about it, either."

"Does Marianne say that to you?"

In the orange sweatshirt, layered over her lilac turtleneck, he had the coloring of an exotic orchid, a delicate one requiring special care. Jonathan had built walls around his feelings. No intruders allowed.

"I talk about them when *I* feel like it," he said. "Not when someone else does."

"I understand," Vrai said, and she did. This was his way of keeping his balance. "I didn't mean to pry."

His face flushed, Jonathan turned around. "Why didn't you tell me Skip gave Frank a black eye?"

"I don't know that it was Skip. Let's not jump to conclusions here."

The phone rang, startling them both. It was Dave. The restaurant was open.

"But first," Vrai said, "I want to call Frank."

Jonathan just stared at her.

"Here's why. If his wife answers, then we'll have a pretty good idea of who's been trying to find Justin."

"Maybe you should eat first."

Did he think *she'd* come unhinged? "Let me at least see if Information has Frank's home phone number, OK? You can be putting your slacks on."

Her finger was sore from so much dialing. She tried using a ballpoint pen, then flung it to the floor. "This place needs to transform itself. Prepare for the twenty-first century."

"Take a deep breath," Jonathan said. "Count to ten."

An Information operator she hadn't spoken to before said that Frank's number was indeed listed. Vrai wrote it down.

"Your decision," she said to Jonathan. "Shall I call him now, or after dinner?"

"Oh go ahead."

A woman answered. "Is this Mrs. Leigh?" Vrai asked.

"Who's calling please?" the woman snapped.

Vrai explained that she worked in the library but had become stranded in the blizzard and was calling to ask Dr. Leigh for a few days off.

"Don't worry about it. The library's closed."

Vrai took a chance. "Celeste? This is Vrai Lynde. Is Frank there? I need to talk to him."

Jonathan, looking worried, sat down on his bed facing her.

Finally Frank's voice, pitched even lower than usual, growled "Hello."

"I'm so sorry to bother you. This is Vrai Lynde. I just wanted to let you know that I'm snowbound in Tennessee."

"You could've called Doug Duesberg," Frank said.

"For some reason Information didn't have his number," she lied. "I'm afraid I won't be able to come to work tomorrow."

"No one will, myself included. Don't know when the library will re-open." Frank's voice was like a tape being played at the wrong speed. Vrai had heard that he brewed beer as well as tea. On this Sunday afternoon he sounded like he'd had a little too much of his own pale ale.

"I'm glad you made it back to Baltimore OK," she said.

"Where did I go?"

"To a conference in New York."

"Oh, that." Frank coughed. "I wasn't able to attend. Seem to have caught the flu or something. Luckily, my dear wife's here to nurse me through it."

"The reason I'm in Tennessee." Vrai hesitated, looked

over at Jonathan, whose eyes were less wary now. He gave her a slight nod. Finish what you've started.

She forged ahead. "I went to Skip's funeral. Skip Howard. Did you know he died?"

Silence from Frank. Then, "I did, yes. A trad-egy."

Was he mixing alcohol with flu medicine? "Did the memorial service for Gussie take place?" Vrai said.

"The what?"

"Gussie Morgen. The psychology librarian who retired last year? She had a fatal heart attack."

"She was elderly," Frank said, his enunciation suddenly perfect.

"Her service was supposed to have been in the Poole Room. I would've gone, but Skip's was the same afternoon, and I'd known him longer. He and Gussie were such good friends."

Frank coughed. Said his wife had some medicine ready for him to take. Vrai heard a click. A teaspoon against a glass? She waited.

A female voice told her that if she'd like to make a call, she should please hang up. Vrai slammed down the receiver.

"What'd he say to you?" Jonathan demanded. "Did he cuss you out?"

"He hung up on me."

Inspector Clouseau cocked his head. "That means we're getting close."

"I learned two things. His wife's there with him. And he was in Baltimore when Skip died."

There was an ominous whir. Jonathan beat Vrai to the window. A helicopter, flying north along I-81, buzzed out of sight.

"Probably searching for stranded cars," Vrai said. She tested the moccasins and judged them dry enough to wear. "Here you go."

"Frank knows star-69," Jonathan said when the phone rang. "He's calling you back."

Vrai lifted the receiver, offered a cautious hello. It's my husband, she mouthed to Jonathan, who took his slacks into the bathroom.

"What's wrong?" Bob asked. From the other side of the country he could tell she was upset. "You've been on the phone. Everything OK?"

"We have some new information. Skip's death might not have been an accident."

Jonathan came out wearing his slacks. He sat down on the floor to put his moccasins on.

"We're going up to Boston," she told her husband, "as soon as they plow the interstate. Jonathan wants to see his parents' graves."

"Poor kid. Is he listening?"

"I don't even know where Laramie's buried." Tears arrived with no warning. Everything she'd felt since learning of Skip's death had liquefied and was streaming down her cheeks. "She was my best friend," Vrai sobbed into the receiver. "I never told her good-bye."

"Then go," Bob said. "Why let the Blizzard of the

Century stop you? But don't count on a snowplow. You may have to wait for nature to take its course."

"Nature is," she blubbered. "The sun's out. The restaurant's open."

Jonathan let out a groan and threw a moccasin against the radiator.

"Good," Bob said. "I've been worried about you."

"There's a spot by the restaurant," Vrai sniffled, "where jonquils are blooming in the snow." She dabbed at her eyes with the sheet. "Two days ago they were, anyway. You should be here, with your cameras. It's incredible."

"Wish I could be." Bob sounded like he meant this. "Call me when you leave for Boston, and along the way. I'll want to know where you are."

The phone radiated a warm glow. A magic wire carried her voice to Seattle. She told Bob everything—about Skip's meeting with Frank by the tennis courts, Frank's black eye, his fake flashlight filled with pepper spray. About the sunglasses in the snow, and the glasses she'd found in Skip's apartment. "Remember I told you Gussie Morgen died? Two days before Skip?"

"Sounds suspicious," Bob agreed. "How're you going to find out what really happened?"

"I just talked to Frank."

"Not sure that was wise," Bob said.

"He hung up on me. That speaks volumes, don't you think?"

"A regular *Britannica*."

"I also talked to Gussie's son in Hagerstown. We're going to stop there on our way north."

"A good librarian can find out anything," Bob said. "My wife once told me that. Larry's here. Wants to say hello."

Vrai wasn't ready for the conversation to end. She longed to make plans to fly out to Seattle.

But Larry was on the line. "You're driving to Boston in a blizzard? What's the deal?" He sounded worried, protective. Had he been protecting her in other ways as well? Did he know about Daphne?

"My friend Laramie's son is here with me," Vrai said. "He wants to visit his parents' graves." Her voice seemed strong enough to continue. "And so do I."

"Where was Skip buried?" Larry said.

"I took his ashes to Knoxville, to his mother. We put them on a bookshelf in her living room."

"Oh." Larry cleared his throat. "Hard to think of Skip like that. He was such a cool guy, always joking around."

"Then cherish your memories. He'd want you to." Even to her this sounded sappy.

"Jeez, Mom."

"How're your classes going?" Vrai said. "I'd like to come out for your graduation."

"The ceremony? I don't do graduations, remember?"

She did remember. "Hey."

"Hay is for horses, Mom."

"I just thought of a name. For Dad's puppy. Indigo. Pass it on."

After she and Larry had said good-bye, Jonathan showed her how much his moccasins had shrunk. "No way I can wear these. No way I'm putting on those ice skates."

Vrai stuffed one of her sneakers with toilet paper. Jonathan tried it on, then pushed more wadding into the toe.

"How come you never told me about the pepper spray?" he said.

"I'm just guessing. I could have it all wrong."

"I bet Frank sprayed Gussie, too. That's why she had a heart attack."

"We may never know. Prepare yourself for that possibility."

Vrai slipped her heels on. The black wool coat completed her outfit. Only two days ago, this had been funeral attire. Now she felt wildly hopeful.

Justice for Laramie and Miguel's assassins seemed unlikely, but she and Jonathan had identified a possible suspect in two other deaths. Hadn't they?

"What happened to Justin?" Jonathan leaned down to tie the sneakers.

"He stepped on a land mine in Viet Nam."

"Uncle Lloyd was in Viet Nam."

"He and Skip were there together. They were very, very lucky."

A half-formed idea shimmered like a mirage, then disappeared. A clue? A hole in her logic? A missing piece of the puzzle?

"Justin must have a pretty boring life." In the stuffed sneakers, with a blanket wrapped around him, Jonathan waddled toward the door like a penguin.

"He plays the clarinet or oboe or something. With a trio, I think." She handed Jonathan her newly dry socks to wear as mittens.

"Cool." Jonathan turned the socks into hand puppets. "We can't wait to meet him."

Vrai opened the door. The sky was preparing for a spectacular sunset, rehearsing its repertoire of hues. "Ready for this? You go first."

Jonathan silenced the puppets in order to pull the blanket tight and stepped out into the snow. "Does Justin like staying with his aunt and uncle?"

She closed the door but didn't bother to lock it. Her breath was visible. "He didn't say."

"Maybe he can move in with us. If things work out, I mean."

"Don't push your luck." Vrai pointed at Uncle Bud's bootprints. "Follow those."

Jonathan took a giant step forward. The snow was taking on pastel tints of pink and violet.

Slowly they stumbled past her car. The air was so cold it hurt to breathe. Jonathan hopped down from the ridge of snow into the plowed parking lot, nearly losing a shoe as he went. He re-wrapped the blanket around him and offered Vrai a hand.

The trek to the restaurant would have been easier

on ice skates. Vrai, in her heels, fell twice, Jonathan only once. He was also better at getting up again.

"On our way back." Jonathan spoke in short gasps. "We can see. Orion and his dogs."

From the hammock on Lloyd's patio Vrai had seen Orion, flashing his star-studded belt. "Dogs?"

"Canis Major. Canis Minor."

"Know what that is?" She pointed. An oval mound had replaced the swimming pool.

"Helicopter pad," Jonathan said.

Her ears hurt. "Prehistoric monster bird. Laid an egg."

They stopped trying to talk and concentrated on staying upright.

At first the sound was faint. Vrai glanced over at Jonathan.

"Snowplow!" He screamed it.

Vrai named the more likely source. "Uncle Bud's tractor."

"Look!" Jonathan gestured toward the interstate.

Below them, with its lights flashing, there was indeed a snowplow, clearing a northbound lane. Bright orange, of course. They were still in Big Orange country.

Jonathan waved at the vehicle in wide, frantic arcs. The driver saw them and tooted his horn.

chapter 19

❄ ❄ ❄

$\mathcal{J}$t was Monday, the Ides of March, a day for portents and signs. The sun was out, the snow glistening. The license plate on the maroon van ahead of them proclaimed that Vrai and Jonathan had a friend in Pennsylvania.

Good omens all.

Vrai had borrowed Uncle Bud's shovel and, with the Canadian's help, dug out her Toyota. After a terrifying slide down the Smoky View's driveway, she and her kidnappee were back on I-81. Only one lane was open; progress was slow.

From his voice mail Lloyd would learn that his nephew was headed north, explanation to follow. Bob knew Vrai was on her way to Hagerstown.

According to the owner of the kennel, Elsie and Dewey were fine, she wasn't to worry, they could stay as long as necessary. Robbie was safely back in Lincoln.

Chunks of ice occasionally slid down from the car's

roof onto the windshield. *Just ice*, Skip's voice whispered in her ear. *One space away from justice.*

A portion of State Street in downtown Bristol was also the state line. When Vrai was a child, her father had once straddled the border in the family car, placing himself in Virginia, her mother in Tennessee, and Vrai, strategically seated in back, in both states at once. Gleefully in limbo. Here but also there. Anywhere she chose to be.

On I-81, however, there was no time for games. One second she and Jonathan were in Tennessee, and the next they weren't.

"'Welcome to Virginia,'" Jonathan shouted, pointing, and Vrai glimpsed the familiar sign—blue background, white lettering, and a red cardinal, the Virginia state bird, in an upper corner. Good omen or bad?

"Try not to yell. Your driver's a little nervous." Vrai felt as though she'd crossed a jurisdictional line as well. Jonathan's legal guardians wanted him back.

A few miles later a billboard caught her eye. Deer John's promised "everything you need for hunting whatever you want to."

"Can we stop in Abingdon?" Jonathan said. "I'm hungry."

"It's only eleven o'clock. I was thinking Wytheville for lunch."

"I can't wait till then."

"Will you please try? We have a long drive today."

"Uncle Lloyd never minds stopping."

"Is this his car?"

No doubt about it, the next sign had negative implications. "'Interstate closed,'" Jonathan yelled.

"Please. Don't. Yell." Vrai tightened her grip on the steering wheel. "Could be an old sign they haven't taken down yet."

It wasn't. Just beyond the first exit for Abingdon sat two snowplows. A tow truck, too, had been abandoned. Orange cones forced all traffic onto the exit ramp. Vrai had crossed the state line and gotten nowhere.

The historic Martha Washington Inn on Abingdon's Main Street had no vacancies. The frazzled woman behind the desk said she'd heard the Barter Theater was taking in stranded travelers.

"Oh, look." Jonathan pointed toward the Inn's dining room. "White tablecloths and everything."

"I don't want to sleep in a theater seat," Vrai said. "We need to get back on the road, find a place to stay tonight."

From southbound I-81 she took the first exit claiming to have lodging. "Try downtown Bristol," the sleepy woman in the motel office said. "Lots of motels there. We're full up."

Just down the road was Deer John's. Despite the Closed sign in the window, lights were on inside. Vrai parked beside the only car in the parking lot.

"Howdy," a male voice boomed when she ventured inside. "Not open for business today. Sorry."

"You sell boots?"

The man looked her up and down, taking in her dressy black coat, her jeans and heels. "What sort of animal you huntin', ma'am?" He had the jowls of a basset hound and a basset's sad eyes.

Jonathan, her stuffed sneakers loose on his feet, stumbled in behind her.

"You have boys' sizes?" Vrai said. "We went to Knoxville for a funeral and got stranded."

"Sorry. Doing inventory today." He waved the sheets of paper in his hand. "Seemed like a good time for it."

An array of rifles and shotguns filled one wall. There was a circular rack of neon orange hunting jackets.

"Your door's open." Vrai put a hand on Jonathan's shoulder. "He needs boots and a warm jacket. Are you Deer John?"

"The one and only."

"You sell guns to criminals?" Jonathan said.

"I sell rifles, mostly, to men who provide food for their families," Deer John said. "My customers are fine upstanding citizens of the community. Criminals use hand guns."

"Any of those rifles high-powered?" Jonathan said.

"I got some telescopic sights, sure. How old are you, young man?"

"My mom and dad were murdered with rifles. Criminals do so too use rifles."

The hound-dog eyes sought guidance from Vrai. "That the funeral you been to?"

"No," Vrai said. "That one was a few years back."

"So you're not his mother."

"She's my guardian angel," Jonathan said.

"What size boots he need?" Deer John said with a sigh.

Vrai looked at Jonathan.

"Two," he said.

"What size you wear, ma'am?" Deer John said.

"You sell women's boots?"

"Women hunt. No surprise there. This here's an equal opportunity enterprise."

"Eight medium. Do you have anything on sale?"

"No ma'am. Remember, I'm not even open today." Deer John went off to see what he could find in the back.

Jonathan, looking pale, stepped out of the sneakers and walked over to a row of chairs facing away from the rifles. Vrai sat down beside him and patted his wrist. He pulled his arm away.

In front of them was a display of rolled-up sleeping bags. Deer John even sold air mattresses. There was trail mix beside the cash register and a water fountain between the two rest rooms. For a night or two, she and Jonathan could manage quite well here.

Deer John returned with his arms full of boxes. "You're in luck, young man. These here are real nice boots. Only sixty-nine ninety-nine."

"I'm a librarian," Vrai said. "We take inventory all the time. I could help you with yours."

"You'd still have to pay for the boots." Deer John set the boxes down on the floor.

"I could help with the inventory, and you could let us spend the night here in sleeping bags."

"This look like a bed-and-breakfast to you?" Deer John spread his newly emptied arms. "Now, you want to buy some boots or not? I'll sell 'em to you, out of the kindness of my heart, but I ain't the Red Cross."

He got down on one knee, and Jonathan stuck out a foot. "Are they waterproof?" Jonathan said. "My other boots shrank."

"Timberland. Best on the market. 'Course they're waterproof."

"You have a jacket in his size?" Vrai said.

"Ma'am, I'll sell you anything you want, but you cannot spend the night here. We clear on that?" Deer John rose slowly to his feet. "My cousin manages the Tri-Cities Motel, down in Johnson City. I could call and see if he has room for you."

"Thanks all the same." Johnson City would mean crossing back over into Tennessee. Vrai was headed forward, not backward.

. . . .

It was nearly three o'clock when, sporting new boots and neon-orange jackets, they checked into a Howard Johnson's near an unplowed section of State Street. After a lunch of grilled-cheese sandwiches and HoJo milkshakes, they went out to explore.

"If you stand like this, you'll have one foot in Tennessee and the other in Virginia." Vrai demonstrated. "Under the snow, there are brass markers embedded in the pavement."

Jonathan followed her example. "We're nowhere men." He strummed an imaginary guitar, then leaned down to adjust the rolled-up cuffs of his new cargo pants.

Vrai remembered something else from her childhood trip to Bristol. "Which way's the sign?" she called to a man shouldering a heavy bag. The mailman pointed.

After trudging several blocks they could see it in the distance, suspended above the street in the gathering dusk.

BRISTOL
VA   TENN
A
GOOD
PLACE TO LIVE

"Thanks for the new clothes," Jonathan said. "Thanks for everything."

As if in response, the sign's lights came on.

chapter 20

❋ ❋ ❋

V rai took the exit for the motel, south of Roanoke, where she'd planned to spend the night after Skip's funeral. "There's a Shoney's here. Used to be, anyway. I need to see some color." With only four dollars left in her wallet, she also needed to pay with a credit card.

Wytheville had been the most harrowing part of the drive so far—only one northbound lane open, the tractor-trailer in front of them lobbing clumps of dirty snow against their windshield, and on either side, nothing to see but snow, snow, and more snow, under a somber gray sky. She loved these mountains, but not today.

The landscape lacked color, but something else was amiss—that lost piece of the puzzle, the question she should've thought to ask by now, the fact that was staring her right in the face, the crucial bit of information she'd been too professionally inept to locate.

What was it?

The Shoney's sign, crusted with snow, was the bright

red Vrai remembered, but the restaurant's interior was bleakly beige. She feasted her eyes on the colorful menu.

"Are you an artist?" Jonathan said. Last night he'd voluntarily taken a shower, washed his hair, and even used the toothbrush she'd bought for him. Today he was wearing his new drugstore underwear and socks.

"Not a very good one. Why?"

He shrugged. "Colors. Art history. What does an art history librarian *do*, anyway?"

Vrai quoted from her mission statement. "Provide resources and research assistance for students and professors of art history."

"So this is at a college?"

"Stoneham-Knox University. The students call it the school of hard knocks."

"Are there any star atlases in your library?"

Vrai admitted she didn't know what a star atlas was.

He rolled his eyes. "Take a wild guess."

"An atlas of the stars? No, but we do have a few atlases of the earth."

"Bor-ring."

She ordered an omelette with green peppers and ham, a glass of orange juice, and a bowl of bright red strawberries. Coffee, of course.

Jonathan asked for a hamburger and crayons.

The crayons arrived first. On the back of the sheet of paper meant for coloring, he drew seven green dots, then looked up at her.

"The Big Dipper," she said.

He switched to orange and made five more dots in a zigzag pattern.

"No idea," she said.

"Cassiopeia," he announced, then chose a blue crayon for a dot halfway between the two.

She took a wild guess. "The North Star?"

"Bingo!" Jonathan said this so loudly that customers at the other tables turned around. A few of them smiled at her, as if thinking: how wonderful to have such a happy little boy, a child without a care in the world.

. . . .

It was almost dark when they reached Hagerstown. The street where the Papastefanoses lived was rutted ice, sanded in spots, but their driveway was clear, the sidewalk to the front door of the brick colonial neatly shoveled. Vrai parked behind a blue van belonging to Papastefanos & Sons, Painting Contractors, whose slogan was, "Let Papa Do It."

Before she could ring the doorbell, the front door was opened by a tall, white-haired man with Gussie's thin-lipped smile. This was George. His wife Grace, wearing a flowered apron, relieved Vrai and Jonathan of their orange jackets.

From the living room came a deep voice. "Glad you're here," Justin said, rolling his wheelchair into the hall.

Khaki Bermuda shorts hid his stumps. He seemed balder and grayer than Vrai remembered, but his most striking feature, his one and only eyebrow, the right one, was still black.

With his droopy eyelids, Justin reminded Vrai of a meditating Buddha. She'd warned Jonathan not to stare, and he was doing his best. "This is my friend Jonathan," she said. "He's ten."

"You're the one from Boston?" Justin held out his hand, and Jonathan shook it.

"That's right." Jonathan gave Vrai a look that said, I was born there, wasn't I?

George headed upstairs with Vrai's suitcase. "Mama's about ready to serve dinner. Let me show you your room."

The green wall beside the staircase gave way to a blue hallway. The twin-bedded guest room was a different shade of blue.

"Love these colors," Vrai said. "Nothing but gray-and-white monotony on the interstate."

George set her suitcase on a luggage rack with needlepoint straps, colorful flowers against a blue background. "Customers change their minds." He gestured at the walls. "Pacific Calm in here. Talk about redundant. But I didn't name the paints. I just slapped them on."

Past tense. "Are you retired?" Vrai said.

"My sons run the business now. Don't know what we'd do without them. Andre was over here shoveling all day Sunday."

Jonathan pointed across the hall. "That the bathroom?"

"Sure is." George grinned. "True Blue Lagoon in there. Try saying *that* three times."

That, that, that, Jonathan mouthed to Vrai before shutting the bathroom door.

George lowered his voice. "Justin's anxious to talk to you. He's been quite agitated, ever since he heard about Skip."

Vrai stared down at the white chenille bedspreads. "Skip and Gussie both. It's incomprehensible."

"Augusta was . . ." But George couldn't continue.

"How come the water in the toilet's the exact same color as the bathroom walls?" asked Jonathan from the hall.

"One of life's little coincidences," replied George Papastefanos.

. . . .

The dining room's peach walls and maroon tablecloth were a perfect complement for the servings of meatballs, scalloped potatoes, and red wine. Justin, seated across from Vrai and Jonathan, adeptly speared the meatballs with his fork. On the wall behind him was a framed print of a donkey listening to a guitar-playing monkey.

Vrai recognized the prints on the other walls as well. *Los Caprichos* were a nightmarish series ridiculing the repressiveness of eighteenth-century Spain. The etchings so angered the Inquisition that Goya stopped trying to sell them, afraid he might be imprisoned, tortured, even killed.

"Goya's *Caprichos*," Vrai said.

George looked pleased. "Grace gave them to me for our fiftieth wedding anniversary." Behind him was Goya's favorite, *The Sleep of Reason Produces Monsters.* The self-portrait of a nightmare, it depicted grotesque creatures flapping their wings above the sleeping artist's head.

"Vrai's the art history librarian," Justin said to his plate.

The betrayer? Justin's expression was hard to read. He spoke as slowly in person as he had on the phone, reminding Vrai of an executive in an old movie enunciating carefully into a Dictaphone.

"Jonathan," Justin said. "How did you know Skip?"

"I didn't," Jonathan said.

"But you went to his funeral?" Justin's reason was wide awake. "Did you fly down from Boston?"

"He was born in Boston, but he lives in North Carolina now, with his aunt and uncle," Vrai hurried to clarify. "Jonathan's Uncle Lloyd and Skip were childhood friends."

Jonathan glared at her. He was perfectly capable of speaking for himself.

Justin's wine was in a sturdy juice glass. He took a sip. "Later, I'd like to talk to Vrai in private."

"Of course." George and Grace said this together.

Jonathan, with an agenda of his own, tapped his spoon against his milk glass. "Anyone know where Gussie's gold-fish are?"

No one did.

He turned to Vrai. "You said the goldfish were real. You said they might be here."

"They were real," Vrai said. "I *saw* them. Even my sons saw Gussie's goldfish." Embarrassed, she glanced at Justin. "Skip wrote fiction. Did you know? I discovered some of his stories. One of them mentions the celestial goldfish Gussie kept in her office."

"Oh, those," Justin said. "Those were real."

"Someone flushed them down the toilet," Jonathan said. "Right?"

The black eyebrow went up, the mostly bald head turned slowly back and forth. The Buddha was inscrutable.

His thighs covered by a yellow blanket, Justin sat propped against yellow pillows on an opened sleep sofa in the den off the living room. A crimson T-shirt revealed his muscular arms.

"Hi, Vrai," he said as she was preparing to knock on the door jamb. "Did Uncle George remember to leave the light on?"

"He did." She stifled a yawn. The wine had made her sleepy.

The door to a half bath had been removed from its hinges and left leaning against a wall. Justin's wheelchair was next to the sleep sofa. Vrai chose a chair with a view of the living room and sat down. Jonathan, upset at being excluded, was not above tiptoeing downstairs to listen in.

Justin didn't turn his head. Didn't speak.

"You mentioned phone calls," Vrai prompted. "The police knew about them, and Skip did, too?"

"It's difficult," Justin began. "Not a pretty story."

The longer he talked, the more relieved Vrai was that she didn't have to try to hide her increasing uneasiness. Justin claimed Frank had made a series of obscene phone calls to Gussie. The first few times, Gussie simply hung up on him. When the calls continued, Justin insisted she contact the police.

The officer she spoke to asked if the caller was threatening her. If he was just talking dirty, then she should continue to hang up, and the calls would most likely stop. Or, if she knew the caller's identity, then she could obtain a court order requiring him to stop. But probably the best approach would be to get caller ID, so she'd know not to answer in the first place.

Gussie told the cop the caller was her former boss, who'd previously harassed her during a meeting in his office. She'd walked out on him that day, and consequently she was no longer employed.

"Mother decided she didn't want the calls to stop. She got this crazy idea that she would show the world what Frank Leigh was really like." With his maddeningly slow pace and careful diction, Justin explained that Gussie had bought an answering machine, with extra cassettes, and even though the instructions warned her it was illegal without his permission, she started recording Frank's phone calls.

"What sorts of things did he say?" Vrai felt compelled to ask.

What color underwear Gussie preferred. How often she changed it. This was all Justin was willing to disclose. Gussie would press the record button, set the receiver gently down on the table, and allow Frank to incriminate himself. She kept a log with the dates and times of the calls.

A Sgt. Bailey came one afternoon and listened to the tapes. He told Gussie to stop recording Frank herself and let the police take over. That way the evidence would stand up in court. In the meantime, she should simply hang up on the jerk. Or get caller ID.

"When was this?" Vrai said.

"*Months* ago. That was the last we heard from Sgt. Bailey. He took the tapes and Mother's log with him."

Vrai could understand Justin's anger. Still, in a city with a rising homicide rate, nasty phone calls to a feisty old woman, who'd broken the law herself, might not have seemed all that important to a cop.

"And Frank kept calling?" She thought of Bob and his photographs. Exposures. People going about their daily lives, unaware of the photographer. By taping Frank's phone calls, Gussie had been attempting something similar.

"He did. Mother bought more tapes and started a new log. She didn't trust the police. She wanted her own proof." Justin sighed. "When the phone rang, that last time, I was in the kitchen, taking a root beer from the fridge. Mother was in the living room. She said hello, but nothing else, so I knew it was Frank again. Then she said a word I'd never heard her use before. Her dying word, as it turned out. Seconds later, she crashed to the floor."

"How awful for you."

Justin made a sound in his throat.

"Shall I go now?" Vrai was more than ready to head upstairs. Might a jury conclude that by taking Frank's calls Gussie had egged him on, encouraged him to keep calling? Was this even the sort of crime that went to trial?

"No, not yet." But Justin seemed to be waiting for her to speak.

"So Skip was planning to confront Frank, with all this, by the tennis courts," she said.

Justin nodded. "You understand now why I need to get back to Baltimore." His voice had turned husky. "The police don't know Mother's dead. How she died."

Had Jonathan been right all along? Was Frank responsible for both deaths? Vrai told Justin her theory about the pepper spray.

"Pepper spray! Frank should've been locked up *years* ago."

Justin had another story, this one from Skip, who'd talked to a librarian at the college in Pennsylvania where Frank had taught history. The day after Frank was denied tenure he'd stayed home, didn't bother getting dressed. A Girl Scout selling cookies knocked on the door. Frank recognized her as one of his department head's daughters and opened his bathrobe.

"A Girl Scout?" How true was this story? "But Frank has a daughter of his own."

"Keats was wrong, you know. Truth and beauty aren't one and the same. The truth can be ugly as shit. The girl's father," Justin went on, "decided not to put her through the ordeal of having to testify. On the condition that Frank leave town immediately."

The Greek olive who'd ruined Frank's life.

"Maybe we should talk to Bev," Vrai said. "See how a lawyer would approach this." Pass the buck, she meant. She wished she'd steered clear of Hagerstown. How could she share such sordid details with a ten-year-old? This was getting way too complicated.

"I thought about that, too," Justin said. "Some legal advice would be helpful."

"You said Bev and Skip had broken up?"

"Not sure what happened there," Justin said. "Skip didn't want to talk about it."

"Another thing. Jonathan's parents were murdered. No one was ever arrested. He's all caught up in this. He wants justice for Skip and Gussie, and I'm not sure that's even possible."

"Poor guy."

"I'm so sorry, Justin." Vrai got to her feet. "Anything I can do for you before I go upstairs?"

Justin folded his arms. "You mean like kiss me good-night?"

Vrai moved quickly to the light switch.

"My mother always did." Justin touched his forehead. "Right here. I really miss that."

It seemed a small thing. Vrai leaned down and gave Justin a quick kiss. "I'll turn out the light now."

"Suit yourself," Justin replied.

chapter 21

❄ ❄ ❄

Vrai woke with a start. Someone was breathing on her chin. "Jeez," she said. "What?"

"What do you mean what?" Jonathan turned on the lamp between the beds. "What did Justin say is what. Are you going to tell me or not?"

It was five past six. "Now?"

"I can't go back to sleep till I know."

Vrai closed her eyes.

"No fair," Jonathan said. "Wake up."

"I am awake. Can't you wait a minute?"

Jonathan, surely counting to sixty, waited.

She pushed herself up on one elbow. "Frank made some phone calls to Gussie," she whispered. "The last one upset her so much, she had a heart attack and died."

"But what did he say to her?"

"Ssshhh. Please. You can't say anything to George and Grace, OK? They're upset enough already."

"I won't. So what did Frank say to her?"

"Justin didn't go into details." This was true. "All I know is, Gussie made tapes of the phone calls. I think the police have some of the tapes."

"Good for her."

"Ssshhh. The problem is, Gussie was breaking the law. Recording Frank without his permission."

"But Frank was breaking the law," the Inspector reasoned, "wasn't he?"

"I don't know. Justin wants to talk to Skip's old girlfriend, Bev. She's a lawyer."

"So we're going to Baltimore?"

"Where I'm going is back to sleep." Vrai rolled over to face the wall. "Please. Turn off the light and get back in bed."

An obedient click, and the room went dark. She closed her eyes. How could she get out of this mess?

. . . .

At nine o'clock Vrai woke from a nightmare in which she, Skip, and Gussie were tied together at the wrists with barbed wire. Identical eyes on the tops of their heads looked into the future. What the eyes saw there was death.

In dreamlike fashion, the surrealists and the cubists had realigned the real world. Escher turned one shape into another, joined one dimension to the next. But an actual dream was made up of memory fragments. A dream pointed back to the past. It did not predict the future.

The room was empty. Jonathan's bed was made. She examined her wrists. No blood. Touched the top of her head. No eye.

Justin wanted her help. Jonathan, too, was expecting her to act.

But what if she did nothing?

She found Jonathan seated on the stairway landing, listening in on a fierce family argument taking place below. Someone named Winsome, who was a nurse at Johns Hopkins Hospital in Baltimore, had just returned from visiting her family in Jamaica. Winsome was willing to move into the apartment Justin had shared with Gussie. Justin felt comfortable in that apartment. He knew his way around. There was a shower he could use.

George and Grace were adamantly opposed to his leaving. They'd buy one of those shower chairs. George and his sons would carry Justin to an upstairs bathroom, anytime he wanted.

Justin appreciated their concern, he really did, but he needed to go home now. Vrai would drive him.

Round and round they went, until a compromise was reached. The wheelchair was too large for Vrai's car. George and Grace would drive Justin to Baltimore in the van. That way they could meet Winsome before deciding to leave Justin in her care. If she didn't seem capable, then Justin would return with them to Hagerstown.

"Fat chance of that," Jonathan whispered.

"Not sure Winsome's a real person," Vrai whispered back. "He's just determined to get to Baltimore."

A sudden silence from the dining room. Vrai motioned to Jonathan to stand up. They'd barely started down the stairs when Grace appeared.

"Good morning, you two," Grace said. "Sleep well? Breakfast is ready."

....

Once again they were on an interstate, I-70 this time, headed east toward Baltimore. After three cups of Grace's excellent coffee, Vrai was seeing the situation more clearly. To run from the truth would be cowardly. Miguel had known this. So did Skip. Not to act would be condoning evil.

Justin wasn't exactly an eyewitness, but he had heard, and could report on, how and why his mother had died. As for Skip's death, Vrai had concocted a logical scenario, but at this point it was more fiction than fact. Was Frank in any way responsible? How could she find out?

"What're we going to *do* in Baltimore?" Jonathan said.

"I guess that depends on whether Justin stays there or goes back to Hagerstown. If he stays, he may want a ride to the police station." Without his wheelchair? "Or maybe he'll just talk to the police by phone."

"He could've done that from Hagerstown," Jonathan pointed out.

"True."

The magic word. *Brew rhymes with true.* Given the right circumstances, Frank might be willing to reveal what had happened that fateful afternoon. While drinking tea with his wife, wouldn't he feel compelled to tell the truth?

Vrai used the last of her money to place a call from a gas station in Frederick, an hour west of Baltimore. Celeste answered. Vrai invited herself for tea.

"Tea?" Celeste made it sound as though she never drank the stuff.

"Is Frank there? Maybe I should speak with him."

"Let me check," Celeste said.

"Hello, Vrai," Frank said finally. "Tea sounds lovely. Maybe sometime next week? Surely the University will have reopened by then."

"I'd like to come today," she said. "I'll have a young friend with me."

"You want to come to my house for tea?" Frank did not sound pleased. "May I ask why?"

"Justin, Gussie's son, has been in touch with the police. In the interest of fairness, I'd like to hear your side of this."

"My side of what? I have no idea what you're talking about."

"Then I'll explain when we get there. I'm hoping Celeste will join us. Would three o'clock be convenient?"

"I'll look forward to it." And Frank hung up.

Vrai returned to her dirty, salt-caked Toyota, her heart hammering in her throat. "Want to have tea with Frank and his wife?" she said. "This afternoon?"

Jonathan's mouth fell open. "Really?"

Vrai couldn't resist. "*Vraiment*. But I'll do the talking. Is that understood?"

"I can't say *anything*?"

"I'd really rather you didn't." She described the elaborate tea-brewing ceremony to which Frank attributed his long and happy marriage. If all went well, then, in front of Celeste, Frank would tell the truth. Either he'd played a role in Skip's death, or he hadn't. Frank Leigh would not lie to his wife while drinking tea.

"But what if Celeste brews the tea?" Jonathan said. "Does Frank have to tell the truth then?"

"I'm not sure," Vrai admitted. "All I want to know is, what really happened? Why did Skip run out in front of that car? Maybe Frank doesn't know, but then again, maybe he does. He'd never tell the police, but he just might tell us."

"And then we can tell the police."

Vrai hadn't thought that far ahead.

"At least I'll get a good look at the creep," Jonathan said. "Did he sound scared?"

"He pretended he didn't know why on earth I would want to talk to him."

"Does Baltimore have a harbor?"

"A big one," Vrai said. "Might be frozen over at the moment. Why?"

"Ice is good. If he won't cooperate, let's just dump Frank in the harbor."

"Instead of dumping the tea, you mean?"

Jonathan glowed with pleasure. "I knew you'd get it."

. . . .

Mr. Tony's Pizzeria occupied the first floor of a corner row house across the street from Gussie's apartment building. Vrai decorated the bare coat tree with two bright orange leaves, and she and Jonathan sat down in the booth by the front window. From there they could keep an eye on George's van, which was parked in a space for Emergency Vehicles Only. If a police officer happened by who didn't consider painting an emergency, Vrai was to hurry over and assure him that the van would be moved ASAP.

By leaning into the bay window she could also see her own car. After circling block after block she'd done the unthinkable—moved a rusty lawn chair to the sidewalk and backed into the space the chair was meant to reserve. Every car owner in Baltimore knew the rules. The person who'd shoveled out the space retained clear title to it. If the owner of the space she'd stolen should return, she planned to dash down Mr. Tony's steps and move her car pronto.

"Ready to order?" the waitress asked.

"Where's Mr. Tony?" Jonathan wanted to know.

"He be dead," the waitress replied.

"Do you have a phone book?" Vrai said.

"I can ask. You want to order first?"

Vrai explained that they would soon be joined by at least three others and ordered what Justin had suggested. How, she wondered, would he get his wheelchair up Mr. Tony's steps?

About ten minutes later, George came out of the apartment building and held the door for Grace. The Papastefanoses got into their van and drove off.

"But that's the only parking space for miles!" Vrai said, worried the lunch would drag on forever. Before having tea with her boss and his wife, she wanted to stop by her own house and change into something appropriate.

The pizzas arrived, the lumps of sausage glistening with fat, the mushrooms as appetizing as chopped liver. Colorful as it was, Vrai had never much liked pizza, the dirty-socks smell of it.

She asked again for a phone book. "I promise to return it."

Jonathan was on his second slice of pizza when a black woman came out of the apartment building, followed by Justin in his wheelchair. While waiting at the corner for a break in the traffic, Justin took the woman's hand, and she bent down to kiss the top of his head. White slacks were visible beneath her gray parka. Justin turned his face up to hers, and she gave him a long, lingering kiss on the lips.

Jonathan had seen it, too. "Is that the nurse? What's her name again?"

"Winsome."

"Like Dim Sum? She doesn't look Chinese."

Vrai spelled it. "Winsome means so cute and charming as to win your affection."

The lovebirds crossed the street and disappeared. The waitress brought out a shiny new phone book with yellow covers.

"Thanks," Vrai said. "I should've been more specific. Could I see the white pages instead? I want to look up someone's home address."

"I'll leave this here, case you change your mind again."

Minutes later the waitress, holding the precious white pages, prevented the kitchen door from swinging shut on Justin's wheelchair. Soon the coat tree had acquired two new leaves: a gray suede parka with a fur-lined hood, and Justin's tan leather jacket. Justin had changed his clothes, perhaps even taken that shower he'd made such a fuss about.

Did he know how beautiful Winsome was? How graceful and poised? More likely, he'd been charmed by her musical, lilting voice. "I'm Winsome," she sang. "Justin has told me everything."

Jonathan moved over, and Winsome slid in beside him. After Justin had positioned his wheelchair at the end of the table, the waitress took their drink orders, plopped the phone book down in front of Vrai, and returned to the kitchen.

"Why did George move the van?" Vrai said.

"They wanted to get back before dark." Justin sounded only slightly triumphant.

"To Hagerstown? But I didn't get to thank them for their hospitality."

"I'll tell them, next time we talk," Justin said. "I spoke to Bev just now. She'll be joining us."

Vrai looked at her watch. It was after two. "What did she say?"

"She was with a client," Justin said. "I told her Frank was responsible for both deaths. We can explain the rest when she gets here."

"Jonathan and I have to leave soon." Vrai opened the phone book. "I need to find Frank's address. We're going to his house for tea."

"Nooo! That'll screw everything up. Let's talk to Bev. I thought you agreed."

"I do think we should talk to her. After we have all the facts." Vrai made a mental note of the address: 4802 Brandywine. Approximately fifteen minutes away.

"You've gone completely nuts," Justin said. "Frank won't tell you anything. Wait for Bev. She'll advise us, and then we'll go to the police. All of us together, in her minivan."

Jonathan remained uncharacteristically silent.

"Aren't you eating?" Winsome said to Vrai.

"I had a huge breakfast. Justin's aunt is a wonderful cook."

Winsome tore off a slice of pizza and placed it in Justin's

hand. "A lot of people I know don't trust the police," she told him. "Sometimes those coppers get it wrong."

"But the police have the tapes," Justin reminded her. He put the pizza aside, reached into his shirt pocket, and brought out a cassette. "This has Frank's final conversation with my mother on it."

"I tried to listen to it," Winsome said, "but the answering machine's broken."

"Part of the crash I heard when . . . " Justin, visibly upset, returned the cassette to his shirt pocket.

"Frank might tell *us* the truth," Jonathan chimed in. "If the police try to talk to him, he'll just ask for a lawyer, and the lawyer will tell him not to say anything."

"You watch too much TV." Justin turned to Vrai. "Isn't it a little early for tea? Please wait for Bev."

"She's a corporate, not a criminal lawyer."

"She went to law school, didn't she?" Justin said. "Therefore, *a fortiori*, she knows a lot more about the law than we do. There was a definitely a crime, probably two of them. Without the legal system involved, there will be no punishment."

"Frank's killed two people," Winsome said to Vrai. "You sure you want to take a little boy to that man's house?"

"I'm not so little," Jonathan said.

Justin accepted another slice of pizza from Winsome. "Let's just sit tight," he said. "Bev will be here soon."

At two forty, Vrai stood up. She put on her jacket and removed Jonathan's from its hook. "You two talk to Bev, and we'll talk to Frank. It's more efficient that way. Then we can all meet up and compare notes. I'll pay you then for the pizza, if that's all right."

"You'll regret this," Justin said.

"Coming?" Vrai said to Jonathan.

"Someone needs to go with her," Jonathan said.

Winsome turned to him. "Here in Baltimore, people keep rat poison under the sink. If Frank offers you sugar with your tea, refuse it."

"Frank uses sugar cubes," Vrai said. "He has these dainty little tongs."

Winsome stood up and let Jonathan out of the booth.

✳ ✳ ✳

chapter 22

*I*t was three o'clock, and Vrai was hopelessly lost in a maze of one-way streets.

"Brandywine!" Jonathan shouted it.

Perched atop the street sign was a red cardinal, perhaps the very bird Vrai had seen glaring at her, in an accusatory way, the afternoon Skip died. As she made the turn onto Brandywine, the cardinal flew off.

Directly opposite Frank's house was an empty parking space. The parking gods, at least, looked favorably on this visit. But her first attempt at parallel parking was a miserable failure, her second only slightly better.

She removed the key from the ignition and sat staring at it. How could she have been so blind? The missing piece of information had nothing to do with the deaths of Skip and Gussie. It had to do with her.

Why hadn't she warned Skip?

After Frank brewed tea for her that afternoon, she should have stopped by Skip's office, called him at home, gotten word to him somehow. "Frank knows about Melody," she could have, should have told her friend. "I didn't tell him, but I think he knows."

She was indeed a betrayer. Hers was a passive betrayal, but betrayal it was. A character flaw of the worst kind. That cardinal had seen right through her.

"Let's go," Jonathan said.

"I'm not feeling so good."

"You're just nervous."

"Worse than that." Would she ever be able to tell Jonathan the truth? "I need to organize my thoughts."

"You want me to be quiet."

"If you would, please." But all she could think about was the cowardly way she'd let a dear friend walk into a trap.

Too late, now, to make it up to Skip. Or was it?

"Let me do the talking," she said.

"I know, I know," Jonathan said. "I'm here to do the remembering, so I can testify in court."

"I hope you're not worried about the sugar. The kind of rat poison I use comes in little green pellets."

"You have *rats* in your house?"

"Not any more."

. . . .

Frank's sidewalk and steps had been sloppily shoveled. A short, round woman in black slacks and a deep pink velour top opened the door, admitted to being Celeste, and without enthusiasm allowed Vrai and Jonathan to come inside.

At the end of a hallway was the back door and, beside it, the kitchen sink. The sparsely furnished living room was dominated by yet another portrait of Napoleon.

Footsteps on the stairs. Frank appeared, wearing corduroy slacks and a cardigan with suede elbow patches. Mr. Rogers with a badly bruised left eye and a scab on his left cheek.

Vrai introduced Frank to Jonathan, and they shook hands. Frank then looked at Vrai. The visit was her idea. Vrai looked at Frank. It was his house. He was the host.

"What can I do for you?" Frank said, studying the bannister.

"I wanted to talk to you about Skip," Vrai said.

"An old friend of yours, as I remember. Such a terrible shame."

Jonathan unzipped his jacket. Vrai did the same. When no one took the hint, they set the puffy orange creatures on the stairs.

The left sleeve of Vrai's turtleneck had a tomato sauce stain from Grace's meatballs. Her jeans were knee-sprung and wrinkled. In his new T-shirt Jonathan, a walking advertisement for BRISTOL VA TENN, looked far more presentable than she did.

"Would you like for us to take off our boots?" Vrai said.

"No need," Frank replied.

"Where shall we sit?"

Frank's reluctant gesture toward the dining room im-
plied the obvious. The four of them would hardly fit on
the wicker love seat. Living alone, in a temporary rental,
he didn't do much entertaining.

Jonathan walked around the dining room table,
pulled out a chair, and sat down. Vrai stood behind the
chair opposite him and asked if there was anything she
could do to help. She directed her question at Frank, the
brewer of tea and truth. Or was his story about marital
tea parties pure fiction? Did Frank only brew tea for his
most naive and gullible employees?

Vrai turned to blonde, blue-eyed Celeste. "Frank
once brewed tea for me in his office. It was delicious."

By the way Celeste sat herself down in the chair far-
thest away from the kitchen, it was clear she didn't in-
tend to serve anything to anyone this afternoon. She examined her bright pink fingernails.

Frank settled into the fourth chair, opposite his wife.
"Do sit down," he said to Vrai, so she did.

"Now what's this all about?" Frank said. "I'm sorry
your friend's dead, of course, but I'm not sure how I can
help you deal with your sorrow."

What total crap! He knew she hadn't come for grief
counseling.

"I was wondering," Vrai began. "Could you tell me?
When did you last see Skip?"

Frank didn't need even a second to think this over.
"I haven't seen Skip Howard since the day he called me

a . . ." He glanced at Jonathan. "A terrible name. In my own office, no less."

Vrai turned to Celeste. "The afternoon Frank brewed tea for me, he told me it was the reason for your long and happy marriage. Because brew rhymes with true. 'One cannot lie while drinking tea.'"

Celeste's look of pained disbelief said it all. Brewing tea was indeed a private ritual for this couple.

Behind Jonathan was an old card catalog, its oak surfaces scarred and faded from years of use. The labels on the drawers appeared to be dates: 1800-1850, 1900-1915, etc. This must be The Napoleon Project—Frank's massive bibliography—arranged by date of publication.

"That eye must be painful," Vrai said to Frank. "What on earth happened?"

He clasped his hands, set them on the table, and stared at them.

"When did it happen?" Vrai said. "Looks like it's healing nicely."

Frank continued to stare at his hands.

"Jonathan and I have spoken to Justin," Vrai said. "Justin Morgen, Gussie's son." She glanced at Celeste, to see if the name rang a bell, but Celeste was intent on tracing a semi-circular blemish on the table's surface.

Vrai turned back to Frank. "Justin said Skip was planning to meet you by the tennis courts . . ."

"As I just said," Frank cut in, "I haven't seen Skip Howard in over a year. And never once by the tennis courts."

"Were you here when he hurt his eye?" Vrai asked Celeste.

Celeste shook her head.

Was she lying? How much did Celeste know? If she'd been the one calling around in search of Justin, then Frank must have told her at least some of the sordid story.

"What's going on?" Celeste chewed her pink lipstick. "Why are you here?"

"For tea," Vrai said. "Empereur Chen-Nung, or whatever you have on hand."

"I love tea," Jonathan said.

Slowly, deliberately, Frank stood up. He would not be provoked, his body language said, into revealing anything. With great reluctance, however, he would play the polite host and brew a pot of tea. He strode into the kitchen.

Vrai listened, her eyes on Jonathan, as cupboard doors were opened and shut, cups met saucers, lids connected with teapots. "The day after he died, the library staff made a memorial for Skip in one of the elevators." She spoke loudly enough for Frank to hear. "There's a bust of Dante down on Level Four. Students often put him in the elevator and let him ride up and down. One of the staff must have done it this time. And somebody slipped a T-shirt over Dante's head. A white T-shirt with blue letters that said, 'We have been transformed.'

"People brought flowers," Vrai went on, speaking to Frank's empty chair, to the kitchen behind it. "The floor of the elevator became a sea of flowers. There were cards and photos pinned to the elevator walls." She paused, steadied her voice. "Everyone was so sorry Skip had been killed."

"Did you take flowers?" Jonathan said.

Vrai frowned at him. She would do the talking. "A rose." One long-stemmed red rose.

. . . .

The florist shop was on the other side of Olmsted Parkway from the library. Before crossing over, she'd walked north, to the scene of the accident. With Bob's old Washington Diplomats umbrella shielding her from needles of sleet, she'd tried not to look for bloodstains on the pavement, tried not to wonder if Skip had sailed through the air or been crushed beneath the optician's car.

A tall hedge of azaleas hid the tennis courts from the sidewalk. At a gap in the hedge was an unshoveled path. Some of the icy footprints in the snow could have been Skip's, the last steps he took in his life. Vrai had left prints of her own as she headed toward the chain-link fence surrounding the tennis courts.

On the courts themselves the snow was untouched. No one, not even Skip Howard, had tried to play tennis there.

It was on her way back to the street that she'd spotted the sunglasses under the azaleas. By then, any traces of pepper spray on the lenses would have been washed away by rain and sleet. The subsequent blizzard would have obliterated all footprints on or near the path. The only way to place Frank at the scene was to get him to admit he was there. By the tennis courts. With Skip.

Which he'd already denied. Twice. Before anyone had tasted so much as a drop of tea.

chapter 23

❄ ❄ ❄

*a*t a normal tea party, polite conversation with the hostess would be appropriate. "Is your son here with you?" Vrai asked Celeste.

"Both our sons are in New York."

"Oh," Vrai said. "I thought your younger son wanted to finish high school in Philadelphia."

"This is his spring break. He went up to New York to visit his brother. You're just full of questions, aren't you?"

"Celeste," Frank bawled. "I can't find a tray."

Celeste pushed back her chair and scurried into the kitchen. After a long silence, something clattered to the floor. There was the rattling of china, followed by another silence.

"Now he can't find the rat poison," Jonathan whispered. He put his hand to his throat and mimicked gagging.

It was Celeste who brought in the tray, set it on the table, and distributed the steaming cups, each with a tiny teaspoon on the saucer. Frank followed with a sugar bowl and tongs, which he handed to his wife.

"How many lumps?" Celeste asked Jonathan.

"Those look like cubes to me," Jonathan said.

"One or two?" Celeste leaned toward him.

"No thanks," Jonathan said, covering his teacup.

"One lump please," Vrai told Celeste, who then sat down and dropped two lumps into her own tea.

Frank, back in his chair, raised a cup of unsweetened tea to his lips. "Too strong?" he asked his wife.

Celeste sipped. "Just right, as always, dear."

"Very good," Vrai agreed, taking a second sip to prove it. She hesitated, unsure of the protocol. "Your eye," she said finally to Frank. "You don't remember when it was injured?"

Frank studied his teaspoon. He stirred his unsugared tea.

Celeste, suddenly talkative, explained that the previous tenants, students, had left their brewing equipment behind, in the basement, and Frank had taken up a new hobby. While checking on his pale ale one night, he'd fallen down the stairs. Or maybe up. He had no memory of the incident and so, Celeste surmised, must have knocked himself unconscious.

"Could this have happened a week ago Monday?" Vrai said to Frank. "Dr. Brill told me he saw you that night at the grocery store. He thought the steak you were buying might have been for your black eye."

Frank glared at her. Bingo! she thought.

Emboldened, she turned to Celeste. "Your husband

made a series of phone calls to a librarian who'd retired. Gussie Morgen was her name. He said some unpleasant things to her, and the last time he called, she had a heart attack and died."

"I don't believe you," Celeste said.

Frank's eyes were on the card catalog, his mammoth undertaking, his life's work. Had Celeste typed the catalog cards? Inserted the labels in the drawer-fronts? Was the bibliography as much her work as Frank's? Maybe she shared in his disappointment at not receiving tenure and felt they'd both been treated unfairly.

"Here's what I've put together so far," Vrai said to Celeste. "Gussie died a week ago Saturday, after receiving a phone call. When she slumped to the floor, her son phoned Skip, who came right over. Skip called an ambulance, and he also gave the *Sun* an obituary. The following Monday, Skip was planning to talk to Frank. On Mondays, Frank always goes to the Faculty Club for lunch. He takes the short cut, beside the tennis courts, and Skip knew this."

"They never clear that path," Frank said, "so I don't go that way in the snow. Skip may have been there. I was not."

"But you did have lunch that Monday at the Faculty Club?" Vrai said.

"I was feeling unwell," Frank said, "so I came home."

Unwell due to having caused a fatal accident? Vrai turned back to Celeste. "It may be of some relevance that Gussie's family is of Greek heritage."

Celeste carefully returned her cup to its saucer.

"Skip seemed to think there was an incident once with a little girl," Vrai went on. "A Girl Scout? Whose family was Greek?"

Celeste closed her eyes, the better not to see, and Vrai knew that particular story was true.

"What I'm certain about is this," Vrai said. "Two days after Gussie died, Frank ended up with a black eye, and Skip ran into the street, where he was hit by a car and killed."

Frank pushed his cup and saucer away. "Quite frankly, I think you two should leave now."

Vrai heard Skip's voice. *Quite Frank Leigh is not quite willing to be frank.*

"Just one more question, please," Vrai said. "The flashlight Celeste gave you, the one that's not really a flashlight?"

Frank reached into his pocket and withdrew his key ring, from which dangled only keys. "I lost it," he said.

"When?" Vrai said.

"A while ago." Frank's eyes were on his wife. "I didn't say anything, dear, because I knew you'd worry."

"I'll get you a new one," Celeste said sweetly.

Vrai looked over at Jonathan. He wasn't buying their charade, either. Even Inspector Clouseau could figure this one out. A criminal disposes of the murder weapon.

"Here's what I think," Vrai said to her boss. "I think you blinded Skip with pepper spray, by the tennis courts, and that's why he ran out into the street."

"That's enough," Celeste said. "You've had your tea. Now go."

Frank's cheeks were even pinker than his wife's velour. "You've got some nerve. Have you forgotten who you work for?"

Vrai couldn't resist. "Whom," she said. "How did you learn of Skip's death?"

A sly smile touched Frank's lips. "Margot told me. I was at home, and Margot called to give me the terrible news. Ask her, if you'd like. I'm sure she'll remember."

Vrai took another sip of tea. Empereur Chen-Nung was sharpening her mind. There was no need to ask Margot. Frank was telling the truth this time.

"So," she said. "Monday afternoon. After skipping lunch at the Faculty Club, you called Margot, maybe to tell her you'd be taking the rest of the day off because you were feeling unwell, or maybe to ask her to cancel Tuesday's staff meeting so you could attend a conference in New York. Anyway, Margot knew you were at home, so when she learned Skip had died, she called to tell you. Then you started feeling even worse, like maybe you were coming down with the flu, but you wanted a glass of ale, so you went down to the basement and fell and knocked yourself unconscious, and then sometime after midnight, even though you were too sick to travel, you left the house and walked to the grocery store."

Across the table, Jonathan's eyes did a victory dance. She'd scored a spectacular goal.

"You think you're so damn smart," Celeste said.

"Did you hear the impact?" Vrai was close to tears.

"When the car hit Skip? Why didn't you go out to the street to help him?"

Frank's face was crimson.

"You were there," Vrai insisted. "Maybe you never meant for Skip to die, but you were there when he did. Admit that much at least."

Frank stared at his teacup. "I'll say it one more time. I never saw Skip Howard by the tennis courts. Not the day he died. Not ever."

"He was my friend," Vrai said, "and you turned him against me."

Frank's eyes were hard as steel. "Not true."

"We've both asked you to leave," Celeste said. "Why are you still here?"

A loud knocking, and Celeste's hand went to her heart. Frank seemed frozen, unable to move, so it was Celeste who answered the door. Seconds later, she escorted two uniformed policemen into the dining room.

Jonathan looked elated. Vrai wished Justin hadn't been so hasty.

The policemen unzipped their jackets, revealing holstered guns. With their dark hair and ruddy cheeks, the officers looked enough alike to be brothers. "Sir, are you Frank Leigh?" the younger one asked politely.

Frank nodded. Slowly he rose from his chair.

"We don't want to disturb your family," the older one said, eyeing Jonathan. "I wonder if you could step outside with us for a minute?"

"We're not his family," Jonathan said. "Thank goodness."

"I am," Celeste said. "I'm his wife. I'd like to hear what you have to say."

"We'd just like you to come to the station," the older man said to Frank. "Sgt. Bailey wants to talk to you. He would've stopped by himself, but he's had a busy afternoon, so he asked us to."

Frank grabbed the edge of the table. "If this is about those tapes, then you must know they were recorded illegally."

Vrai raised her hands, palms forward, like a traffic cop. "Stop right there," she said to Frank. "How do you know about the tapes?" He had indeed spoken to Skip that afternoon.

But Frank, realizing he'd said too much, said no more.

"Remember what you heard just now," Vrai said to the officers. "He knows about the tapes. Gussie didn't tell him, and neither did her son. Skip did, though, just before he died. Skip Howard."

The older man gave her the calm, professional nod of someone who's used to dealing with hysterics.

"We don't know what Sgt. Bailey wants," the younger man said to Frank. "All we know is, he'd like to talk to you. You can follow us in your car."

"Am I under arrest?" Frank said. "I'm fairly new in town. I don't have an attorney as yet."

"Bailey would like to get a statement," the older man

said. "That's all. If we were arresting you, we'd have to say so and read you your rights."

Jonathan could hold back no longer. "I can give you a statement." He stood up, the better to command the attention of his audience. "I'll tell you exactly what happened. You won't get the truth from this asshole. Two people are dead because of him. Skip and Gussie. Gussie and Skip. Count 'em. One and one are two."

The older man studied the ceiling. "My mother, if I ever used language like that, would've washed my mouth out with soap. Palmolive."

The younger man was smiling. "Sir, are you coming?"

Frank's cheeks were dangerously scarlet. "I don't have to, do I?"

"No, sir, we can't make you," the older man said. "We're just asking if you'll be a good citizen and help Sgt. Bailey with an investigation he's working on. Your wife may come, too, if she'd like. If you get there and change your mind, you can always leave."

"What about us?" Jonathan said. "We know what really happened. He killed two people."

"Nonsense!" Frank snapped. "I'm a library director."

"If it was a murder investigation," the older man said, "then Sgt. Bailey would've come himself. All he wants is a statement."

"My wife took the train down from Philadelphia," Frank said. "We don't have a car here. So I'm afraid we can't go anywhere today."

"I'll take you," Vrai said. "My car's parked just across the street."

"That'll work," the younger man said.

. . . .

Where were the newspaper photographers when you needed them? No photo would appear in the *Baltimore Sun* with the caption, "Library Director Taken to Police Station for Questioning." A few neighbors, alerted by the presence of a police car double-parked on their block, watched from their porches as Frank and Celeste followed the officers down the steps.

To make room for the two liars to ride in back, Vrai moved Skip's computer with its true stories to the trunk. She apologized for any dog hairs.

The policemen took a different route to Keswick Road than Vrai would have, but she stayed with them all the way. "You're right about the tapes," she said over her shoulder to Frank. "Gussie should have told you what she was doing."

Frank said nothing.

"You were there, weren't you?" she said. "You didn't push Skip into the street. I'm not saying you did. You used your pepper spray, in self-defense. He'd hit you, after all. At least tell me I have that much right."

But Frank would not.

. . . .

The Northern District police station was in an ancient building known as the Castle. Vrai found a parking space and turned off the engine. "Want me to wait here for you?"

Frank was silent on the subject of what he wanted Vrai to do. He and Celeste got out of the car, slammed the doors, and followed the older policeman inside.

"I wish Justin hadn't called the police." Vrai felt drained. "We were so close." She wanted to believe this. "All we can do now is go home."

She stared up at the Castle's turrets. Too bad there wasn't a guillotine inside to coerce a confession from Frank.

Jonathan's cheeks were wet with tears.

"Oh, please don't." She knew better than to mention his parents, the unjust world they, too, had inhabited. "Frank's not worth it."

"I know." Jonathan sniffled. "It's not that. It's what you said."

"What I said when?"

"Just now." He wiped at his eyes. "Let's do it. Let's go home."

chapter 24

❄ ❄ ❄

Vrai felt her grip on the steering wheel loosen, her shoulders relax. In this maze of one-way streets, she already knew which way to turn. The snow-laden branches of each maple and poplar and sycamore seemed like welcoming arms. After a painful, life-altering week, she was home.

A shoveled-out parking space awaited her, claimed by a chair from her front porch, the sidewalk and steps to which had also been cleared of snow. Vrai's heart grew wings and soared. Bob still had a key to their house. Concerned about her, he must have flown in from Seattle. The neighbors would have something new to gossip about. Were the Lyndes back together again? Would Vrai be moving now? Would she take that new little boy with her?

Another possibility raised its ugly head. Lloyd knew about the spare key hidden under a loose porch tile. Had he suddenly realized he loved Vrai, not Marianne? More likely, the shoveling was a type of ransom, in return for which Lloyd would take Jonathan back to Asheville.

"Could you move that chair, please?" Vrai said. "Looks like some Good Samaritan found my snow shovel."

"This is it? We're home?" Jonathan unbuckled his seat belt. "Which one's your house?"

Vrai pointed. She was home. Jonathan was still in limbo. He set the chair under a tree, and she parallel-parked like a pro.

Before starting up the front walk, she scanned the parked cars. Not a BMW in sight.

A note taped to her door identified the shoveler. "My mom's idea," it read. "You can pay me if you want."

She showed the note to Jonathan. "Bryan McQueen, next door."

"Some Good Samaritan."

She tested the door to see if it was locked. It was.

The house was empty. The only entries during her absence had come through the mail slot. A visitor would have picked up the envelopes and put them on the hall table. She did this herself, then turned up the heat.

Jonathan set his jacket on the larger of the two settees and surveyed the living room. Pre-Raphaelite props, Bob had dubbed the settees, both of them covered in turquoise brocade, with two preening peacocks woven into the fabric of the smaller one. Above the fireplace hung a large oval mirror in an ornate gold frame. The mirror had come with the house and would stay here when she moved out.

She followed Jonathan into the dining room, where

the French doors to the back patio provided a snow gauge. Total accumulation: above the first pane.

"These are my sons." She pointed to the wall filled with photographs, most of them Bob's, moments he'd waited with loving patience to capture. Her favorite was the one Larry had taken of Bob attempting to photograph Robbie. Robbie was holding a lacrosse stick taller than he was, and Bob, crouching off to the side, was waiting for the perfect configuration of light and shadow. What Larry had captured was his brother's alert, amused awareness of both cameras.

"Larry's older, right?" Jonathan said.

She nodded. The boys' presence in the room was almost tangible. A past presence.

"Nice house," Jonathan said.

"Just make yourself at home while I check on a few things, OK?"

The answering machine in the kitchen displayed a red PF. Power failure. Therefore, no messages.

She flipped on the basement light and hurried down to the half bath beside the furnace. No evidence of frozen sewer pipes.

Back in the kitchen, she poured spoiled milk down the sink drain and retrieved the unopened half-gallon she'd stored in the freezer nearly a week ago. There were frozen flounder filets for dinner. With maybe some rice? Did Jonathan like fish?

Where was he? As she started down the hall, Vrai heard

the second-floor toilet flush. Jonathan then clumped up the stairs to the third floor.

Exhausted, she sat down in the white leather La-Z-Boy that had belonged to her parents. The recliner didn't really go with the antique settees, but it was far more comfortable. She adjusted the lever, elevating her feet, and lay back.

There was so much to do.

Phone calls to make. Her parents. Bob. Lloyd. The kennel.

Maybe Justin?

Groceries to buy. Laundry to do. Mail to sort. A bed to make up with clean sheets.

Trips to plan. Boston. Seattle.

A trip to the bank.

. . . .

Someone was squeezing her shoulder. "Chicken noodle soup's on," a familiar voice said.

Jonathan was grinning, proud of himself. "I made myself at home. But I wasn't sure which bedroom's mine."

Vrai adjusted the La-Z-Boy and sat up. It was after seven. "Third floor, either room you'd like."

"I can choose?"

"For now. Till we get all this sorted out."

Jonathan gave her a look. "You must be hungry. Want a PBJ with your soup?"

"Sounds good." She smiled up at him. "The bread's in the freezer."

"Not any more."

. . . .

The obituary for Laramie and Miguel, hidden away at the back of a dresser drawer, was still painful to read, but it did give the name of the cemetery. In another drawer Vrai came across a forgotten but still-valid credit card.

Something made her turn around. Jonathan, in what had become his GO VOLS nightshirt, was standing in her bedroom doorway.

"Ready for bed?" she said.

"You can sleep up there with me if you want."

Was this why he'd chosen Robbie's twin-bedded room? "I will if you get lonely." She waved the credit card. "Let's take the train up to Boston. I'm tired of driving. Maybe this weekend?"

But Jonathan shook his head.

"I thought you wanted to see your parents' graves."

"I do, but the snow will be too crusty now for making angels. Besides, what about the police? What about Justin?"

Vrai wondered if his grandparents were entirely to blame for his never having visited the cemetery. She didn't push it. Travel-weary and discouraged, she was only too glad to stay home.

"Then tomorrow we'll go pick up Elsie and Dewey," she said.

Jonathan padded into the room. He gave her a wordless hug.

"Sleep well." She smoothed his hair. "Want me to come up and tuck you in?"

"I'm ten years old."

"Well, let me know if you need anything. I'm going downstairs for a while."

After all the telephone conversations he'd overheard at the Smoky View, it seemed silly to worry about his listening in. Still, she longed for privacy.

. . . .

By touching the tones on the kitchen phone, she called Florida.

"Finally!" her mother said, sounding more angry than relieved. "Where *are* you?"

"Back in Baltimore." Vrai explained about having to stop in Bristol. She didn't mention Hagerstown, wasn't yet ready to divulge details of the Gussie/Skip/Frank saga.

"We knew you'd checked out of your motel. Your father finally called Bob. He told us not to worry, you were headed north. So we've been calling and calling, but your phone just rang and rang. We couldn't even leave a message."

"The power's been out," Vrai said. "But everything's fine now."

"We had no way of knowing that. Daddy's gone out to buy groceries. I stayed here in case you called."

"I'm sorry. Really I am. It's been a rough week."

"Is Jonathan still with you?"

"For the time being. Can we talk later? I'm exhausted."

"Good-bye then, sweetheart. We only worry because we love you."

"I love you, too." After hanging up, Vrai unplugged the answering machine and plugged it in again. A red 0 replaced the PF.

It was nine thirty, six thirty in Seattle, but Bob wasn't home. We're back in Baltimore safe and sound, she told his answering machine. Thanks for reassuring my parents. No trip to the cemetery planned, not yet, so give me a call.

Next she called Lloyd's office. While his voice was encouraging her to leave a detailed message, she gathered her courage. "We're in Baltimore now and glad to be here," she said as calmly as she could. "Jonathan's an extraordinary child. Do you ever wonder what his mother—Laramie, I mean—would want for him?"

Her hand shook as she replaced the receiver. Her heart was racing. Tired as she was, she knew she'd need help falling asleep, so she began heating some of the thawed milk for hot chocolate.

When the phone rang, she just knew it was Bob. "Hi there," she said, giddy as a teenager.

A businesslike voice said, "Vrai, this is Bev DeFazio."

"Bev. Hello," Vrai managed.

"Have I called too late?"

"Not at all. I'm really sorry about Skip."

"Not the sort of news you want to hear from your secretary, that's for sure. But I'm mainly calling about Justin. What's going on with him?"

Vrai's brain was so scrambled, she couldn't imagine how Bev and Justin even knew each other. Then it came to her. "Was Justin the one who sent the police to Frank's house?"

"Did he? He's called me twice now. First he wanted me to meet him at some pizza place. I'm just back in town after visiting my parents in Albuquerque. I had clients to see today." Bev had always been a fast talker—the polar opposite of Justin; tonight her words were tumbling out at an alarming rate. "I was sorry to hear about his mother, but Justin knows I can't just leave work like that."

"I was making progress with Frank, until the police showed up." Vrai was beginning to wonder if this was true. Without the police there, Frank might not have mentioned the tapes at all.

"Frank Leigh? You went to his house? But why?"

For tea, Vrai almost said. "Wait a sec." The milk was boiling over. She grabbed for the pan and turned off the stove.

"Justin kept going on and on about the two deaths being related," Bev said. "He didn't sound quite right in the head. I've always thought Justin has to have at least some brain damage."

Vrai filled the attorney in. "That's why I went to Frank's

house," she added. "To try to find out if he really did meet up with Skip by the tennis courts."

"Did he?"

"He won't admit it," Vrai said, "but he knows about the tapes, so he must have."

"Everyone's getting a little crazy here. You and Justin know nothing about the rules of evidence."

Vrai knew something about the methodical steps for authenticating a painting, the most crucial one being the connoisseur's initial gut reaction. The experts referred to this talent as their "eye," their "sixth sense."

"You have a theory of what happened," Bev went on. "And you may be right. But there's not a shred of evidence that a crime was committed. Unless. Wait. I wonder if Frank ever threatened Gussie."

Vrai thought of Skip's story, "Slipping." But evidence had to be based on fact, not fiction. Even she knew that.

"Poor Skip," Bev rambled on. "I wasn't at all surprised to hear he'd run out into traffic. Losing his job really affected him. Thanks for your messages, by the way. My father's in the hospital, that's why I went to Albuquerque. Otherwise I would've tried to come to the funeral."

"Is your dad going to be all right?"

Bev didn't answer right away. "We hope so."

Vrai poured the scalded milk into a cup and stirred in some cocoa.

"Skip and I had put our relationship on hold," Bev said. "I don't know if you knew or not. I was afraid to break things off entirely, Skip was acting so weird. He needed professional help, but he wouldn't go. He was angry at you, of all people. I thought maybe a change of scenery would do the trick, so last summer we went to Bethany Beach for a week. Lisa, my daughter, was going to stay with her father, but at the last minute he had an emergency business trip, so she came along with us. Skip wouldn't let Lisa out of his sight. She's twelve, an excellent swimmer, but he didn't want her out beyond the breakers. He'd walk along the beach, following her, yelling at her to come back. I was even more upset with his behavior than Lisa was."

The onslaught of words, with its swirling implications, was making Vrai dizzy. She pulled over the kitchen step-stool and sat down.

Didn't Skip ever tell you about Melody? she wanted to ask. Was Bev even aware that Lisa resembled Skip's little sister? At one point he'd talked about marrying Bev, yet he hadn't trusted her with his most painful secret.

Had his accumulated losses driven Skip over the edge? Within the space of a few years, his sister, his father, and his childhood sweetheart had died. More recently, he'd lost his job, because a trusted friend had betrayed him, and then his fiancée dumped him. Finally, his substitute mother, who was being tormented by their former boss, had a heart attack and died.

Did Skip cover his eyes and start across Olmsted Parkway as a way of tempting fate? Was he thinking, I can't take it any more, so please, be my guest?

Was Frank blameless?

"I wish I could've convinced Skip to talk his problems over with someone." Bev let out a sigh. "But I called you about Justin, didn't I? He's so persistent. He called me at home tonight, wanting me to come to a meeting with a Sgt. Bailey at the Northern District."

"I'd like to be there." Vrai owed this to Skip.

"Good," Bev said. "You can go in my place. Saturday morning at ten."

"A young friend's staying here with me. He'll want to come, too."

"How young?" Bev said.

"A very mature ten. His parents were assassinated. He wants justice this time. So please try to come. You know more about the law than we do."

"Justice. An abstract and elusive concept. Everyone wants it, but no one's quite sure what the hell it is." And Bev hung up.

. . . .

The hot chocolate hadn't made her the least bit sleepy. She lay in bed wide awake, her mind churning.

Skip had been angry with her, but he never told Bev why. Never told Bev about Melody.

Frank knows, Vrai should've said to her friend. Two simple words. Why hadn't she said them?

Would Skip still be alive if she had?

This thought propelled her up the stairs to the third floor. Jonathan had left the hall light on, the bedroom door open. Standing beside his bed, Robbie's bed, she whispered, "Tiles in Lugash," but Jonathan was too deeply asleep to hear.

"The Art History Library?" she said softly. "A betrayer works there."

Jonathan slept on.

. . . .

The library re-opened on Friday. Vrai arranged for Jonathan to stay with Linh Nguyen, who lived on the corner. Years ago Linh had provided afterschool daycare for Larry and Robbie, who were her own sons' ages.

"Glad to help out," Linh said. "Like old times."

Dr. Brill didn't come in. His secretary said he'd hurt his back carrying a load of firewood into his house.

Did Frank come to work with his bruises? Vrai made no effort to find out. She intended to keep a low profile until all this blew over, or blew up, or whatever was going to happen.

When she returned home at five thirty, a red *1* was blinking on the answering machine. Sounding unusually serious, Lloyd said he had something very important to discuss with her. He would call back.

She put the dogs' leashes on and walked down to the Nguyens' house. There were no messages when she and

Jonathan returned from Poe Park. No one called during dinner. Or after dinner.

Not Lloyd.

Not Bob.

The phone in the room at the Smoky View hadn't stopped ringing. What did all this telephonic silence mean?

chapter 25

❄ ❄ ❄

*a*s directed, Vrai and Jonathan took the elevator up to the third floor of the Northern District police station. There, in a dimly lit hallway lined with buckets into which the ceiling was actively leaking, they found Justin in his wheelchair. Beside him, on a wooden bench, sat Bev.

Vrai touched Justin's arm. "OK with you if Jonathan and I sit in?"

"You think we can pin *anything* on Frank?" Justin sounded discouraged. Perhaps the attorney had been lecturing him on the rules of evidence.

"We have to try," Vrai said. She introduced Jonathan to Bev, who looked tired, her short brown hair in need of a shampoo.

"How's your father?" Vrai asked her.

"About the same."

"Is Winsome coming?" Vrai said to Justin.

"She wanted to, but she has to work today."

Vrai and Jonathan sat down on a bench across the hall, too far away from the others for easy conversation. Water plopped into buckets. Occasionally a phone rang.

"You sure we're in the right place?" Jonathan whispered.

At ten fifteen a white-haired man wearing khakis and an Orioles jacket negotiated his way down the hall. "Good morning, Mr. Morgen," he boomed. "Sgt. Bailey here. Would you like to come into my office?"

Justin moved his wheelchair forward. Bev stood up. Vrai and Jonathan joined the party.

"Whoa now," Sgt. Bailey said. "Not sure there's room for everyone. Is this a family meeting? I can't stay long. My grandson has a soccer game today." He looked at Jonathan. "What's your name, young man?"

"Jonathan Santiago. I play soccer, too."

"Beverly DeFazio." Bev's hand shot forward. "I'm an attorney."

Sgt. Bailey shook Bev's hand. "Mr. Morgen's attorney?"

"No. I was Skip Howard's . . . fiancée."

"Skip Howard?" Sgt. Bailey looked confused.

"The man who was hit by a car on Olmsted Parkway," Bev said. "Two days after Gussie Morgen died. We believe the two deaths are related."

"Oh, yes," Sgt. Bailey said. "I think Mr. Morgen mentioned that." He turned to Vrai.

"Vraiment Lynde. I was a friend of Skip Howard's. Also his and Gussie's former co-worker. Jonathan's with me."

"Well, now." Sgt. Bailey looked up and down the hallway. Only a few office lights were on. "Let me get the file. Maybe we can have a quick meeting out here."

He returned with a file folder and two metal folding chairs. Vrai and Jonathan sat in the chairs, facing Bev and the sergeant on the bench. Justin completed the circle.

"I owe you an apology, Mr. Morgen," Sgt. Bailey began. "I should've been in touch with you long before this. I did ask my lieutenant to listen to those tapes of your mother's. I asked him about authorizing a tap on her phone. He had the same question I did. Your mother didn't have to listen to the caller. Why didn't she just hang up?"

"She didn't listen," Justin said. "As soon as she knew who it was, she put the receiver down on the table."

"I see. The problem now is, with your mother being deceased, I think any criminality pertaining to the phone calls died with her."

Vrai expected Bev to object, or ask a question, but it was Justin who spoke up. "My mother *died* because of one of those phone calls." He touched his shirt pocket. "I have the last tape right here."

"We could charge this Frank Leigh with homicide if he'd shot her, sure. But didn't you say your mother died of a heart attack?"

"That's what Skip and I were told."

Justin was speaking even more slowly, more distinctly, than usual. Jonathan turned his head from Sgt. Bailey to Justin and back again, as if watching a tennis match.

"It may very well be that the heart attack was brought on by the nature of that last phone call. But there's no way to prove cause and effect." Sgt. Bailey put his hand on his chest. "A heart attack's in here just waiting to happen."

"You told her to stop taping Frank," Justin said. "You promised us the police would gather evidence that would stand up in court. Are you telling me you did nothing?"

"I'm telling you I tried. Phone taps are expensive. I tried to get authorization, but I failed. I also failed to report back to you and your mother. Once again, Mr. Morgen, I do apologize."

"She was just a silly old woman to you," Justin said. "And now she's dead, because of the very phone calls you agreed to investigate."

Sgt. Bailey closed the folder. "I also want to report on my meeting Wednesday afternoon with Frank Leigh and his wife. Mr. Leigh did come in to the station, but he declined to give us a statement, written or otherwise. He was polite about it, I'll give him that. He did say that he hadn't spoken to your mother in over a year."

"In person, maybe," Justin said. "But he definitely spoke with her by phone."

"Gussie kept a log of the calls," Vrai said. "Couldn't we back that up with records from the phone company?"

"I suppose we could," Sgt. Bailey said. "But with her being deceased, as I said, it would be difficult to bring charges."

Finally Bev spoke. "Could we talk about Skip Howard? Frank Leigh was at least indirectly involved in

Gussie Morgen's death. We believe he may have been physically present when my fiancé died."

When Bev didn't elaborate, Vrai jumped in. "The two officers who came to Frank's house Wednesday afternoon heard him mention the tapes Gussie had been recording. The only person who could've told Frank about the tapes was Skip Howard, right before he was hit by that car."

"Skip Howard." Sgt. Bailey frowned. "The pedestrian fatality, right?"

"That black eye Frank has?" Vrai said. "We think Skip gave it to him, and then Frank blinded Skip with pepper spray, and that's why Skip ran into the street."

"Any witnesses? Any evidence at all?" Sgt. Bailey said.

"There was an autopsy," Vrai said.

"An autopsy?" Bev cleared her throat. "I didn't know."

"And surely," Sgt. Bailey said, "somewhere, there's a police report." He turned to Bev. "Was Skip a nickname?"

"I suppose it must have been."

"Jasper Pascal Howard, Jr.," Vrai said. "Date of death March 8, 1993."

Sgt. Bailey re-opened the folder and wrote this down. "It's usually thirty days before an autopsy report becomes available. Did anyone see Mr. Leigh at the scene of the accident?"

"Skip did," Jonathan said.

"Skip can't testify in court," Sgt. Bailey said. "What you'd need is someone who can. And will."

"Could I listen to the tapes you have?" Bev said. "Even though they were made illegally, if Frank Leigh threatened Mrs. Morgen, then there might be charges we could bring."

"Since we never officially opened a case, those tapes weren't marked as evidence," Sgt. Bailey said. "I think I could put my hands on them, but not today. Maybe in a week or so?" He turned to Justin. "Mr. Morgen, I am deeply sorry for your loss. I admired your mother. Full of spunk, she was. Not the least bit silly, not to me, anyway. You're wrong to think that. And just between you and me and the fencepost, that Frank Leigh's guilty of something."

"Guilty of double murder," Jonathan said, his voice trembling.

"I'm afraid there's no proof of that." Sgt. Bailey spoke with grandfatherly patience. "Before we can charge a person with homicide, we have to have irrefutable evidence. Evidence that's sure to stand up in court. Our detectives are very busy these days. Baltimore's homicide rate has been on national TV. *World News Tonight*, I think it was. Peter Jennings."

Vrai wondered why an officer capable of such courteous and articulate stonewalling hadn't risen above sergeant. Maybe the police force was a second career for this man. "What if the autopsy shows traces of pepper spray?" she asked him.

"You'd still need a witness, someone who actually

saw Mr. Leigh using the spray on . . ." Sgt Bailey glanced down at his notes. "Mr. Howard. Understand what I'm saying?"

She did.

"Anything else I can help you folks with before I go cheer for my grandson?" Sgt. Bailey stood up. He returned the file to his office and, after a silent ride with them in the elevator, said he'd be in touch.

"In touch about what?" Justin asked when the four of them were outside. He wiped at his eye, the one with the eyebrow.

"The autopsy, maybe?" Vrai said.

"He's basically finished with us," Bev said. "Unless we can come up with 'irrefutable evidence.'"

"I thought the police collected evidence," Vrai said. "Isn't that what we pay them for?" She touched Justin's shoulder. "Don't give up, not yet. I'd like to try to talk to the optician whose car hit Skip. Think that's a good idea?"

Justin nodded. "Worth a try."

"What do you think?" she said to Bev.

"Honestly? I'm sorry to say it, but I think this meeting was a complete waste of time. But sure, go ahead if you want."

Bev and Justin headed toward the handicapped parking spaces. "Anyone remember the optician's name?" Vrai called after them.

No one did.

"You think they've cleared the snow off that soccer field?" Jonathan said on the way to her car.

"Maybe his grandson plays indoor soccer." Vrai put her arm around him. "I'd like to stop at the library. Do you mind? You don't have to come in."

"Your library or Skip's?"

"Skip's. The John Joseph Stark Library. JJ's for short."

"I wouldn't miss it for anything."

"I left my copy of the newspaper article about the accident with Skip's mother," she said. "I think it gave the name of the optician."

....

Twenty minutes later she waved her ID at the guard seated by the turnstile on Ground Level. "We'll just be a minute."

The guard eyed Jonathan. "He still has to sign in."

While Jonathan dutifully added his name to the list of Saturday visitors, Vrai asked if there had been a service in the Poole Room for Gussie.

The man gave her a blank look.

"Gussie Morgen," Vrai said. "Sorry to give you bad news, but she died two days before Skip Howard did."

"Oh." The guard looked stricken. "I hadn't heard." He shook his head. "There was a service? Here?"

"I guess not. Otherwise you would've known about it." Vrai followed Jonathan though the turnstile.

It felt odd to be in JJ's, which hadn't changed, when so much else in her life had. She led Jonathan to the elevators and pushed the button to bring one up from below.

"Where was the memorial for Skip?" Jonathan said. "Which elevator?"

The left one is the right one. The right one is the wrong one. Skip again. "The left one, I think."

The elevator on the right arrived, clanking, and they rode down to Level Six. Current Periodicals.

Vrai went first to the newspapers displayed on wooden rods. But Skip had been dead for more than a week now. She found the March 9 *Sun* in its stack on a neatly labeled shelf and spread the newspaper out on a table.

"You don't have to read this," she said to Jonathan. "Yes, I do."

Pedestrian Killed on Olmsted Parkway
By Martin Sheppard

A Baltimore man was struck and killed in the northbound lane of Olmsted Parkway at approximately 1:15 on Monday afternoon. According to Baltimore City Police, Jasper Pascal Howard, Jr., 50, was hit by a 1990 Volvo driven by Nicholas Grassley, an optician from Cockeysville. The victim was taken to Maryland Memorial Hospital where he was pronounced dead, said Lt. Alonzo Adams, a city police spokesman.

The accident occurred near the tennis courts on the campus of Stoneham-Knox University, where Mr. Howard had been employed as a librarian. The driver, who remained on the scene and summoned an ambulance, has not been charged. The victim, according to Mr. Grassley, ran into the street with his hands over his eyes. No other witnesses have come forward. Lt. Adams said speed did not appear to be a factor in the incident but that an investigation is ongoing.

While Vrai photocopied the article, Jonathan stood staring out through the wall of windows at the snow-covered ivy. Six stories underground they were. Not as bad as six feet under in a coffin, but still. The library's design was more hospitable to books than to humans.

After she'd re-folded the newspaper and returned it to its place on the shelf, Jonathan wanted to see where Gussie had kept her celestial goldfish.

"Some other time," Vrai said. "I need to go home now."

"So we can look this Grassley person up in the phone book?"

She nodded. A lie. The library had phone books. But where she felt an urgent need to be, and very soon, was on the steps to her front porch, with a cold wind in her face and her keys at the ready.

chapter 26

✳ ✳ ✳

Maybe being underground was conducive to ESP. On her porch stood a man with crutches, his right toes peeking out from a white plaster cast.

"Uh oh," Jonathan said. "I know that man."

As she started up the walk, Vrai felt a rush of adrenaline. No way Jonathan was going back to Asheville.

On the porch sat two suitcases and two duffle bags, with BWI labels affixed to their handles. No way Lloyd was moving in, either. She hoped he'd tipped the cabbie well.

From the other side of the door came excited barking. Elsie and Dewey loved Lloyd.

"Where the hell have you two been?" Lloyd sounded frantic. "I need to use the bathroom."

Either he'd forgotten about the key under the loose tile, or the ruse was for Jonathan's benefit. Vrai unlocked the door, worried the dogs' eager greeting would make it clear to Jonathan that his uncle was no stranger here. But clever Lloyd brandished a crutch at them, and Elsie and Dewey, their feelings hurt, slunk away.

"I'm afraid the nearest bathroom's upstairs," Vrai said. "First door on the right."

"Damn," said the master of deception.

While Lloyd, his right knee bent, climbed the stairs on crutches, Jonathan carried the luggage into the living room. Before unzipping the larger duffle, he glanced up for permission. Vrai, equally curious, nodded at him to go ahead.

Elsie padded over to sniff at the bag's contents. Dewey was keeping watch by the stairs.

"This is *my* stuff," Jonathan said, wide-eyed.

"All of it?" Vrai said.

He opened a suitcase and gave her a hesitant smile. "What's going on?"

"I'm as surprised as you are."

"Oooh, I hate these." Jonathan attempted to tie plaid pajama legs around Elsie's neck, but the dog wriggled free.

The crutches came sliding down the stairs, frightening Dewey off. Lloyd followed, slowly, on his butt.

Vrai waited until he was balanced on one foot again and could see the opened bags. "What's this all about?"

"Damn it all," Lloyd snapped. "You had no right."

"It's my stuff," Jonathan said. "Why shouldn't I see it?"

"For the same reason you should wait till Christmas to open your presents." Lloyd swung himself into the living room. "I *told* you I had something to discuss." He glared at Vrai.

"Discuss away," she said.

"Not sure this is the best time."

"Then give us a small hint," she said.

Lloyd looked from Vrai to Jonathan and back again, his expression changing from irritation to concern. "It's just that we've been wondering." He pivoted toward Jonathan, who was kneeling beside a duffle bag. "Would you like to stay here for a while? On a trial basis? If it's all right with Vrai, of course."

Jonathan seemed reluctant to tear back the rest of the wrapping on this surprise gift, and Vrai understood why. It was one thing to want to leave home. It was quite another to be shown the door. Evicted, along with your belongings. Her sense of duty toward him—the promise she'd made in the shower to his mother—was overshadowed by a stronger emotion: the desire to protect a loved one from harm.

"That's the first option," Lloyd said quickly. "Here's the second. I take you, and all these bags, back home with me tomorrow. We miss you and hope that's what you'll decide to do."

Jonathan got to his feet. "I *am* home." He went to Vrai and wrapped his arms around her waist.

At the Smoky View it was Vrai who'd come undone, sobbing into the phone, with her husband at the other end of the line. Now it was Jonathan's turn to fall apart. She hugged him to her, patting his heaving shoulders.

Lloyd looked to her for guidance, and she saw the uncertainty in his eyes. Letting Jonathan decide for himself seemed a cruel variation on the theme of leaving the boy alone to think things over. What was wrong with Marianne? Why couldn't Lloyd say no to her?

"Whose idea was this?" Vrai said.

Lloyd's shrug spoke volumes.

"He can stay here forever," she said. "Or for as long as he wants."

Jonathan disentangled himself, removed his eyeglasses, and dried his eyes on a sleeve. "Did you bring my soccer stuff?" he sniffled.

"Not sure what all she packed."

"What do *you* want?" Vrai said to Lloyd.

"We want Jonathan to be happy."

"Not we. You. What do you yourself want?"

"I want the best situation for Jonathan." Lloyd looked away. He seemed bewildered by this scene he'd created. "I know there's been, well, tension at home."

"Does he have to decide right this minute?" Vrai said.

"Of course not."

"I already decided," Jonathan said. "Give it a rest, you two."

. . . .

While preparing sandwiches for lunch, Vrai noticed a red *1* blinking on the answering machine. She set the mayonnaise jar aside and pressed play, hoping to hear Bob's voice. But the message was from Lloyd, giving her his flight number and arrival time at BWI.

"See?" Lloyd called to her from the dining room. "I *tried* to let you know I was coming. I was planning to discuss this with you on the ride in from the airport. That way the bags could've stayed in your car."

Vrai strode to the dining room door. "This isn't a B&B with airport shuttle service, you know."

"But where *were* you?" Lloyd was seated in his usual chair. They'd often had breakfast together at this table, Lloyd in his underwear and Vrai in her green robe.

"At the police station," Jonathan said, and Vrai returned to the kitchen while he filled his uncle in on the meeting with Sgt. Bailey. How mature was Jonathan? Mature enough to sit there having a normal conversation with his abandoner.

When she took them their tuna salad sandwiches, Lloyd looked up at her. "Are we talking about your boss? Is this the 'heads will roll' Frank? What is he, some sort of psychopath?"

"The department head who denied him tenure was Greek," Vrai said. "Gussie was Greek."

"But that's completely bonkers."

"How do you know about Frank?" Jonathan said.

Mr. Smooth Talker described the dinner at Skip's apartment. "Skip and Vrai and I go way back," he said. "So this Frank person killed my oldest friend?"

"We think Frank was responsible for both deaths," Vrai said. "What we lack, according to the police, is irrefutable evidence."

"Wait!" Jonathan cried. He went to the kitchen and returned with a phone book.

"What would you two like to drink?" she said.

"Vrai makes really good milkshakes," Jonathan said.

Lloyd gave her an approving smile—she and Jonathan had developed an obvious rapport—and asked if hot tea would be too much trouble. Vrai had to remind herself that this was a man she could not trust.

"You want tea, too?" she said to Jonathan.

"Tea? Never again. Got any chocolate ice cream?"

"Sorry. I could do chocolate milk."

"Sounds good." Jonathan busied himself with the phone book, and Vrai let the drinks wait. "No Grassley." He looked up in dismay. "Nothing even starting with Grass."

"Mind if I look?" Vrai said, but Jonathan was right.

"Who's Grassley?" Lloyd said.

"His car hit Skip," Jonathan said. "So he was a witness. We want to talk to him."

"Shouldn't you let the police handle this?"

Vrai shook her head. "They have zero interest."

"We'll find Mr. Grassley," she told Jonathan. "Don't you worry."

"Find him how?"

"He has a driver's license, doesn't he? If we can't locate him, then Bev will."

"I'd like to help," Lloyd said. "I knew Skip even longer than you did."

"Maybe you could talk to a lawyer," Vrai said. "Criminal law isn't Bev's area of expertise."

"Did Skip have a lawyer?" Lloyd said. "Did he have a will?"

"No idea." Why hadn't this occurred to her? What would happen to Skip's furniture and other belongings? Maybe Bev would know.

"Bev and Skip had called off their engagement," she said.

Lloyd didn't even know Skip had been planning to get married. Couldn't remember when he'd last heard from his longtime friend.

Did Lloyd know how Melody died? Vrai had never asked him. Now she never would.

. . . .

"You two jumped the gun on me," Lloyd said when lunch was over. "I didn't do a very good job of explaining. Please understand that this arrangement doesn't have to be permanent." He looked at Jonathan. "Marianne and I will welcome you home at any time. Tomorrow, if you want."

"I like it here," Jonathan said.

Lloyd looked as though he wished it had all turned out differently. "Well then, I have two reasons to talk to my lawyer. About Skip, and about you. Vrai will need some sort of temporary guardianship, in case there's ever a medical emergency."

The four bags contained the opposite of ransom. The kidnapper was being allowed to keep the kidnappee. It was hardly the way Vrai had anticipated taking on the role of Jonathan's mother, but it had definite advantages. No divorcing, for one.

"I can have your school assignments sent up by mail," Lloyd said. "Think that'll work?"

Jonathan rolled his eyes. "I'll still have school?"

"Of course you will." Lloyd turned to Vrai. "I guess he can just go in to work with you? Do his assignments there in the library?"

"Sorry." Contrary to popular opinion, libraries weren't free day-care centers. This was especially true of the Art History Library. "We'll have to make other arrangements."

"Mrs. Nguyen?" Jonathan said. "She let me play games on her computer."

"Maybe. I'll ask how much she'd charge."

"Oh." Lloyd seemed surprised that there might be costs involved. "I'll come visit as often as I can. If that's all right."

Would Lloyd visit them in Seattle? Vrai didn't need to cross that bridge just yet. But it seemed wise to let him know what sort of hospitality he should expect in Baltimore.

"You can sleep in Larry's room," she said. "Jonathan's in Robbie's."

Lloyd glanced meaningfully at his crutches. "Is Larry's room up on the third floor?"

"Tonight you can have my bed. I'll sleep in Larry's."

"Kind of you."

"Will Marianne be visiting, too?" she asked.

"To be determined," Lloyd said.

. . . .

That night, after Jonathan had gone to bed, Lloyd made himself comfortable in the La-Z-Boy. Vrai joined the peacocks on the smaller settee. "I need to know what's going on," she said.

Had he and Marianne argued? If so, did it have anything to do with her? Or had they simply realized, after a few days without Jonathan, that they preferred not having him around at all? Jonathan deserved a loving home, and Vrai was only too glad to give him one, but she wanted to understand the circumstances under which this rather drastic decision was made. Had they talked it over in a rational way, or had petite little Marianne come up with the bright idea all by her tiny little self?

Lloyd understood her frustration. It was unforgivable that he'd told her unkind and, admittedly, untrue details about his wife. Laramie had never much liked Marianne, so it wasn't the least bit surprising that Vrai felt the very same way.

"You evasive, lying shit," Vrai said.

"If that's how you feel, then I don't want to sleep in your bed. I'll stay right here. Pee in the kitchen sink if I need to."

Vrai found the dogs' leashes, put on her trench coat, and stormed outside with Elsie and Dewey. When she returned, Lloyd was either asleep or pretending to be. She left the kitchen light on and went upstairs.

chapter 27

❄ ❄ ❄

*a*t work on Monday, Vrai thought to look in the Yellow Pages. Nicholas Grassley was listed under Opticians, with a phone number identical to that of an optical shop in Towson. She decided not to tell Jonathan until there was something to tell.

The next day she left her assistant in charge and took a long lunch hour. The Eyes Have It was next to a Chinese restaurant in a strip mall. Inside the shop, behind a glass counter, sat a curly-haired, barrel-chested man wearing a white foam neck brace. Vrai took a seat in the row of chairs by the door.

"Is that Mr. Grassley?" she whispered to the woman waiting beside her.

"Don't know his name, hon, but he's a sweetie. You'll see."

Hundreds of empty eyeglass frames stared out from the cream-colored walls. Red frames, blue frames, black frames, and tortoise shell. It was unnerving. Vrai felt as though she were being watched.

You'll see, Skip whispered.

Finally it was her turn. The optician apologized for the long wait. And for not getting up from his chair. "Now, how can I help?"

"Are you Nicholas Grassley?" she said. "There's something I'd like to ask you."

"Uh oh." He turned off the courtesy. "Business hours are for customers only."

She lowered her voice. "That accident you were in? I was good friends with the man who died."

"I don't have time for this. Police, insurance investigators. I even had a lawyer come in."

The police had been here? "It's nothing like that." Vrai showed him her University ID. "Skip and I worked in the library together."

"Maybe you'd better come back to my office." Slowly, gingerly, Nicholas Grassley stood up. He ushered her into a small room at the back of the shop. One desk, one file cabinet, and two chairs, but he didn't invite her to sit down.

"Here's my question," Vrai said. "Did you happen to notice anyone else at the scene?"

"I barely had time to notice him. Your friend."

"Skip," Vrai said. "That's what everyone called him."

"So this is personal for you. Well, it is for me, too. This Skip fellow just ran out into the street. He had his hands over his eyes." Nicholas Grassley demonstrated. He'd slammed on the brakes, he said, and was immediately rear-ended by a taxi. It was the taxi driver who'd called for an ambulance.

"Was Skip rubbing his eyes?" Vrai said. "It's possible he'd been blinded by pepper spray."

The optician stared at her. "Pepper spray? I guess that would explain it."

"That's why I'm wondering if you saw anyone, maybe near that hedge of azaleas?"

He started to shake his head but winced with pain.

"A short man with a gray beard?" she said. "With the beginnings of a black eye?"

"I was too concerned about the man I'd hit." He fingered the top of the foam collar.

"The irony is, I'd just given blood at the Red Cross." This was something he did several times a year, he said. It never affected his vision or caused him to be the least bit lightheaded.

"The accident wasn't your fault."

"Then why do I feel this terrible guilt? Why did this have to happen to me?"

Why indeed? "Can I leave you my phone number," she said, "in case you remember something?"

"You're saying someone with pepper spray was responsible?"

"I believe so," Vrai said. "I'm just having a hard time proving it. The police say I need a witness."

"So the police know about this?"

Towson was in the county. "The city police. One of them, anyway. A Sgt. Bailey."

"I need to get back to my customers." He turned around

with care. "I wish I could help, I really do, but I saw no one. Maybe you could talk to that cab driver. Sam something. Or was it Stan? The police would know."

. . . .

But, as Jonathan pointed out, neither of the two drivers would have been there to see Frank aiming the little red flashlight at Skip. So, instead of wasting time trying to find out if the police had even talked to the cabbie, Vrai began spending her lunch hours on the path by the tennis courts, asking passersby if, on Monday, March 8, anyone had seen something unusual. An argument? A fistfight in the snow? A man running toward the street?

No one she spoke to remembered a thing.

Nor did Vrai see Frank on the path. If he was still lunching at the Faculty Club on Mondays, then he was taking the long way around.

Finally she told her father the whole story and asked what he would do. Absolutely nothing, he said, and you shouldn't, either. Accept defeat and move on. "It took real courage to go to Frank's house," he added.

"I was afraid you'd think that was stupid of me."

"You took a chance, and it paid off. You learned something. But the most important thing right now is to find another job. You don't want to work for a man like that. Get away from that monster. What about Tallahassee? Lots of libraries down here."

Good advice, and Vrai knew it, but she still had Seattle on her mind. Thinking she'd like to be her own boss for a change, she applied for the directorship of an art museum library in Tacoma.

"References available upon request" she stated in her application, intending to ask Dr. Brill for a reference only if she became a serious candidate. She didn't. Had someone in Tacoma spoken to Frank?

She was both disappointed and relieved. Jonathan had settled in. He enjoyed his days with Mrs. Nguyen. Why uproot him again so soon? Besides, the closer she stayed to the scene of the crime, the more she could make Frank squirm. He knew he was responsible for two deaths. He knew Vrai knew. People did crack. Even hardened criminals sometimes confessed their crimes and asked for forgiveness.

Not long after the tea party at Frank's house, Vrai's name had been deleted from all library routing slips. She was no longer informed about staff meetings. Her assistant stopped showing up for work.

But the books Vrai ordered for the Art History Library continued to be purchased, cataloged, and delivered. Her paychecks were still deposited in her bank account. In many ways she had the perfect job. She didn't have to serve on committees or attend staff meetings or endure performance appraisals.

Later she would wonder if this irrational thinking was a sign that she was finally grieving for Skip. Grief and guilt, that double whammy.

. . . .

Isolation breeds ideas. Vrai acted on what seemed like her best one.

After a clandestine meeting with the head of current periodicals, a new label, *True Stories*, appeared on one of the shelves down on Level Six. Above the label sat an innocuous manilla folder. Even though Skip's stories weren't listed in any catalog, word got around. They disappeared quickly, only to be replaced by fresh photocopies. The stories were left on tables in the cafeteria, on classroom desks, in the student union coffee shop. It was JJ's own version of *samizdat*.

Before printing the stories out, Vrai had made a few editorial changes. She deleted the reference to the Art History Library and the betrayer who worked there, and she deleted all mention of Miguel and the ways he'd been tortured. Appropriately placed footnotes explained that material had been deleted due to privacy concerns.

She'd then read the stories to Justin and asked if he'd prefer to have Gussie's name deleted as well. Justin said he wanted the whole world to know how Frank had treated his mother. His own plan had been to try to play Gussie's tape recordings over the library's public address system. Distributing Skip's stories, Justin agreed, was a much better approach.

One afternoon Dr. Brill appeared in Vrai's office. "Have you read these?" He waved copies of the stories.

Vrai could not tell a lie. "I have."

"Who wrote them, do you happen to know?"

"Not for absolute certain."

"Possibly the former head of reference?"

Vrai nodded. Entirely possible.

"But he's not distributing them."

"No," she agreed.

"Be careful," Dr. Brill said. "These paint an ugly picture. I'd hate to lose you."

. . . .

Jonathan, of course, came up with an idea of his own. He wanted to picket the library with signs reading FRANK LEIGH IS A DOUBLE MURDERER.

"Ever heard of libel?" Vrai asked him. "It's against the law."

"Ever heard of freedom of speech?" he shot back.

"Pinochet's a murderer. Frank's mean, and he's sneaky, but he doesn't kill people on purpose. We have no proof that he does, anyway. You heard Sgt. Bailey."

So Jonathan tore up the signs, threw the pieces in the fireplace, and lit a match.

chapter 28

✳ ✳ ✳

On Memorial Day weekend Vrai drove Jonathan up to Boston, to the cemetery, north of the city, named for a grove of long-dead chestnut trees. The cemetery office had sent her a map of the plots, with 205 A and B circled. Jonathan had eagerly studied the map. He'd even joked about plotting their way to the plots. But once they were actually there, he hung back, his expression gloomy and disinterested. So Vrai went off to search for the graves on her own.

The tombstone, vaguely heart-shaped, said only:

MIGUEL JOSE SANTIAGO   LARAMIE DAWN EISEN SANTIAGO
      1940—1986   1946—1986

Vrai was disturbed by the starkness, the brevity. She'd expected, at the very least, a line from one of Miguel's poems. Some indication that their lives, and their deaths, had been extraordinary.

She touched the curved marble. Never once during their long friendship had Laramie revealed her full name. Laramie Dawn. The place *and* the time of conception? A secret well worth keeping.

I'm taking good care of him, Vrai wanted to whisper. But her friend was in no way *presente*. Like everyone else on this hillside, Laramie was forever absent. With a tombstone to prove it.

Jonathan was a good distance downhill, admiring a bronze dog—the cemetery was a virtual sculpture garden. When Vrai called to him, he looked up but made no move to join her.

He was ten. They were his parents.

Finally he trudged up the hill, came to a stop, and raised a hand to shield his eyes from the bright sunlight. A dutiful soldier, saluting, awaiting further orders.

"Is it what you expected?" she said gently.

Jonathan shook his head.

"They have a really lovely view." In the distance were rounded blue foothills, reminiscent of the Smokies.

"They can't *see*," he said with some force.

"Of course not," Vrai agreed. "But someone picked out a beautiful spot for them."

"Oh yeah? Look." He pointed at a nearby monument. The angel on top of it had oversized wings, the sort of wings that flap in nightmares. "Would you want to look at that thing all day?"

"At least now we know where they are," she said.

"Where they are, is up there." He pointed skyward.

Did he mean in Heaven? Or among the stars, his beloved constellations?

"And here." Vrai put her hand on her heart.

"So let's go," Jonathan said. "Please, can we just go?"

. . . .

He spent most of July, as usual, with his grandparents on Cape Cod. Mrs. Eisen had invited Vrai to come up, too, for as long as she'd like. But Vrai was afraid a request for vacation days might be granted permanently. If she returned to Baltimore to find that her paychecks had been stopped, how would she pay the mortgage?

Jonathan called her from Cape Cod several times a week to ask if there had been any new developments. "Nothing so far," she'd say. "Please stop worrying about me. I'm fine."

But she wasn't fine. And there *were* new developments.

During the phone conversations with her husband at the Smoky View, he'd told her the truth as he knew it. He didn't yet know that Daphne was pregnant. After months of dithering about what to do, Bob chose Independence Day to break the news to Vrai and ask for her advice.

So this is why you pretty much stopped calling, she wanted to say. Why you sounded so vague and distracted when you did call.

You'll just have to make up your own stupid mind, she nearly said. Either you love me or you don't.

"I think the decision's up to you," she told him.

"C'mon, be a friend, help me out here," Bob pleaded. But she wouldn't.

. . . .

In the fall Jonathan enrolled in sixth grade at an Episcopal school with an after-school daycare program. This was Lloyd's idea, and he paid for it, whether out of his own pocket or from Laramie's estate Vrai neither knew nor cared.

For Jonathan's eleventh birthday, at the end of September, Vrai gave him the two *azulejos* she'd designed and fired herself during a weekend ceramics class (a weekend when Lloyd was in town). She'd come up with the patterns after researching the tile-makers of sixteenth-century Portugal, who'd combined elements of Moorish design with Flemish, Dutch, and Italian influences. The word *azulejo*, she'd learned, came from the Arabic for "little polished stone."

Jonathan was polite about the gift but not overly enthusiastic. Still, she kept at her new hobby. At first her failures outnumbered her successes, but occasionally she ended up with tiles she was downright proud of.

A few of these were displayed in the studio's gift shop, where, miraculously, they sold. A woman who lived in a Spanish-style house in Guilford, Baltimore's ritziest neighborhood, commissioned Vrai to make a backsplash for her kitchen. It wasn't long before another commission materialized, this time for a guest bath in Roland Park.

. . . .

At Thanksgiving, Vrai's bedroom was the only one without a houseguest in it. Both her sons were in town, plus her pregnant daughter-in-law, Charlotte. In lieu of attending their college graduation ceremonies, Larry and Charlotte had decided to elope. They'd kept their marriage a secret until Labor Day, when Larry had called to tell his mother that in April she would become a grandmother.

The part of her that felt left out, that wished she could've been there for the wedding, kept quiet. "How exciting!" Vrai said, and she meant it. This surprise pregnancy nearly made up for the other one.

Bob, despite the fact that Daphne had recently given birth to their daughter, was still dithering about what to do. As Vrai watched Larry carve the Thanksgiving turkey, all she knew for certain was that she and Bob were still husband and wife.

Jonathan was shy, at first, with his new "siblings." He seemed especially subdued around Robbie, whose attention Elsie and Dewey quite obviously preferred to his. But Sunday morning, on the ride to the airport, Jonathan sat happily squeezed in between Larry and Robbie, so that queasily pregnant Charlotte could ride up front.

This, Vrai realized, was her family now. Three sons, a daughter-in-law, and a grandchild on the way.

．．．．．．．．．．．

Again Dr. Brill showed up in Vrai's office. "I can't remember the last time you took a vacation," he said.

"It's been a while," she agreed.

"I think we could close the Art History Library between Christmas and New Year's," he said. "I think no one over at JJ's would even notice. What do you think?"

Vrai wanted to stand up and give this wise Santa a hug. "It's always very quiet here that week."

"Then's let's do it."

"Thank you," she said, blinking away tears.

So she and Jonathan, interstate travelers once more, spent Christmas in Tallahassee with her parents, both of whom seemed delighted to have a new grandson. Her mother, perhaps relieved that Vrai was no longer living alone, didn't offer a single word of advice. Her father quietly handed her the employment section from the Sunday newspaper, where he'd already circled the only two ads for librarians.

On the way back to Baltimore, at Lloyd's request, Vrai made a detour to Asheville. She was even less enthusiastic about staying in Jonathan's old house than he was, so they checked into a motel for the night.

During dinner at a noisy restaurant, Marianne ordered one glass of wine after another and switched her gaze from Jonathan to Vrai and back again. "You happy now, darlin'?" she said finally to Jonathan.

"As a lark." Arms bent, hands at his shoulders, Jonathan flapped his fingers.

While Marianne was in the ladies' room, Lloyd reported that he'd finally spoken to an attorney about Skip. After listening intently, the man had leaned back in his big chair and told Lloyd a story. Oliver Wendell Holmes, Jr., the famous judge, once had a lawyer in his court who kept pleading for justice. "This is a court of law, young man," the judge admonished, "not a court of justice."

"Is that a true story?" Jonathan said.

"Better be," Lloyd said. "I paid good money for it."

"Did the guy who wanted justice win?" Jonathan said.

"What do you think?" his uncle replied.

From an inside pocket of his sport coat Lloyd withdrew an envelope and handed it to Jonathan. "Open this later, OK? Merry Christmas."

The generous check, Vrai knew, was to be spent on new clothes. Jonathan was growing.

. . . .

Eventually the *Sun* did run photos of Dr. and Mrs. Franklin Benjamin Leigh, accompanying a long article about their new digs. In June of 1994, after extensive negotiations with the state, Frank and Celeste moved into an historic country estate near Reisterstown.

The mansion's original residents had been none other than Jerome Napoleon Bonaparte and his bride. In 1803, while visiting Baltimore, the Emperor's younger brother, Jérôme, had fallen in love with and then married a young woman named Betsy Patterson. The Emperor was not pleased. He ordered the marriage annulled and forced Jérôme to return to France and marry someone whose lands could be added to the empire. By then Betsy had given birth to a son whom she called Bo. Napoleon offered Betsy a home in Europe for the rest of her life if she would give Bo up and allow him to live with his father and be educated in France. Betsy, who was as wise as she was beautiful, refused. In 1826 Bo's wealthy grandfather gave him the estate near Reisterstown as a wedding present.

According to the article in the *Sun*, the mansion's newly refurbished library would soon be open to the public. Any resident of the state of Maryland would then have access to bibliographic information contained in "an antique card catalog." Eventually, The Napoleon Project would be available for purchase on CD-ROM.

"Un-be-liev-able," Jonathan pronounced after reading the article. "Guess we could write to the governor," he added without enthusiasm.

Vrai, too, was out of ideas.

In gathering information for a possible civil suit,

Bev had determined that Gussie's last phone call had been placed not from Frank's office, not from his home, but from a pay phone outside a small grocery store near his house.

Vrai did a little investigating on her own. The grocery sold Empereur Chen-Nung tea.

chapter 29

✳ ✳ ✳

*J*n August, after Rupert Brill had returned from a trip to Italy, Vrai wrote Frank a short letter of resignation, saying that she'd accepted a job in Seattle and would be leaving in two weeks. Before putting the letter in the campus mail, she walked down the hall to give a copy to Dr. Brill.

"Beating the Little Corporal to the punch, are you?" Dr. Brill didn't seem at all surprised. "Do sit down. Any possibility I could talk you into staying? Skip Howard was right, you know."

The back of her neck prickled. "Skip? About what?"

"About you. I didn't think undergraduate art history courses at the University of Tennessee would be adequate preparation for our librarian. Skip asked me to give you a chance. I'm so very glad I did."

Vrai had a hard time keeping her composure. Without Skip, she would never have been offered this job. Without her, Skip might not have lost his own job.

Dr. Brill deserved an honest explanation for her leaving. "Remember that morning you saw Frank Leigh at the grocery store with a black eye?" she said.

"Buying a steak. What an idiot!"

She told him her theory: who'd given Frank the black eye; why Skip had confronted Frank that day by the tennis courts; what had caused Skip to run out into the street. Dr. Brill listened with growing dismay.

"I do wish you'd confided in me earlier," he said when she was finished.

"There were no witnesses, at least in Skip's case, so the police said nothing could be done."

"There are ways. I'm from Texas, remember?"

"It's time for me to move on," Vrai said. "Doug Duesberg will probably send one of the humanities librarians over here part-time until you hire my replacement. I'll leave detailed instructions."

"You are not to worry. Let's hope your new boss won't display criminal tendencies."

This made Vrai smile. Her current boss, the real one, was a gentleman through and through.

Dr. Brill turned to gaze out his window at the hazy, hot, and humid afternoon. It wasn't long before he swivelled back around. "Do you remember the police officer's name?"

"Sgt. Bailey. He's at the Northern District."

Dr. Brill wrote this down. "First name?"

"I don't know. If you think you might be willing to

talk to him, then I have an idea." It was actually a variation on Justin's idea.

"Let's hear it."

. . . .

A few days later, she helped Dr. Brill set up a lunch meeting for the following week. Vrai asked if she could bring
Jonathan along. Bring anyone you'd like, Dr. Brill replied.

So she didn't feel the need to explain Jonathan's deep
involvement in this saga. Or to mention how brave the al-
most-twelve-year-old was being about their move to Seattle.

He'd made friends in Baltimore. This was home for
him now.

In Seattle, Vrai kept telling him, he'd have new friends,
plus a whole new family. It'll be an adventure. You like ad-
ventures, don't you? I like it here, he said at one point. So
do I, she admitted, but this move has all sorts of advantages. Besides, you'd be changing schools this year anyway.

Not once did she suggest the possibility of his returning to Asheville. Jonathan never brought the topic up,
either. Nor, more tellingly, did Lloyd.

. . . .

The Faculty Club, built long before Knox College merged
with Stoneham Women's College, still had the original
draperies at its tall windows. On the wood-paneled walls

hung portraits of unsmiling men in dark suits and ties. The dining room, designed for a small membership, was cozy, intimate.

Twenty years ago, Vrai wouldn't have been welcome here for lunch. Back then, the males-only rule had been relaxed on specified evenings, for faculty wives who wished to dine with their husbands.

Vrai's first visit had been eleven years ago, on the day of her interview, when she'd been escorted by Skip and the other members of the search committee. Today's visit would be her last.

Dr. Brill had reserved the large round table for ten. Vrai and the others were already seated when he and Frank came in.

She hadn't seen Frank in nearly a year and a half, not since the tea party in his rented row house. Life in a country mansion with his devoted wife seemed to agree with him. He was smiling as he sauntered toward one of the smaller tables by the windows, perhaps anticipating a friendly *tête-à-tête* about hiring a new art history librarian.

Dr. Brill, the tall Texan bent on justice, quickly caught up with the Little Corporal. He steered Frank over to the round table and its assembled posse.

Sgt. Bailey, in uniform, stood up. "Nice to see you again, Mr. Leigh."

Frank ignored the sergeant's extended hand.

"Dr. Brill, I presume," Sgt. Bailey then said with a smile, and the two co-conspirators shook hands.

Vrai handled the rest of the introductions. In turn, Justin, Winsome, Bev, and Jonathan shook hands with Dr. Brill.

"Won't you please have a seat," Dr. Brill said to Frank, indicating the chair directly opposite Sgt. Bailey.

Frank's metallic eyes darted back and forth, as if looking for an exit. But he did sit down.

Dr. Brill took the chair between Jonathan and the officer of the law. As planned, Sgt. Bailey had his back to a wall plug.

"Have you ordered yet?" Dr. Brill inquired politely.

"We were waiting for you," Vrai said.

The menus were encased in black pseudo-leather covers. Frank opened his and studied it intently, like a preacher searching for a favorite line of Scripture, an advantageous adage, a get-out-of-hell free card.

"My treat," Dr. Brill said jovially. "Too bad they're not serving the braised goose today. It's one of my favorites."

Frank ordered a bowl of vegetable soup and closed his menu.

"Dieting?" Dr. Brill said. "Don't let me off so easily. This is a very special occasion, a farewell luncheon for Vrai, an opportunity for all of us to wish her success and happiness in Seattle."

Frank looked only slightly relieved. While everyone else ordered, he pretended to re-read the menu. "Soup will do me, thanks," he told the waiter.

"Another reason for our luncheon today," said Dr.

Brill, "is that all seven of us are in agreement. At the very least, Frank owes Justin here an apology."

"I don't understand," Frank said.

"I think you do," Dr. Brill said. "I'm quite sure you know that Gussie Morgen was Justin's mother."

"I'm sorry for your loss," Frank said to Justin. "Of course I am. Perhaps I should've sent a sympathy card."

"You *caused* it." Justin was on Frank's left, his wheelchair touching the empty chair between them. "It's a little late for sympathy. Even an apology's not enough. But I'm willing to listen."

"I have no idea what you're talking about," Frank said.

His soup arrived. No one else had ordered a first course. "Mind if I go ahead?" Frank lifted his spoon.

"Maybe this will refresh your memory, Mr. Leigh." Sgt. Bailey set a black, rectangular boom box, a Sanyo, on the white tablecloth. "Thanks to Mrs. Morgen's excellent record-keeping and to her son's insistence that she involve the police, I'm prepared to play back for you, and for every table in this room, telephone conversations from 14 October and 19 November of 1992. In my opinion, those two are the most damning."

Vrai, seated next to the vacant chair on Frank's right, saw him swallow. He hadn't yet touched his soup.

She'd asked Jonathan to save his anger for later, to try to keep quiet, be polite, and let Sgt. Bailey handle this. After some discussion, Jonathan had solemnly promised not to call Frank an asshole, or anything else, to his face.

If this scheme worked, then Frank would be both publicly humiliated and, according to a colleague of Bev's, legally liable, at least in a civil suit. Maybe not for homicide, but for a lesser crime.

Sgt. Bailey looked over at Jonathan, then at Vrai, and she remembered that the sergeant had a soccer-playing grandson. "Go ahead," she said, and Sgt. Bailey hit Play.

"Me again," a scratchy voice said. In "A Magical Library Tour," Skip had described Frank's voice as deep and sonorous. The boom box elevated the pitch somewhat, but it was clearly Frank. *"Comment allez-vous, aujourd'hui?* All morning I've been thinking about pubic hair. How curly it is."

"Stop!" Frank said. "Turn that damn thing off."

Sgt. Bailey complied.

It was August. Classes weren't in session. With fewer people than usual lunching at the Faculty Club, the room had quickly gone silent. All eyes were on their table, as the red-faced library director rose from his chair.

"Sit down." Dr. Brill and Sgt. Bailey said this in unison.

Frank sat. He played with his spoon, studied his soup bowl, and set the spoon aside.

"Is that your voice?" Sgt. Bailey said.

"Are you recording me now?" Frank asked.

"Of course not. I'd have to inform you ahead of time. You know that." Sgt. Bailey shook his head, as if amazed by Frank's stupidity. "Is that your voice on the tape?"

"No, it is not," Frank said. "What that man said is disgusting."

Conversation at the other tables had not resumed. The entire room was listening. Despite the air conditioning, Frank was sweating profusely. Vrai was certain that Justin could smell it, too. But Justin couldn't see Frank's beet-red face. She'd have to remember to tell him.

"I'll play the rest of it," Sgt. Bailey said. "Listen carefully now."

"No," Frank said. "Please. I don't know who that is."

"Listen, then." Sgt. Bailey hit Play.

"In older women . . . " the scratchy voice continued.

"Turn it off," Frank said. "You're trying to intimidate me."

"Duh." Jonathan, on Vrai's right, whispered it.

Sgt. Bailey ejected the first cassette and inserted a new one.

"No, don't," Frank said quickly. "It might've been me. I'm sorry," he said to Justin.

"Yes or no," Sgt. Bailey said. "Was that your voice?"

"Yes. I said I'm sorry. Can I go now?"

Sgt. Bailey raised his abundant white eyebrows at Bev. Here was a freely given confession, duly witnessed. Was it sufficient? Bev nodded.

"Where you can go is straight to hell," Justin said to Frank.

"As you surely will." This was Winsome's lilting voice.

"Mrs. Morgen didn't listen to your filthy mouth," Sgt. Bailey said. "She simply recorded you."

"Illegally," Frank said.

"It's not illegal to record a crime," Bev said.

Frank was on his feet. Jonathan grabbed Vrai's wrist.

"We're not finished." Vrai, too, stood up. "In case you've lost track, there were two deaths. Gussie died during one of your despicable phone calls. Two days later you blinded Skip with pepper spray."

Frank was embarrassed to the core but still capable of lying. "I've already told you. I was at home that afternoon. Ask my secretary. She'll verify it."

"First you sprayed Skip, then he ran in front of that car, then you left the scene of a fatal accident and slunk home and called Margot." As Vrai enumerated these events on her fingers, Frank kept shaking his head. So she told the lie she'd cleared with the others, including Jonathan.

"Someone saw you. I have an eyewitness."

She wasn't expecting a full confession. A guilty look, a quick intake of breath would be just fine. Sgt. Bailey would then take Frank in for questioning. At the Castle. By expert interrogators.

"The hell you do," Frank snarled. He glared at Dr. Brill. "*Et tu, Brute*? I won't forget this."

"See that you don't," Dr. Brill said.

Frank stormed out of the room, and Vrai sank back into her chair. "How could I have said that differently?"

"He was there, all right," Sgt. Bailey said gently. "That's how he knows there were no witnesses."

"At least we can put together a civil suit for Justin," Bev said.

"Is it *always* legal to record a crime?" the sergeant asked her.

"Beats me," the attorney replied.

"Thanks, everyone," Justin said. "I wish Mother could've been here for this."

"It was your idea," Vrai reminded him. "We just tweaked it a little."

The room was abuzz with conversation. How much had the other guests heard or even believed?

Dr. Kraus, a history professor who specialized in the Visigoths, sat down in the chair Frank had vacated. "I'm a little hard of hearing," he said. "Think you could play that tape again? Maybe I could act as this young lady's eyewitness."

"The tape's a private matter, Fritz," Dr. Brill said. "The young lady is Vraiment Lynde, our art history librarian, at least for a few more days. She's moving to Seattle. We've gathered to bid her *adieu*."

"I see. A private party." After tasting Frank's cold soup, Dr. Kraus returned to his table.

With a wry smile, Dr. Brill raised his water glass. "Even a partially cooked goose is worth celebrating."

"A toast," Winsome whispered to Justin, and he raised his glass along with everyone else.

"Hear, hear," Sgt. Bailey sang out. "I wasn't at all sure this scheme of yours would work."

He then set the boom box on the floor.

The waiter brought their plates. As Vrai squeezed lemon juice on her crab cake, Jonathan picked up a French fry.

"There's ketchup." She pointed to the bottle.

Jonathan nodded, keeping quiet, being polite.

So Vrai knew. He was every bit as disappointed as she was.

chapter 30

❄ ❄ ❄

Epilogue

*g*etting off scot-free originally meant not having to pay a tax, or *skot* (from the Old Norse).

Is justice the first cousin of revenge?

How much can a private citizen do?

Seated on a damp bench in the Liliuokalani Gardens in Hilo, Hawaii, waiting for sunrise, Vrai is besieged by these thoughts. It's March 8, 2000. The seventh anniversary of Skip's death.

The outline of a pagoda is visible beside an arched bridge. Two joggers appear in the mist. There are fishermen with poles. The gray Pacific, as calm as its name, laps gently against the shoreline.

The first Hawaiians relied on only two directional words: *makai* (toward the sea) and *mauka* (inland, toward the mountains). As the sky begins to lighten over Hilo Bay, Vrai heads *makai*, to a front-row seat on the seawall.

She has been on the Big Island for two days but, due to persistent clouds and rain, has yet to catch so much as a glimpse of Mauna Kea, the huge mountain looming over the town of Hilo in nearly every travel-guide photo. The best time to see it, someone suggested, might be sunrise.

The sun neither rises nor sets. The sun, a star, is stationary. The earth, a planet, is what's moving. This, Galileo deduced by looking through his telescopes. For proving Copernicus was right, Galileo was tried and convicted by the Inquisition. After his trial, Galileo went blind.

A large yacht drifts past, abruptly comes about, and veers out to sea, its sails black against the gradually lightening sky. Her own life changed course just as quickly, the afternoon of Skip's funeral, that storm-clouded day she drove off with Laramie's child.

Now a new millennium has been announced. Vrai's not buying it. The new millennium will begin, like all the others, with the year one—2001, to be precise.

Yesterday she bought a dictionary. The Hawaiian word for justice is *kaulike*, which must be three syllables, at least, but is easy to read as cow-like. Old Bossy chewing her cud, thinking things over.

Truth is *oiaio*. She will ask for help in pronouncing that one.

There are six words for defeat. The Hawaiians (like the Indians Columbus so mistakenly named, believing he was in India) were defeated again and again.

The palm trees along Hilo's waterfront have become

visible. Soon, from her perch on the seawall, Vrai can make out a few shops and businesses. Less distinct are the houses climbing the hill behind the town. Determined to see as much as possible of Mauna Kea, she follows a footpath across a narrow causeway to a small island.

In the travel-book photos the sky above Hilo is always blue. A snow-capped Mauna Kea towers over the town. The White Mountain's true height, when measured from its base on the ocean floor, is 32,000 feet, making Mauna Kea the tallest mountain in the world.

Travelers to Paris see the Eiffel Tower. Vrai has come to Hilo expecting to see Mauna Kea.

Her disappointment is as oppressive as the cloud cover. That she is unable to detect even a hint of such an enormous entity seems a personal failure on her part, one reminiscent of, but dwarfed by, the ways in which she failed Skip.

Frank Leigh was never arrested for or even charged with anything. He did have to pay a sort of *skot*, the $50,000 awarded to Justin in a civil suit. The suit was settled out of court, its terms kept private. But Justin immediately called Vrai in Seattle with the news. As long as Frank forked up $10,000 a year, no one else would ever know about his tormenting phone calls to an elderly woman. It wasn't enough, Justin said, but it was better than nothing.

He then swore Vrai to secrecy. She has told no one, not even Jonathan.

By now Frank must be *skot*-free.

. . . .

Vrai crosses back over from the tiny island to the Big Island and returns to her hotel for the buffet breakfast. In the lobby she buys a postcard depicting a cloudless day in Hilo, with the massive Mauna Kea showing off its snowy top. The woman who takes her ninety cents insists the postcard's photo is real and even claims to have seen Mauna Kea from Hilo herself.

Stairs lead from the lobby down to the restaurant, a large room open to the island breezes. This pleasant architectural detail has a serious purpose: to prevent structural damage from tsunamis.

The shape of Hilo Bay invites tsunamis. On April 1, 1946, the tsunami warnings were ignored as an April Fool's joke, and many people died. Much of downtown Hilo was destroyed. Before the town had entirely rebuilt, along came another tsunami in 1960. That one was precipitated by a powerful earthquake in Chile, where, in 1960, twenty-year-old Miguel Jose Santiago was a student of poetry, and Augusto Pinochet was a Professor of War.

Homes are no longer built in the most vulnerable areas of Hilo, which have been turned into parks. Still, it takes courage to live here. The entire town could be buried forever if Kilauea, an active volcano, should erupt in this direction.

In the chilly, open-air room, Vrai spots her travel

companion. She stops at the coffee urns, fills a mug with the local brew, and joins him at his table.

Jonathan adopts a mock-parental tone. "You're sopping wet."

"We're in Hilo. It's raining."

"*I'm* in Hilo. I'm bone-dry. Where've you been?"

"Witnessing sunrise." She won't mention Skip, the anniversary of his death, the justice sought and denied. Their trip to Hawaii is a happy occasion. In September, Jonathan will enter the University of Hawaii at Hilo, where he'll major in astronomy.

He's seventeen now and a bit of a nerd, a wiry soccer star with an offbeat sense of humor and an unwavering loyalty to what he holds most dear. By learning the chords for "Blowin' in the Wind," he taught himself to play acoustic guitar. He still sings Dylan's words very slowly, turning them into a dirge.

"Couldn't sleep?" Jonathan says. "Still on Seattle time?"

Vrai nods. She swallows more coffee. "I was hoping to see Mauna Kea."

"But we're going up there this afternoon."

"Not the same." She pulls the postcard from her pocketbook. "This is how I want to see it."

On Mauna Kea's summit are observatories operated by eleven different countries. Jonathan's interest in astronomy intensified during his first months in Baltimore, when one of the school assignments he received in the mail asked him to visit and report on a local institution.

He chose the Space Telescope Science Institute and wrote three pages about the Hubble Space Telescope's defective lenses, which distorted the initial photos taken in space. After Shuttle *Endeavour* was launched in December of 1993 to install new cameras, he was invited to the office of an astronomer who'd befriended him. At the age of eleven, Jonathan Santiago was among the first to know the repairs had been successful.

"Earth to Vrai." He waves his fork in front of her face. "Sorry."

"Do. You. Have. Another. Jacket?" He touches her damp sleeve. "There's snow up there."

"On Mauna Kea? I'll believe it when I see it." She drinks the last of her coffee. "Maybe the hotel has clothes dryers."

"Maybe there's a Deer John's in Hilo."

Vrai will miss this kid when he moves halfway across the Pacific. "I wonder if Deer John would remember us."

"He kept telling you he wasn't the Red Cross. As if the Red Cross sells high-powered rifles." Jonathan rolls his eyes. "Saw some sweatshirts yesterday. They have my size. I wasn't sure about yours."

"Let me guess. The sweatshirts say University of Hawaii."

"Well, they sure don't say GO VOLS. My treat this time, OK?"

A waiter offers Vrai more coffee, but Jonathan declines for her, insisting she eat something instead. Visitors to Mauna Kea's 14,000-foot summit risk altitude sickness. Caffeine is contraindicated. But once Jonathan has gone off to build her an omelette, Vrai waves the waiter over and allows her mug to be filled to the brim.

....

In Seattle, the framed photographs of Laramie and Miguel sit upright on Jonathan's bedside table. After he finally revealed his secret hiding place—a large crawl space between his bedroom closet and the bathroom pipes—Lloyd carefully wrapped the photos and put them in the mail. It was nearly a year before Jonathan opened the package.

"Your mother was beautiful," Vrai said to him that day.

"I wish I could remember her better," he replied. "I've forgotten them both."

Lloyd's claim that he would get a divorce when his daughters finished college turned out to have been prophetic. After the proud parents attended the younger daughter's graduation ceremonies at Mary Washington, Marianne left on her annual trip to France. This time she didn't return. His name is Maurice. He owns a vineyard in Alsace. Marianne and Maurice are now husband and wife.

Lloyd has not remarried. He was, and still is, devastated by Marianne's departure from his life. Instead of employing some of her perverse psychology, Lloyd immediately flew off to France and tried to win back the only woman he has ever loved. There are times when Vrai feels almost sorry for him.

When his divorce was final, Lloyd asked Vrai to sign a complicated legal agreement, consistent with the laws in both states, assigning Jonathan two legal guardians, one in North Carolina and one in Washington. The document will expire when Jonathan turns eighteen and was, in Vrai's view, unnecessary. The person responsible for Jonathan Santiago has always been Jonathan Santiago himself.

Lloyd has been a good uncle to his nephew, visiting him several times a year. He'll return to Seattle in June for Jonathan's high school graduation. Larry and his family, who live nearby, will attend the ceremony, too. As will Robert, who's in graduate school in Oregon. Vrai's parents are thinking about coming, but Lloyd's mother is in poor health, so his parents won't be able to make the trip.

Bob may even come up from Texas for the occasion. Vrai hopes Daphne will have the good sense to stay home.

Not long after Vrai and Jonathan arrived in Seattle, Bob stopped his dithering, quit his job, and moved to Austin. Daphne had named their little girl Nike. The goddess of victory. When Nike was three years old, her parents tied the knot.

So there was divorcing after all. Followed by remarrying. Vrai, who'd been less surprised by Bob's defection than Lloyd was by Marianne's, managed to keep her balance. Lloyd developed a taste for scotch—no more wine for him—but due to liver problems has now sworn off alcohol altogether.

Vrai seems to have sworn off men.

. . . .

Dr. Tomás Rosales, an astronomy professor, is driving, with Jonathan in the passenger seat and Vrai in back. Tom, as he prefers to be called, is listening politely to Jonathan's excited predictions as to when Betelgeuse, a star in Orion, will explode.

The road is barely visible through the heavy mist. Random tree limbs float by. Vrai stifles a burp flavored by her multi-ingredient, "some-of-everything" breakfast omelette. The Jeep is warm, too warm, but she's reluctant to complain.

Seattle has mists and fogs aplenty. Even so, Mount Rainier is almost always visible for at least part of the day.

Her job offer (nearly six years ago, that was) came not from a library in Seattle but from Larry and Charlotte, who needed a nanny for little Muriel and then, a year later, baby Penelope. In exchange, Vrai and Jonathan received free room and board. Vrai's father was so pleased with this arrangement that she still wonders if he had something to do with it.

Elsie and Dewey survived the long car trip from Baltimore to Seattle but then died within months of each other. Vrai often wonders about Cassi. Nancy has stopped replying to Christmas cards, so Vrai has stopped sending them. Either something has happened on Bittersweet Way, or Vrai's multiple address changes were too much to keep track of.

Once she became the sole owner of the row house in Baltimore, she stopped renting it out and put it on the market. When the house finally sold, she bought a bungalow three blocks away from Larry and his family. Muriel is now in first grade, Penelope in pre-school. Jonathan's so smitten by the girls that he lets them call him Jon.

One career change led to another. Her new blue-and-white business cards read: *Iberian Tiles by Design, Vraiment Stevens Lynde, President.* She's a fifty-four-year-old entrepreneur. Business was slow at first, which suited the full-time nanny, but eventually she began receiving more orders than she could handle. Now the tiles are painted and fired in Puebla, Mexico, with Vrai responsible for their design and marketing.

Ceramic tiles speak to her, challenge her. Remember how much you loved geometry? they say. Here, solve another puzzle, they say. Use as many colors as you like. And while you're at it, create a secondary pattern involving multiple tiles, a pattern capable of repeating itself.

In Islamic mosques these repeating patterns appear to go on forever, a representation of infinity. A glimpse of heaven on earth.

Or so she's read. She's been inside only one mosque in her life. What she remembers from the huge structure in Córdoba, Spain, is not its tiles but its magical forest of pillars, the most beautiful of them translucent alabaster.

Jonathan has taken every Spanish class available to

him. His best friend and soccer teammate grew up in Ecuador. On Vrai's first trip to Puebla, Jonathan accompanied her as translator, but he refused to go again, insisting she learn to get by on her own. For months the two of them spoke nothing but Spanish at home. She doesn't yet consider herself bilingual, but she's able to communicate well enough with her *artistas*, whom she pays well. Most years she earns less than she did as a librarian. On the plus side, she's her own boss.

Although Jonathan has had a year of French, he no longer mentions Interpol. The failure to achieve any real justice in Frank's case seems to have discouraged him from going after the far more evil Pinochet.

But Jonathan does keep up with the news, often printing out articles from the online Chilean newspapers. Vrai's own file of clippings from the U.S. includes a description of Pinochet's collection of Napoleana.

In 1993, the year Skip and Gussie died, Manuel Contreras, former head of Pinochet's secret police, was convicted of arranging for the Washington, DC, car-bombing of a former Chilean diplomat (who'd publicly condemned Pinochet) and his assistant. The date of this double assassination is significant: September 21, 1976. Ten years later, to the day, Laramie and Miguel Santiago were gunned down on Cape Cod.

Contreras avoided prison at first but is now serving a seven-year sentence in Chile. He has claimed the car bomb was Pinochet's idea. The men who did the dirty work made careless mistakes and were arrested, tried, and convicted in the U.S.

Did Contreras, at Pinochet's urging, hire more competent assassins for the job on Cape Cod? Perhaps a wealthy yachtsman who, as soon as the fatal shots were fired, set sail for home?

Back when Vrai and Lloyd were sleeping together, they never talked about Laramie, but now that they aren't, Vrai has some new information. Mr. Eisen retired from the FBI involuntarily. Yes, he was sixty-five at the time, but he wasn't ready to stop working. It seems his attempts to look into his daughter's murder encountered some curious dead ends. Something to do with the CIA, Lloyd thinks, and he could be right. That the CIA played a role in bringing Pinochet to power is indisputable.

. . . .

Tom and Jonathan are now chattering away in Spanish. Vrai lacks the energy to try to follow their conversation. Her new UHH sweatshirt has a peculiar odor, in the overly warm vehicle, as they float along through heavy mist. Again, ominously this time, she tastes undigested tidbits. Desperate, she lowers a window.

"Too warm?" Tom says. "I'll turn off the heat." His curly brown hair and beard, soulful eyes, and kissable lips look so familiar that she feels certain she's met this professor before.

"Drink some water," Jonathan urges.

Water helps to prevent altitude sickness, which is not the problem. Her queasy dizziness is due to jet lag and lack of sleep.

"Jonathan's right." Tom turns around to hand her a bottle.

"Got any aspirin?" Her head is pounding.

"In the glove compartment," Tom says to Jonathan, who gives her two white pills and watches her swallow them down. "Drink *all* the water," he says.

She drinks until Jonathan is facing forward again. The water makes her want to gag. If this trip up Mauna Kea weren't so important to him, she'd ask to go back to the hotel.

At the summit Tom will give them a tour of the new Gemini North observatory. Gemini South is in the Chilean Andes. Together the two telescopes can see the entire sky. Vrai has trouble imagining such vastness.

When Jonathan began applying to colleges, she thought he might look in North Carolina. Or Colorado, halfway between Seattle and Asheville. She should have known better. The only distances Jonathan cares about are measured in light-years.

There are good astronomy programs in the Pacific Northwest, but their observatories don't compare with the ones on Mauna Kea. The University of Hawaii at Hilo accepted Jonathan immediately. The reference from his friend at the Space Telescope Science Institute surely helped.

So Vrai was surprised when, out of the blue, he asked if they could visit Hilo during his high school's spring break. She wondered if he might be having second thoughts.

. . . .

They stop at a visitors' center, where they'll spend an hour adjusting to the altitude at 9,000 feet before continuing on up to the observatories. Tom has brought camouflage-green parkas for them to wear. Neon orange would've made more sense, if they're ever going to find each other again in the fog. Vrai puts the musty-smelling parka on but, grateful for the cool air, doesn't zip it.

"Do you have a fever?" Tom sounds worried.

Vrai touches her forehead. "Don't think so." She studies Tom's face. He looks older; his hair is shorter. Maybe that's why she can't place him. He's not wearing a wedding ring, but then Latino men often don't. Is he Latino?

Tom uncaps another bottle of water and hands it to her.

"I'm fine," she says.

"Drink it anyway," Jonathan orders. "The whole bottle this time."

Vrai takes a sip.

"Another," Jonathan says. "This is serious."

She forces down another swallow. The water tastes metallic and stale.

The two stargazers head down the sidewalk to the men's room to pee out all that water they've been guzzling. Vrai walks around to the observation deck. There's a railing to hang onto but, other than thick gray mist, absolutely nothing to observe.

Inside the small building are displays and brochures. A map of the night sky. A few people sipping hot chocolate from paper cups. Anyone headed down to Hilo? she wants to call out.

Back outside, she wanders over to a monument near the parking lot. The visitors' center, she learns, is named in honor of Ellison Onizuka, an astronaut and native Hawaiian, who died in the 1986 *Challenger* disaster.

A disastrous year, 1986.

Jonathan, waving a sandwich, calls to her from the Jeep. Time for lunch.

But I had such a huge breakfast, she will tell them.

. . . .

An hour and a half later the Jeep emerges from the clouds into blinding sunlight. Ahead loom strange structures of various shapes and sizes. Blizzards occur atop Mauna Kea, but today only a few patches of snow dot the ground. The speed limit on the dirt road is five miles per hour.

The air is thin and dry and pure, uncontaminated by city lights at night and therefore optimal for telescopic viewing. Vrai has listened to Jonathan's excited explanations. She has even seen photos of the area. Still, she is unprepared and overwhelmed. It's like landing on another planet.

Gemini North resembles the domed head of a gigantic, shiny robot. They park beside an aluminum shed at its base.

Vrai is the first one out of the car. "Mind if I don't go inside?" She takes a few steps *makai*.

"You'll freeze," Tom says.

"Don't you want to see the telescope?" Jonathan says.

Both of them sound hurt.

"I'll keep moving, I promise." She will do this backwards—look down at Hilo from the snowy summit. "I need to see the Pacific."

Tom has a musical, baritone laugh. "Not today. The cloud cover's too massive." He points. "That's the top of Mauna Loa. The peak over there is Maleakala, on Maui."

Vrai goes further *makai*. When she was at sea level, she couldn't see the mountain. From the top of the mountain, she cannot see the sea.

Tom's right behind her. "In the Andes the clouds are not so dense. Always, if you wait, there are beautiful views."

"Tom will be in the Andes next year," Jonathan says. "On sabbatical."

There's a familiar lilt to his voice. Vrai turns around. Jonathan's dark eyes, Laramie's eyes, glow with excitement.

"Tom has a brother who's a judge in Santiago." He's grinning now.

"I see," Vrai says, and she's beginning to. Jonathan doesn't need Interpol. He can make the necessary contacts on his own. Beginning with the brothers Rosales.

"You're from Chile?" She stumbles toward Tom, who grabs her arm, keeps her from falling.

Something else is becoming clear to her as well. She's never seen Tom before, not in this century, or even the previous one. *Head of Christ*, the paintings are usually called, some by Rembrandt, some by his students, all depicting the same model, a resident of fifteenth-century Amsterdam. A man who could have known Spinoza as well as Rembrandt. A man who looked a lot like Tomás Rosales.

"Why didn't you tell me?" she says to Jonathan, who takes her other arm. Together he and Tom guide her *mauka*.

"Didn't want to get your hopes up," Jonathan says. "I still don't. What if we find out absolutely *nada?*"

Pinochet has recently returned to Chile, after having been under house arrest in England. The General thinks he has immunity from prosecution. He claims he's medically unfit to stand trial.

"All this is making me dizzy."

"Let's go inside," Tom says to her. "Astronomers work strange hours. You can rest up on one of our cots."

. . . .

There's a large crowd in the parking lot of the visitors' center. The clouds are gone. The night sky is clear. Tom's inside making a phone call. Vrai doesn't know where Jonathan is.

Telescopes are available, but with millions of stars visible to the naked eye, why bother with extra lenses? The sky is a mammoth fireworks display, a blizzard of light. Orion seems close enough to touch. Where have these stars been all her life? Dante and Virgil must have felt like this the night they emerged from hell and could once again see *le stelle*.

Astronomy students from the university point with small lasers as they name the component stars of the various constellations. A nebula pulses below Orion's belt.

The Hawaiian name for Orion means "cat's cradle of the children." Vrai can see this. Rather than a hunter's belt, the irregular line of stars represents a series of crossed strings. She remembers making string figures with Laramie. Cat's cradle required two people. Vrai usually left the trickier transformations to her more nimble-fingered friend.

Jonathan comes up and puts an arm around her. A hug from him is rare these days. "Will you come with me to Chile?"

Didn't he suggest just such a trip seven years ago, as they were heading east on I-40? Not for the first time Vrai wonders: who kidnapped whom that snowy afternoon in Knoxville?

"When?"

"Don't know." He gives her shoulder a pat and steps away. "I need to talk to Tom's brother first."

"It's been fourteen years," she reminds him.

"There's no statute of limitations on murder. Someone there must know who actually killed my mom and dad, and who gave the orders."

"Shall we invite Pinochet and Contreras to tea?"

Jonathan makes a sound that's half laugh, half snort.

"Kidding," she says. "I doubt the two of them ever tell the truth. Not even after a few *cabezas*."

"*Cervezas,* you mean?"

Vrai throws back her *cabeza* and launches a guffaw into the cosmos. Uncountable eyes twinkle back at her. They see everything, Jonathan once told her, and there are so many of them.

She links her arm in his.

acknowledgments

※ ※ ※

efore Brooke Warner at She Writes Press accepted my manuscript, a number of readers had given me valuable feedback. Elizabeth Wagenheim pointed out what was and wasn't working in the earliest versions, which ended with the arrival of the snowplow. "Don't we get to go with them to the cemetery in Boston?" she astutely asked. At the time, I didn't realize the novel wasn't quite finished, but eventually I came to my senses. In 2010 I took a much longer version to John Dufresne's Master Class in the Novel at the Taos Summer Writers' Conference. After further revisions (including a title change), the novel was a finalist in the 2011 Washington Writers' Publishing House Fiction Contest. In 2013, as part of the Queens University of Charlotte MFA Program's One Book semester, I worked for six months with Jenna Johnson, senior editor at Houghton Mifflin Harcourt, on making further revisions.

Readers of a chapter or two include Lillian Martin, Fred Leebron, and my son Brad. Brad's expert help with tech support issues merits a very special thank you from his mom.

I am extremely grateful to all of the above, as well as to those who helped without even intending to: my parents, Hope and Stewart McCroskey (both of whom were avid readers and beautiful writers), Mrs. Snelson (my 7th- and 9th-grade English teacher), the other Brad Coupe (with whom I spent many hours in art museums), Carola Montt, Marvin Ellison, Richard Peabody, Judy Ball, Donna Barr, Donna Feliciano, and Elisavietta Ritchie. Thanks also to my publicists, Rick and Caitlin Hamilton Summie, for guiding me through the maze of first-time publishing, and to Barbara Morrison, for leading me to She Writes.

A Nation of Enemies: Chile under Pinochet, by Pamela Constable and Arturo Valenzuela (New York: W. W. Norton, 1993) gave me insight into life in a country where one's friends and neighbors could suddenly disappear. Also inspiring was John Dufresne's *The Lie That Tells a Truth* (New York: W. W. Norton, 2003).

about the author

❊ ❊ ❊

Jill McCroskey Coupe's first job was gathering (collating) at her father's printing plant in Knoxville, Tennessee, in the foothills of the Great Smoky Mountains. A former librarian at Johns Hopkins University, she has an MFA in Fiction from North Carolina's Warren Wilson College, in the heart of the Blue Ridge. The Southern Appalachians feel like home to her, but so does Baltimore, where she lives now. She's hard at work on her next novel, a series of linked stories.

SELECTED TITLES FROM SHE WRITES PRESS

She Writes Press is an independent publishing
company founded to serve women writers everywhere.
Visit us at www.shewritespress.com.

The Rooms Are Filled by Jessica Null Vealitzek. $16.95, 978-1-
938314-58-2. The coming-of-age story of two outcasts—a nine-
year-old boy who just lost his father, and a closeted young woman—brought together by circumstance.

Stella Rose by Tammy Flanders Hetrick. $16.95, 978-1-63152-
921-4. When her dying best friend asks her to take care of her
sixteen-year-old daughter, Abby says yes—but as she grapples with
raising a grieving teenager, she realizes she didn't know her best
friend as well as she thought she did.

Shelter Us by Laura Diamond. $16.95, 978-1-63152-970-2. Law-
yer-turned-stay-at-home-mom Sarah Shaw is still struggling to
find a steady happiness after the death of her infant daughter when
she meets a young homeless mother and toddler she can't get out of
her mind—and becomes determined to rescue them.

How to Grow an Addict by J.A. Wright. $16.95, 978-1-63152-
991-7. Raised by an abusive father, a detached mother, and a loving
aunt and uncle, Randall Grange is built for addiction. By twenty-
three, she knows that together, pills and booze have the power to
cure just about any problem she could possibly have . . . right?

Things Unsaid by Diana Y. Paul. $16.95, 978-1-63152-812-5.
A family saga of three generations fighting over money and obligation—and a tale of survival, resilience, and recovery.

Wishful Thinking by Kamy Wicoff. $16.95, 978-1-63152-976-4.
A divorced mother of two gets an app on her phone that lets her be
in more than one place at the same time, and quickly goes from zero
to hero in her personal and professional life—but at what cost?